GREEN'S DISCOVERY 2

CREATING A FAIR AND JUST SOCIETY

Green Meets the Visitors — the Protectors of the Universe
Our First Contact with Another World

R.W. Karp

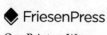 FriesenPress

One Printers Way
Altona, MB R0G 0B0
Canada

www.friesenpress.com

Copyright © 2022 by R.W. Karp
First Edition — 2022

All rights reserved.

No part of this publication may be reproduced in any form, or by any means, electronic or mechanical, including photocopying, recording, or any information browsing, storage, or retrieval system, without permission in writing from FriesenPress.

ISBN
978-1-03-914067-7 (Hardcover)
978-1-03-914066-0 (Paperback)
978-1-03-914068-4 (eBook)

1. FICTION, SCIENCE FICTION, HIGH TECH

Distributed to the trade by The Ingram Book Company

20.	Learning More About the Visitors	111
21.	Implementation Begins—Elections	114
22.	Continuing to Get Organized	117
23.	The Changing Role of Money, Technology, and Innovation	123
24.	Preparing for the Blue World Government	130
25.	Green Welcomes Joy to New York	137
26.	Green and Joy Discuss Her New Role	145
27.	Welcoming the Regional Government Representatives	153
28.	The First Meeting of the Blue World Government	156
29.	Joy Presents the Education Protocols	166
30.	The World Government Discussion Continues	172
31.	Preparing for the Broadcast	180
32.	The Global Broadcast	183
33.	Preparing for Interstellar Travel	189
34.	The Work Gets Done	194
35.	Preparing for First Contact	199
36.	First Contact	205
37.	Summary, and a Few Last Words	219

THE NEW SYDNEY GREEN

FOR MOST OF HIS LIFE, SYDNEY GREEN HAD BEEN A QUIET, RATHER reclusive person, focusing all of his attention, even as a youngster, on his dream of finding extra-terrestrial intelligent life. He became an astronomer and astrophysicist, dedicating all his energies to that search. Days on end, he could be found in his lab, studying charts and graphs, searching. He sat at his desk, knowing there must be life in the dark vastness of space, hoping he would find what he was searching for—it was his obsession. However, Green was always approachable and willing to discuss his research with anyone interested—even those who questioned his dedication. He was always available to his students; they appreciated his support, respected him, and trusted his opinion beyond question.

Green kept on going because he knew that he just needed to discover the key that opened the door, so he kept searching, year after year. Often, as he entered a room for a meeting, people would smile, ask if he found anything, then chuckle. Many of his associates thought he was wasting his time, his genius, but he persisted—and then, one day, it happened.

His students' sighting, followed by the arrival of the aliens—the visitors, as he was to call them—changed his life. It wasn't easy for him, coping with going from being an academic (buried in his research and dreams) and a quiet and socially hesitant professor (who focused on his students and his research) to being thrust into the role of figurehead by the visitors. The visitors had chosen him, they explained, because it was his technology that was reaching out to discover extra-terrestrial life, because he was a scientist, because of his determination, persistence, and curiosity, and because of his potential. They had studied Green and knew they could work with him, that he would come on side and be able to do what they needed from him.

The visitors called him Sydney, his friends called him Green, and his sister, a teacher in the north of Canada, called him Syd; when he travelled, people addressed him as Dr. Green. During the early years, wherever he appeared, he was recognized as the face, the physical being of the aliens. All the heads of government, in all regions, learned to respect his authority and fear the powers the aliens had given him.

Green was never really good at being told what to do, but he was highly organized and focused on his task. When the visitors promised him that he would actually meet them, one of his dreams coming true, it was too much for him to resist. And when they told him why he was the individual they needed to represent them, he felt obligated and co-operated with them, becoming both judge and jury for segments of humanity. He had to do more than just participate, as the circumstances he found himself involved in were often so demanding that he had no choice but to follow the instructions of the visitors. As they hoped would happen, Green slowly settled into his role, not that he liked it, but because he hoped he was having a positive impact on the future of the world. But he became impatient, nervous, and anxious to see some constructive results emanating from his actions. The visitors knew it; they sensed his anxiety, so they tried to alleviate his concerns by repeatedly telling him all would be well in the end, and to trust them.

But the visitors needed Green, and so, from previous experience, they were patient and supportive of him. They needed a face that humans would recognize and trust, and a reassuring voice to which they would listen. They knew what would come to pass; that the people of earth eventually had to participate, and ultimately take control of the changes needed to develop a fair and just society — with equal opportunity for all of humanity.

What Green faced, his tasks, the powers he was given, and what he witnessed, all reframed who he was. He was exposed to the abuses of power, the greed and corruption of the corporate industrial sectors, of labelling segments of society—the pervasive racism—and he saw the extreme disparity between the entitlement of the wealthy, the power mongers, and the lived experiences of everyone else. He learned to become disciplined and demanding during what he called his cleanup work. It would have been difficult for anyone, to say the least, but for a reclusive, focused professor, it was the opposite of who he was, who he wanted to be, and what he had expected in making contact with extraterrestrials.

In the early stages, Green travelled the world, using the unique powers bestowed on him, and with the added support and unlimited powers of the visitors themselves, he worked to start implementing the social, political, and economic changes that were required. During these initial years, he struggled to understand the consequences of his actions. When he took the time to consider what he was doing, he questioned his role—it was traumatic for him, having to deal with the problems to which he was forced to react. However, Green understood that the changes would happen with or without him, and so he was determined to stick with it and worked hard to cope. Compounding his problems were the remnants, the supporters of how things used to be, who were resisting the changes. The visitors explained to Green that what he was participating in was a process, a series of actions to unify and bring balance to a dysfunctional world, and that in time, all would be well.

On this particular day, as Green was in discussions with the visitors, he made it clear to them that he needed to have a couple of days to think about what had happened, go over his accountability, and gain a sense of normality by talking to and socializing with some of his friends at home. The visitors understood, and Green suddenly found himself transported to his apartment in Florida for a weekend stay.

It was a rainy Saturday morning in southern Florida where Green had lived and worked for NASA since he had started his research and teaching career decades ago. These days, during this time of change, he appreciated returning to his apartment and reconnecting with his previous associates. On this visit, he was hoping to discuss his recent experiences in order to get their support and input and vent his emotions. He also wanted to have some quiet time to reflect; however, this occasion turned out to be different. His friends were busy with a pre-arranged weekend event, leaving him alone to deal with his issues.

There was so much on his mind about what was going on and how to continue to deal with the burden he was feeling. He wondered if the visitors would continue to be patient and answer his questions, and he was also anxious about their new plans and the role he would play moving forward. He thought that it might be the right time for him to step aside and let others take over.

The weekend flew by, and on Monday morning, the visitors transported Green back to his office on their spaceship. As Green walked over to his desk and stood there, holding on to the back of his chair, the visitors explained that it was time to discuss several current issues with him. Green dropped his head, sighed, and then slumped into his chair. The visitors went on to say they had to discuss their plans on how they, through Green, would deal with the issues and share with him the next steps in earth's development. The visitors sensed that he was distracted and upset, so they tried, again, to calm him.

Sydney, we know that a lot has happened during these initial years and that it's difficult for you to imagine that it's been for the best. But this is a process, and the first stage is always difficult. Let us be clear with you that we've seen some positive results, and soon we'll talk about those. But, Sydney, there was, and still is, a lot to overcome to pave the way ahead. The next steps will solidify the sequence of events, like the pieces of a puzzle fitting together, and you'll start to see some very exciting developments. Be patient as we discuss with you the current state of affairs on the planet, what we have to do, and how we're going to move forward. As well, we'll answer all of your questions as we go.

Sydney, we have to mention to you now, after the work we've completed so far, and before we continue, that your world's current disposition, it's social, economic, and governance models, are like viruses that we cannot allow to infect other civilizations. Even though we've worked to make some preliminary changes your world is still far too primitive, and that is what we'll work on as we move forward - you have a long way to go. Sydney, one last thing before we get started.

Please keep in the back of your mind, always remember, that as we review the issues in front of us, no matter how difficult that is, and as we work together to resolve those issues, remember that your world is headed toward a time when one's contribution, whether in the sciences, sports, music, entertainment, community services, as a teacher or a manager, whatever one does, that their contribution to society will be recognized. And in return for their service, whatever it is, their day-to-day needs will be met, and much more. That is where we're headed.

Trust Sydney, trust us that we're preparing your world to transition into a whole new age. All will be well and we will always be with you. Right now, Sydney, your world is still in a position within which there is work to do to facilitate those changes. So, let's go over the details of where we are right now, and how we're going to achieve that end point.

2
THE VISITORS DISCUSS EXISTING CONDITIONS WITH GREEN

GREEN GOT UP AND WALKED TO THE FRONT OF HIS DESK. HE stood there waiting, flushed with expectation. He knew the visitors would review and analyse what had happened, where we are right now and the current issues, before discussing the next steps. Green was anxious to get on with whatever was coming, not to go back over what had happened, so he tried to curtail that discussion and have them get right to outlining the plan ...

"Of course, I trust you. We've been working together for several years now, and I can see some progress. It's just that getting to where we are has been tough. I've seen so much, had to do a lot of difficult things that have profoundly affected me, and I'm tired, stressed about what is to come, and concerned, wondering if it's all really worth it. Can we just get on with the next steps?"

Sydney, we know that you're anxious, but please understand that there are no shortcuts in what we're doing. We have to be thorough to know where we are in order to understand and implement the steps to get us to where your world has to be. We also know that you need an extended break, more than just a weekend, and we'll make sure that happens so you can regain your composure and prepare for implementing the next steps. Let us reassure you that what you've done on our behalf will pay off. Your contribution to get us to this point has been amazing, well beyond our expectations, and you'll soon start to experience the benefits for the people of earth.

But Sydney, before that happens and before you have an extended break, we have to clean up some residual issues, talk about a few pressing concerns, and establish the path forward. We need to fully define those issues and problems that are confronting us now, in order to create a baseline to determine the appropriate actions as we solidify the plan to move forward. Systemic changes like this takes time, persistence, collaboration, and meeting established goals and thresholds. Sydney, we were confronted with a broken world order that we had to fix. Together, we've started that, made some fixes, and now must continue our work.

Green accepted the notion of what the visitors were saying. "A baseline," Green responded, "That I can understand …" So, a little relieved by what he just heard, he went back to his desk and sat down. "It's been essential in my research." He moved forward in his chair as he continued, thinking about the first thing that came to mind. "To create a baseline in order to study the movement, the trajectories of planets, and objects in space, to know where they are, their direction forward, so I can figure out where they're headed. Okay, if this is what we have to do, then let's get started."

Thank you, Sydney, that's exactly what we need to do before we move forward. At this point we'll review what we're seeing, and then go over and share with you, and others, how to implement the required priorities and actions. Green got up, and made himself a cup of tea as the visitors were talking, then went back to his desk and sat down.

So, Sydney, together we've made some progress, but we have to deal with the difficult parts, to understand the threats to sustaining our progress. The ultimate purpose in all of this is to bring your world into the future, to fix what is wrong so you can create a balanced and fair society, and then, in time, join with other worlds.

Hearing this, Green shuffled in his chair, pulled himself closer to his desk, had some tea and then grabbed tightly to the arms of his chair as he prepared himself for hearing some difficult news. The visitors started to explain.

You see, Sydney, during the past several years, we realized that on your world the pre-existing structures in society were deeply engrained. Removing the top layers of the problematic leadership as we did, simply exposed what was below. There are followers of the previous extreme leadership still using ideologies, religious and otherwise, trying to maintain their control. Remnants of groups like the Taliban, al-Shabaab, al-Qai'da, and ISIS in the Middle East. The LRA (Lord's Resistance Army) and Boko Haram in Africa, and there are many other examples around the world, such as the powerful elite groups in the U.S., India and China fighting to hold on to their money and power. We've established a foothold, something to build on, but it's still a challenge to continue the progress we've made. All of this is part of the baseline we've observed.

Okay, thought Green, even with all of these issues, there seems to be a desire to continue to fix things, but he was thinking, wondering to what extent the visitors will go, and Green was concerned. The visitors, hearing his thoughts responded.

Sydney, relax. We're not thinking about more extreme measures. We just have to know where we're at in our timeline in order to pave the way for future actions.

Again, Green was feeling a little reassured, but cautious, as he prepared himself to hear what was to come. He made himself a fresh cup of tea, took a muffin to munch on, and returned to his desk hoping for the best. He was nervous, sensing there was a lot more for him to do so he braced himself — and he wasn't wrong.

Sydney, we find that humans are quite a stubborn, arrogant race that is resistant to change. Even after this first decade of introducing new technologies, improving the standard of living of the general population, there are still recurring efforts by the remnants of the plutocracy and corrupt politicians trying to reassert themselves to sustain their wealth, power, and lavishness.

As well, Sydney, the extreme religious factions, trying to hide in the shadows of social media, keep working hard to restore their influence and maintain control over their followers. These groups must be dealt with. Regrettably, we're also still witnessing issues of women all over the world being denied equal opportunities and treated as second-class citizens within their communities.

Green sat there, listening, getting more and more uncomfortable, and embarrassed that this is how we're perceived by the visitors.

The visitors then went on to discuss more of their concerns, focussing on social issues and the remaining disparity in society. They summarised the luxuries, the entitlement, and the continued benefits of the wealthy and powerful minority, and their absolute disregard for others. They talked about how they felt toward groups that still followed the attitudes that dominated society during the Middle Ages; and residual leaders in Asia and Eurasia resisting changes to social models that recognize the needs of the people. They explained to Green, that eliminating this tribalism, at all social, political, and economic levels, is central to the challenges we face.

Sydney, the influence of these restrictive social behaviours, which don't exist in advanced societies on other worlds, has been reduced here, but they're still around and continue to pose a threat. These are some of the reasons we must move as quickly as possible to the next stage—to prepare your world for the future—socially, environmentally, politically, and economically. Sydney, we need you to help with this.

Hearing that the visitors still needed him, Green started to feel a little more confident, as if he might have an edge. He wanted to speak out, so he got out of the chair and stood, leaning on his desk.

"You must know that we're not all bad, don't you? Many of us care about our neighbourhood and our friends, and work hard every day for our families. We may be stubborn, concerned about changing our way of life, but that's because we don't know what that means, and I suppose many are, to some degree, afraid, afraid of not knowing the impact of what is coming—for sure afraid. But isn't that up to you, and me I guess, to show the way?" He sat back down.

Of course, Sydney. What we were about to say is that we've also learned that there are more good people than bad; but they remain quiet, and distant with whatever is going on, if it isn't affecting them directly. They seem indifferent, blind, and unwilling to act—this is also part of the problem moving forward. It's also a very important characteristic of humanity that makes our work more difficult. We've come to recognize that many individuals in your species are resourceful, and inventive, and that those skills are significant, but these people must get involved, stand up, and be counted. Sydney, please know that we've been active in identifying and developing those individuals not only now, but throughout your history.

The visitors paused as Green got up, and a little confused about the history reference he walked around, then went back to his desk and sat down waiting for an explanation he sat there again feeling guilty.

"This is a flaw in our nature. I know, because I've experienced it myself as I've been aware of situations, and haven't said anything. I felt guilty not doing something, but just continued with my work, my life, thinking I had no power, or support, to speak out."

Sydney, as there are issues and problems caused by certain elements in society, we know that there are good people that will come forward, given the proper leadership. And that's one of the reasons we're here, and our responsibility, our role, in keeping balance in the universe. You see, as you were reaching out to make contact, to find other civilizations, we knew that the time had come for us to step in as we can't permit a primitive, violent society such as yours to have contact and infect others. So, to answer your question about our reference to your history.

Sydney, though we've actively been here for a relatively short time, in your three-dimensional reality, be aware that we've been watching your world's development for thousands of years, thinking that it would progress, as others have. We've injected ourselves every once in a while, helping scientists by providing sparks of enlightenment and direction in developing their innovations. But all of that didn't get us the results we had hoped for.

Green heard laughter in the background, which wasn't unusual when something was mentioned that was ironic—but it made him feel a little better about the visitor's intentions.

Sydney, we were there for all of it, watching, hoping we wouldn't have to interfere overtly as we are now. But simply putting ideas in peoples' minds to create innovations, to improve lifestyles, hoping that your world would move in the right direction—it didn't work. We were wrong.

"What are you saying?"

We're just going back over what's happened to bring you some context as to what ultimately brought us here, especially because of you. But not to worry. You see, there are parts of your human makeup, your character, that we didn't take note of, which have had a profound impact on earth's development. So, let's continue, and we'll explain.

"Okay, sorry for interrupting. Please continue."

Sydney, what we didn't take note of, what we underestimated, was the influence of the greed of those who came to power. It was this greed, the selfish desires of people, the entitlement, that took control and moved your world in an unexpected direction. It was their desires, their lust for wealth, power, and lifestyle, and their authority over others, that abused the hierarchical systems that were in place. The expectations of those high up in the social order—that entitlement—caused all sorts of problems by belittling, even ignoring the needs and desires of others.

The abuses of these privileged classes, the development of the monarchical structures, then the plutocracy, the greed of capitalism, and the disparity that created, evolved to a level that became intolerable to us. As the protectors of the universe, we were concerned about those social inequities, the patterns of behaviour, and their potential impact, if they got out, to infect other worlds. So, we knew we had to do something. We couldn't let the negative characteristics of your world have any influence on other more advanced civilizations. Sydney, as we're the caretakers of the universe we sustain the balance in the entire system, and when a civilization reaches out, we must protect that stability.

At the same time that we were evaluating our potential actions, you … you, Sydney … were reaching out, searching for other worlds that support intelligent life. We reluctantly knew then, that there was no choice, that it was time to step in. We can't tolerate the abuse of so many by such a small group of power brokers, especially when you're working to make contact with other civilizations. Sydney, as we've said and must repeat, we are charged with sustaining the balance in the entire system, and we must protect the stability of the universe.

Please understand that the first step in resolving the issues on earth was to establish the seven regional governments. This action, by continuing our work, will eventually create a time when people live, work, and interact with each other equally. In order for your world to mature, each region needs to partner, rely on each other, and communicate and share resources, innovations, and technology. And as it is on other planets, this can only happen within a fair, just, and balanced global society. Do you get what we're saying?

"I understand what you're saying; however, you seem to be focusing on bad behaviour. But as you said, you know that we do have a lot of good people here."

Yes, we do know there are many good people. We're working with you, aren't we? Green heard some laughing in the background. *But Sydney, it's the bad ones who have had, and are currently doing whatever they can to maintain their control, and that's what we're working to change. With your help, and the help of other "good" people, we'll put the right people in positions of management, people who are caring, accountable, and responsive to the needs of others, and Sydney—change will happen.*

Another point we have to work on Sydney, is that on your planet you have social, environmental, and economic networks, but, for the most part these networks, from local to provincial to national, and even international levels, act independently, and that's a problem. Yes, there is some interaction that occurs, but the interdependence between regions that should exist, that should display the universal connectivity and dependence between the parts of the world that make up the whole, that sustain and protect the whole, just doesn't exist in your world order. Sydney, the connection, the reliance and support between the parts of that global ecosystem, the interconnectivity and balance in social structures that provide for all the people of the world that should exist – just isn't there – at least not yet. And that is also what we're working to provide.

"Yes, I understand that we're more individualistic, nationalistic, and care more about personal and local issues, and because of our competitive nature not so much about others. I also understand what you're saying about our nation–states that have been focused more on themselves rather than making a contribution, participating in a global effort. But again, where is this headed?" Green got up and started pacing.

Sydney, the pacing, please.

Thank you. Again, this is all part of understanding the baseline we're working on, so, together, we can move forward. We need to understand human nature to know what we're dealing with. Sydney, this is a fundamental management technique in introducing and managing change – understanding who and what you're working with, the existing conditions and where you want to be.

Sydney, some news for you ... because of all of your help, we're arranging for a special surprise for you.

"You have a surprise for me ... when do I get it?"

3

THE VISITORS CONTINUE AND PREPARE TO FULFILL A PROMISE

WE'LL EXPLAIN YOUR SURPRISE SOON SYDNEY, BUT NOW IT'S TIME TO look at the details that will prohibit your world from moving forward, and then how we'll transition from what was, to prepare the planet, the people of earth, for the future.

Green, standing in the middle of the office, accepted what the visitors were saying.

Good, we're glad you understand. So, let's get going ... we'll start by discussing your economic structures ...

You see, Sydney, your business sector has evolved to be based not on principled social norms to assist people, as they are on other planets, but on a competitive, profit-driven prototype, designed for the benefit of businesses and their investors. This greed, the gouging for profit, influences politicians who are primarily focused on sustaining their power, and thus are influenced in their decision making by lobbyists representing those businesses and industry. Money as the currency of one's value, and lifestyle, is the downfall of a fair and balanced society—money is at the heart of many issues.

Sydney, you know from experience that nothing happens on your world without talking about the cost. This has led to a breakdown in societal norms, how people deal with each other, and it has also affected global co-operation and international networks. Instead of discussing how something might benefit people, the cost of implementation is the primary factor and the impact on people is ignored. Our work has been to start to establish a global ecosystem putting the needs of people first – and bring to your world the stability, the co-operation required between all levels of society, and all the regions of the world, for the benefit of all.

The visitors stopped to give Green a chance to absorb what they were saying.

He walked over to the table that had the charts showing the dot his students had discovered. He looked down at it and sighed. Then, holding on to the table, he asked, "O.K, but where are you going with this?"

We haven't mentioned this to you earlier, but we need you to understand that when we first arrived and reaffirmed the current information our probes shared with us, in frustration, we were very close to eliminating all biological life on this planet, especially after the failure of trying to deal with your world leaders. Of course, this would be counter to our mandate as the protector of the universe, so we looked for an alternative solution.

Then you, Sydney, you came on the scene and we quickly realized that you could become the key to successfully altering the path of your world. You Sydney, you became the facilitator that saved the little blue planet. Because of you, its population has been given a chance to reform—you, Sydney. It was your response to our arrival, no matter how difficult it was, your understanding, your curiosity, your commitment, your dreams, and the support you gave us, that made the difference. When we saw it in you, we intuitively knew that others must exist as well, and working with you, we could accomplish finding them and working with them, while at the same time working to eliminate the negative forces. Then, Sydney, you became our face, our physical representation.

Green was shocked, "What? I never even imagined such a thing, how is that even possible? I'm only me, one person, I was just an unknown researcher and professor."

That's the point. You see, we realized from your world's history that there have been times when a single person's presence has played a significant role in framing your future—such as in religious theology. Anyway, it doesn't matter right now. It's true, and we'll explain more later. Sydney, please understand that because there are still matters that concern you, and us, we need you to help us to finish establishing a global network – a universal, connected ecosystem. As soon as we finish our discussion and present our plans for the next stage, you'll be able to enjoy some free time, and as a reward for all of your work and commitment, we'll keep a promise we made when we arrived—the surprise we mentioned.

"What promise? A surprise? What are you talking about?"

As we promised you several years ago, we're arranging for you to meet with us, face to face so to speak ...

Green heard some chuckling in the background. It would be difficult to describe how excited he was. "What? I'm going to meet you? To see what you look like? To be in the same room as you? Oh my God ... when?" Sydney could hardly control his emotions as he imagined his lifelong dreams coming true. He walked around the room, trying to visualize what he would experience.

Soon, Sydney, but first, as we prepare for your visit, which is a first for any biological unit, we have to have some discussions about the next stages in preparing your world to continue its progress and preparations. So, we need to examine the baseline we've established, and then share with you the next steps for your world to mature by establishing an active global network and setting up the Blue World Government. We need to discuss your role in all of that, then you can have a well-deserved break, and then you will meet with us.

Green made himself a fresh cup of tea then went back to his desk, sat in his chair still excited about meeting the visitors, but not knowing what was to come he tried to focus his attention by sipping on the tea to calm down.

The visitors continued, *Sydney, in order to find solutions and continue to achieve our goals and move forward, the people of earth must learn to rely on collaboration and sharing instead of competing for power and control; they must learn to participate and have compassion and support for others, instead of fighting for privilege and lifestyles. It's only through accountability, communication, and innovation that the world will mature enough to position itself to develop that interconnectivity and reliance on each other to move forward into the future, ultimately making contact with other civilizations.*

Green got up from his desk and started pacing again, as he thought about how to respond. "I know this will take time, all of it ... especially creating an effective world government," then he continued pacing, placing his hands behind him as he would when addressing a class or an audience, "... getting everyone together, on the same page, won't be easy, negotiating and developing the partnerships between the regions, oh my." He paused again to gather his thoughts, still pacing, but he was interrupted before he could continue.

Sydney, the pacing, please.

Green stood still and took a deep breath.

Ironically, Sydney, the visitors continued, *there is no negotiating; there can be no negotiating with the earthly systems that were, that are still in place ... one does not, one cannot, negotiate with governance models that uphold abuse, entitlement, and poverty—that support profit as a determination of success, rather than servicing the needs of the people. It's wrong to support the accumulation of money and power to establish one's status, safety, and lifestyle. Sydney, as you said in your first speech years ago, we must start to focus on the youth, develop the youth, as they are the future. Finally, as we both have recognized, there are people on your world who resist participating, who are working to maintain their entitlement and trying to hold on to their old ways.*

The visitors made it absolutely clear that people can't fix something if they don't understand, and accept, what is broken, if they don't stand up and face the facts, and then deal with the problems. The formula for success, they explained, the activities needed right now, are to study, and plan to react to the conditions defined in the baseline, and then to work together to develop, then share the path, the required ethics, governance models and systems, to move forward.

As it is said, if you don't learn from history, you're doomed to repeat it. This is what we've also learned from helping many other worlds, so we'll send you back to your Florida apartment for a short rest for tonight and tomorrow to think about our discussion, and then we'll bring you back to the ship and get started. And Sydney, we need your full attention.

Green found himself back in his apartment in Florida. He spent the night weighing the scope of what he had heard, trying to cope with and understand what the way forward looked like. Even with all of that, he couldn't get the idea that he was going to meet the visitors out of his mind.

The next day, he got out on his mountain bike and peddled down a road that followed close to the ocean as he had done many times when he was getting in shape years ago. He used the rhythm and the sound of the pounding of the waves on the shore, to help him focus on his ride and clear his mind. Then, when he found a nice spot, he stopped to have a rest. Sitting on the beach, enjoying the view, and listening to the rhythm of the waves hitting the shore calmed him. Refreshed, he came to the conclusion that there was hope, that the visitors wouldn't show themselves unless there was hope, and because of that, he had to continue to support and work with whatever they were planning. He knew it would be a lot of hard work—stressful, detailed, and consuming—but there was no choice and he had to find the strength to continue. It was his legacy.

The next morning, back in his office on the visitors' ship, he made himself a cup of tea and heated up a cinnamon bun to munch on while waiting for the visitors. He sat at his desk, enjoying his tea and his snack. He started thinking about those initial years and the challenges he'd faced as best he could, but now he knew he had to fulfill his mission. He realized that the work in realigning social, political, and economic paradigms, implementing new innovations, reshaping governments, and aiding youth to come into positions of management, would hopefully overpower the old ways. And he thought about meeting the visitors.

But they interrupted his thoughts.

They explained to Green that all of the work so far was foundational. It would take more time, more elections, and the commitment of the youth, the future generations, for the changes to become the new standard. They explained that generational transformations often take decades in order for the conversions to become the norm in society, and so the work continues. They had been through this process many times with other planets and realized the time had now come for the little blue planet to move forward and complete its transition! They also knew, and hoped that Green understood, that to complete the transition, they relied on him to lead the way as they worked to bring many others into leadership roles.

Green was concerned about what his role would be, but the visitors repeated and reassured him that all would be well. After the coming election, it would be time for the local and newly elected regional officers to take control of the governance and implementation work on infrastructure, communications, and supply chain management systems.

The visitors then continued their discussion so he could listen to their internal dialogue to be reassured that they not only knew what they were doing, but also understand that the progress and the issues he was concerned about would be dealt with. He was requested to listen and participate only when called upon, or if he had a question. So, he settled in and, as usual, refreshed his tea, this time getting a muffin and butter to munch on.

Then the visitors started, specifically for the enlightenment of Green.

As we've done many times for other planets, it's now time for your world to begin to assume control, and to continue the development of a new age for your people. Sydney, your world is for everyone to share, to participate in, not for one group, not for the elite, but for all of humanity to have equal opportunity. Therefore, we've organized this meeting to discuss what we, and you, have to do for your world to move forward, and then how the transition will continue. That's why you're here— to listen, understand, then participate, and with our guidance, be prepared to take over to implement the final stages for all the regions of the world.

Green choked on his tea, put the cup down, stood up, and moved away from his desk. He was shocked and started to pace as he interrupted, "Are you saying that you're leaving?" He'd missed the essence of the last statement made.

No, Sydney, we're not leaving yet. Not until everything is in place. We want you to listen to what we're thinking and then how we'll move forward to prepare your world to continue the process we've been working on, together, with you and others. Please understand that from our experiences through several millennium that it's critically important to evaluate our progress, and to review the changes we've implemented, the impact, and the stage we're at currently—our baseline. In this manner, we're always aware of issues and gaps, and are in a much better position to establish how to deal with the next stage of development. Please, Sydney, stop pacing and get comfortable.

Green went back to his desk, sat down, and then opened up his notebook, prepared to take notes as the visitors continued.

You see Sydney, as we've already mentioned to you, and will explain in more detail when we meet, we are the protectors of the universe. Right now, your world is like a contagion that could upset the balance in the universe if it is allowed to expand beyond your planet. This we cannot allow, and that is why we're working to correct how your world functions.

4

SUMMARIZING WHAT IS TO COME

SYDNEY, WE HOPE THAT YOU REALIZE THAT THE CHANGES, THE TECHnology we've introduced, was the first part of the process of creating a new and an acceptable socio-economic, and governance model for your world. Our intervention in this first phase had to be directed, imposed, but moving forward your new leadership will start to take over. We'll be like a catalyst, injecting ourselves, through you, and others we've been working with, to facilitate the necessary actions to mobilize your world in order to synchronize it with the rest of the universe.

"A catalyst, so that's how you define yourselves. I've been thinking about who and what you are, and I've been wondering why you don't just act to end the resistance of groups around the world and the problems they're causing. When will we see the social, political, and economic changes take root?" Green moved forward in his chair and listened intently.

From this point on, we can't impose ourselves that way. We now act in such a way to give your world the tools, the direction, to progress—that is the only way for it to be sustainable. Sydney, progress is being made. Please understand that the apprehension of going from a social structure that people know, regardless of its makeup, to one that they don't know, one that they don't understand, is a cause for concern and hesitancy. Therefore, introducing new innovations, saving your environment, and changing organizational and societal paradigms to fulfill the day-to-day needs of people is a process that will bring people on side. Sydney, it will happen, but let us explain further ... well, give you a picture, a story of what the goal is, and then we'll discuss the steps to getting there.

"I understand, and I thank you and appreciate the social, economic, and technological changes that you've introduced, as well as the new governance models. I know it's a movement, an evolution, a transformation for our world. I would so like to see where we're headed, to have a picture of what is to come."

Sydney, do you remember when we showed you other worlds and what their societies looked like?

"Yes."

Well, those visions were what just and fair societies look like. They showed where your world is headed; that these societies typically do what is morally right and are disposed to giving everyone a quality of life, and a meaningful existence, while being fair and equal to all, regardless of the work one does or where one resides. The basic principle is that the world belongs to everyone, not one country, one region, or one entitled group. Your world will become one nation, and as we've already started to establish, it will be one nation made up of seven regions sharing goods, services, and resources equally. The people of earth have to understand that you're all the same. Regardless of external appearances, you're all the same— both men and women must be treated equally, and accept that all people in all regions of the world are equal, and must be respected as such.

"This is a huge transformation for us. Not only do I hope we're up to that task, but I look forward to being able to participate, and hope I live long enough to experience it. Sorry ... please continue."

Thank you ... Sydney, you will see and experience it. We've been aware of the limited lifespan for your species, so we've been working on that where you're concerned. But Sydney, the limited lifespan of your species is part of the up-side of the changes we're implementing, as generational transitions take place the changes become the norm, but right now, we have to continue ....

Sydney, first, understand that we've been through this process for thousands and thousands of worlds, and the methodology, the strategy, has been established, proven. We are a race that is of one mind, a unit made up of many. What your world is experiencing is not completely unique. It fits into a pattern, and that's why we have to review the progress from time to time, to keep things on track, and make sure that all of the pieces are starting to fit together.

At this stage, we need to define a few things for you that we know the people of earth can understand.

And so, the visitors started explaining. *As it implies, individuals living within a "just and fair" society are caring, supportive, and of ethical character. This must seem impossible to you right now. It may seem like we're working to create an ideal social order. Perhaps we are, but until now, that has been just a philosophical ideal, a thought, a dream, something authors and philosophers wrote about.*

Sydney, what we're working toward is that all individuals, as part of a universal social structure, are raised and educated to become respectful and dedicated to participating in the governance and social decision making for the world—it's not a dream, Sydney. It exists on many worlds. A just society is one that establishes rational order, and a safe and meaningful environment, with fairness involving equitable distribution of goods and services, of opportunities, of education, and of careers—for everyone. This represents the next step in your progress. Sydney, we know there are issues right now that concern you, and we want to hear about those, but be confident that things are progressing and we'll deal with those issues together.

"Thank you, I know you're focusing our attention in the right direction. I'm just concerned that there are questions that need to be dealt with, and I'm not sure we have the capacity, intellectually and philosophically, to follow what you're describing. I'm just afraid we'll fall back to what was. Believe me when I say that we're a practical race; we see and react to what is right in front of us, concrete and obvious. We have trouble believing stories about the future, especially when those pictures, those stories, are abstract and hard to visualize."

Sydney, your world got side-tracked, broken, but the people of your world absolutely have the capacity, the intellect, and have throughout your history had the desire to make changes and improve their lived experiences. Now they're seeing small but continuing improvements, innovations, and social changes that are impacting them positively—and they're safe. Sydney, let's continue, please ... we'll explain about the divergent philosophies, their impact, and then answer your concerns, be patient.

"Sorry, I didn't mean to interrupt again. Please continue."

During your history, philosophers regarded being "just and fair" as the most fundamental of all virtues for interpersonal relations, as well as sustaining a stable governance model. But in your history, that was translated into various religious and social configurations, which diverted the essence of what was defined philosophically, and caused all sorts of societal problems. Sydney, in order to re-establish that fair and just model for society, leaders must understand that "just," in dealing with society, means respecting persons as free and rational individuals, regardless of their ethnicity or where they live or their work. Leaders must realize that they are responsible and accountable, and that the world is for all humankind equally.

Sydney, universal educational protocols, developing ethical, responsible, and accountable leadership, and an efficient supply chain program for goods and services are big parts of the key to success. You see, when individuals and families have no concerns about meeting their day-to-day needs, when they feel they are safe, when they see that those in management positions listen and respond to them, that opens the door for what we're talking about—we have a hill to climb, but rest assured that we will reach the top.

Green just sat there, thinking about how wonderful that would be and hoping he'd see it happen.

The visitors paused as he reflected on what they had shown him on other planets. Then they continued. *Throughout your history, your philosophers and academics, even the moderate religious leaders, encouraged all people to lead righteous lives. To these people, the concept of governance and human interaction was to promote kindness, benevolence, compassion, a peace-loving disposition, and a truly humble and contrite spirit. However, throughout history, their writings were misappropriated, and their efforts were to no avail because of the hierarchical structures that developed. These structures were supported by the influence of religious leaders. Religion became something that used faith, trust, and beliefs, to control followers, to justify the hierarchical model as being imposed by what they called "god." Then those at the top of the ladder used it to accumulate wealth and power, and by reason of their entitlement, to impose their will on others to control people in order to sustain their lifestyles. Everyone else, Sydney, was told to pray for forgiveness for their sins, that they must accept their position in society.*

Green again heard laughter in the background.

The development of class structures—the self-indulgence and greed of those at the top and the entitlement of those in power—caused your current world order to evolve. We watched in horror, hoping for change, knowing that it was too early, that it wasn't the right time in your development for us to intervene. Oh, Sydney, we're sorry to be so repetitive, but this was so ingrained, so woven into society like the threads in a fabric, it became your picture, your tapestry, and no amount of praying could untangle it. What stands out in the development of ethical societal designs is that a just society, as you witnessed on other planets, requires just people functioning within a fair and equitable society—this is the challenge for your world—and the changes that have to be implemented in order for a new socio-economic age to evolve.

"Well, all of that is fine, and I understand it academically," replied Green. "It's easy to discuss definitions and philosophical statements, but right now, our world is not perfect, as we've seen from the depictions in the baseline—far from it—and as you've outlined, that has caused a lot of issues and confusion with the recent actions." Green paused for a moment to collect his thoughts, then he stood up, leaning against his desk, and continued.

"You have to see that in our daily lives, where we experience the reality of the political and business world that you've described, that this is where our human imperfections get in the way of creating a just society. Even after all of the innovations, all the work we've done eliminating most of the abusers and criminals, resolving social issues, and having the elections, we still have problems."

Green moved away from his desk and started to pace again, frustrated. "I ask ... when will this all end?"

The visitors let him pace. *You're right, Sydney ... your world still has issues that have to be addressed. Taking your world from where it was, to where it is, and ultimately to where it has to be in order to create a new era, to join with other worlds, is a step-by-step sequence – like a puzzle taking shape. Sydney, after hundreds, actually thousands of years of developing a hierarchical and social governance model that relies on the control of a small elite class, it takes time to change. Our intervention, however, is making that process happen more quickly, and the next steps will strengthen the resolve and put into motion the final actions to allow all the people in your world to fulfill their dreams. Sydney, be a little patient, and we'll explain the next steps when we meet after you've had a chance to enjoy some real and extended free time.*

"Wait," exclaimed Green. He stopped pacing and returned to his desk. "How do we achieve the task before us? As far as I can tell, it requires a commitment and paradigm change in our societal, economic, and political structures, and a change in the mindset of the people. And although some change is happening, it's not complete by any means."

Now you get it, Sydney ... that is exactly what we're discussing. The paradigm shift, which is starting to become a reality, has to be in conjunction with the development of a governance model based on democratic equality—people interacting as equals at all levels—to use an earthly term, in a "meritocracy", and this will happen with generational change. People in a just society must be able to function as human beings, to participate, to execute their role as citizens by having all of their basic needs fulfilled, the freedom to speak, to vote, and be safe. One of your recent philosophers, Victor Frankl, said it clearly when he argued that there must be meaning in one's life—that is where your world will be when we finish our work.

Sydney, Frankl's discussions of the impact for people that have meaning in their life is critical in your work moving forward. What we'll work on is empowering individuals who are good at art, or storytelling, or sports, or music, or science, or making people laugh, or doing day-to-day supportive jobs, to find that they have respect for their contributions. And in the new world order they'll receive recognition, be a productive part of society, and find that meaning in their lived experiences. Together, and with expanding help from many others, your world will continue to advance until all people have equal opportunity according to their skills, their desires, and have meaning in their lives.

The visitors stopped as they realized Sydney was tired and needed a break. *We know you've been working hard. We need you to know that at the same time, we've been expanding the abilities of others to participate, operate, and maintain the new technologies we've introduced. Please know that you're not alone, and that the tasks ahead will have shared missions and responsibilities. Just a few more minutes, and you'll get an extended break.*

The visitors paused for a moment and then continued. *We've been working on providing extensive training and arranging the mentoring for the next generation entering into management positions.*

Green went over and made himself another cup of tea, and he returned to his desk.

The visitors continued. *Sydney, the most important task now is to begin to implement the creation of the Blue World Government, to have each region appoint a leader and staff, and then focus on the priorities that we'll be discussing, which have to be executed in order to move forward.*

As he was listening, Green instinctively knew how important that was, and he was anxious to hear more.

The priorities are critical, and we'll give you a detailed outline at a later date, but for now, there are a few examples we can share to give you an idea of what is to come. One, as we mentioned, is establishing a world government organization with representatives from the seven regions. Two is to create a universal education system in order to identify potential in all areas of study and expertise. It's within the educational protocols that educators and managers identify potential future leadership, and also provide opportunities for students to achieve their goals and develop the required expertise in all areas of study. Three is at the other end of the scale. There are two issues we have to deal with: first is that although we've removed the leadership of extremist groups, as we have discussed there still remains the remnants that we have to deal with; and second, we must finally eliminate money as the prevalent currency and the foundation for all transactions, both social and economic, and replace it with a model based on recognizing people and their work, at all levels. The visitors paused for a moment.

"Thank you," replied Green, "This is all reassuring, except for the money part." The visitors ignored that last statement.

The general feeling among the visitors, considering the starting point, was that they were relatively pleased with the progress being made. However, they knew it was time to start transitioning so that the people of earth stepped up and became responsible and accountable for governing as they moved forward. They recognized the importance of the transition from one generation to the next, and the role of the youth to assume power. So, the priority of creating a world government, the elections, the communication technology, the new education protocols, and accountability at all the levels of government in the regions, was absolute. This governance structure was critical to continue to implementing infrastructure, and to solidifying the global supply chain management systems.

The visitors continued their discussion, planning a timeline and creating thresholds to achieve, as Green was sitting at his desk, listening. He became somewhat concerned about some of the details, and was about to speak when the visitors interrupted his thoughts.

Sydney, this is a lot to absorb, so go now and have a break. When you're ready, we want to hear from you as we know you still have concerns, and then we'll present to you the actual plans to resolve those issues and move forward.

5
GREEN'S BREAK

GREEN FOUND HIMSELF BACK IN FRONT OF HIS APARTMENT BUILD-ing in Florida. He stood there, taking in the feeling of the warm rays of sun on his face, and the welcoming environment that he was so used to. The warmth of the day engulfed him as he took in the sight of the palm trees with the well-groomed landscaping around his apartment building, and the flowers and shrubs that lined the walkway to the building's front door. He walked over to an area under a group of trees where there was a patio with a couple of lawn chairs and a small table. He sat down, absorbing the wonderful feeling of being home. He was relishing the contentment of the moment, the sun that was poking through the trees, the view, the warmth that surrounded him. Then his feelings of inadequacy returned and he dropped his head as he couldn't avoid thinking that he wasn't sure if he could cope with it all; perhaps the visitors were just expecting too much of him. He took a deep breath, knowing there was much more to come.

Although Green was somewhat relieved after his meeting with the visitors, he knew this was just the start of a much longer journey. Never could he have imagined what was in store for him when his students discovered that dot in space headed toward earth. Never could he have imagined at that time that he would be contacted by extraterrestrials, that he would become their ambassador. His dreams and fantasies of meeting aliens excited him, but then actually being recruited, and the experiences of the past years, were nothing like what he had expected to happen. He was feeling the weight, the burden of his actions, and what he had witnessed as he travelled the world.

Green was torn between the cruelty, the racism, the abuses of power, the criminality, the disparity between the classes, and the assumed permission that the powerful and wealthy group could do as they pleased. He was frustrated with what he had to do to get rid of the abuses and the criminality, and saddened by how he and so many others had just accepted it as being normal, and how they capitulated to those in positions of power. Then he thought about the positive developments with the implementation of new technologies, of the innovations in governance models, working to prepare the world by focusing on the youth to develop the leadership and the commitment in creating a truly inclusive and fair system - we seem to be on the right track he thought.

But complicating this were the actions of the remnants of those who were at one time in power. Those secondary individuals in the old order were still working to regain their control, their status, and their entitlement—making the transition difficult, to say the least. Green was seeing too many issues pop up all over the world, so during his break, he needed some private time before he could express his concerns to the visitors, and listen to their plans to work toward a resolution of what he was witnessing.

The visitors had taught him how to block their ability to read his thoughts when he needed to, and that's what he did. As he was sitting there, he came back to where he was, enjoying his surroundings at the front of his apartment building. Now he felt free from being part of a collective that was always aware of his thoughts, always probing. He had his privacy and could argue with himself to weigh the pros and cons of how to approach what was to come and how to prepare himself if he had to continue his work.

Green contemplated how he would balance his approach to the visitors. He knew he had to express his appreciation for the innovations that had been implemented, and yet there were the profound concerns he had about the impact on the people and the resulting disruption in their lives, let alone his concerns about whether he could continue. During the next several days, he put everything aside, or tried to, by enjoying the sun, being with friends, and just relaxing. Then, as he realized that his free time was about to end, his anxiety returned.

So, as he had done many times in the past when he needed time to think, he got his bike out and went for a ride down the same remote and hardly travelled road along the seaside near his office. Green needed to use up his energy, get rid of his anxiety, and clear his mind, and so he rode and rode, determined to keep going until he could go no farther. He rode for more than two hours until he had to stop. As he got off his bike, he was out of breath, his legs were unsteady, and his muscles were aching from the exertion, but he felt like he was free, like he was in charge of himself.

As he was slowly recovering, holding on to his bike for balance, he looked at the waves rhythmically splashing on the sandy beach, and he got absorbed by the sounds of the ocean as he walked onto the beach, noticing that he was completely alone. He found a nice spot and sat down in the sand. As he sat there, he closed his eyes, enjoying the rays of the sun and he got control of himself from the exertion of the ride. He heard the waves crashing, the sounds of birds, and after a short time while breathing in the fresh air he relaxed. Then his thoughts turned to reflect on how his experiences during the past several years had impacted and changed him, and what he was going to do.

I hope, he thought as he sat there, *that the next phase will be easier, that the progress we've made will start to have general acceptance in each region, and that the youth coming into positions of authority will make the rest of what the visitors have planned more fluid.* He spent the next hour or so recovering from the ride, and thinking about what he wanted to do.

Then, suddenly, he realized that he had to ride all the way back to his apartment, and he had better get started. He got up, stretched, and sadly realized that he wasn't in the shape he had been a decade ago. It took him a lot longer going back as he had to stop several of times to catch his breath, and recover his strength. As he approached his apartment building he was relieved, but he became anxious as he started to wonder what the visitors actually had in store for him. *I hope I can meet their expectations, can I do it*? he thought. He put his bike away, went up to his apartment, and stood in front of the door as he reached for his key. He was pleased with how far he had been able to ride, that he'd made it back, and he smiled.

Then, as he opened the door to his apartment, he recalled something the visitors had said to him—*We've worked hard to lay the foundation, but that effort is not over. Now we'll focus our energies to complete what success we've had and create the path to the future.*

As he walked in and closed the door, he just stood there in the entranceway. Then, when he bent down to take his running shoes off, he suddenly felt stiff, and his aching muscles hit him like a sledgehammer. He slowly and painfully worked his way into the small washroom and splashed water on his face. He started to feel dizzy and almost fell to the floor as he grabbed hold of the counter and rubbed his sore muscles. He took a hot shower to try to relieve the pain and to come to his senses. After he was cleaned up, he felt a little better and hobbled to the kitchen, got a bottle of water and drank just about all of it as he leaned against the counter, thinking. He worked his way to the living room and plunked himself into the sofa, but thoughts about the visitors and how to respond to them flooded his mind.

He knew that he had to brace himself for what was to come. To Green, it seemed that this was a test of his resilience, his commitment. He knew from the visitors that there was a new crop of young leaders to build momentum, who would be more open to the new economic and social paradigms, better enabling the changes to become rooted in society. Early on, the visitors explained to Green that he could trust the new crop of leaders, that they were there to help, implement the directives, and be responsible leaders. The visitors also explained that getting rid of the political parties, the influence of big businesses and wealthy individuals, and establishing new directives for electing leaders and managers would have a significant impact. He realized that the general elections—the one right at the start of the changes, and then the one five years later—were meant to start that process, to develop new and committed leadership.

Green also knew that the youth were much more adaptable to change, to accepting innovation and working together—he knew that they were the key to success. *The visitors have given us new technologies and expected us to adjust to them. Technologies through which we are revitalizing the environment, building housing and infrastructure, and creating a new governance model. It's now that the younger generation has to come together in order to bring balance and equality to our world.* Green was trying to come to terms with everything he had experienced, everything he was witnessing to this point, and find meaning not only in what he had done, but also in what was to come.

To Green, the visitors had forged the direction for earth to build on, but there were questions, and it was a struggle for people to adjust to a rapidly changing lifestyle, so he was concerned about sustaining any progress that had been made. With all of this running through his mind, Green knew that he had to discuss and resolve his concerns with the visitors before moving into the next phase of the mission. He opened himself to the visitors, waiting for them to contact him.

The next day, while he was just sitting in the living room finishing his tea, he was beyond pleased when they communicated with him, saying that they wanted to bring him to the ship.

Sydney, we're aware of your concerns, and we can discuss those issues before we move forward.

After we do that and go over a few other things, it's time, Sydney. It's time ... they paused for effect and to make him a little anxious to hear what was to come ... *for you to actually meet with us, to see how we live, for you to learn what sustains us, and experience our environment.*

6
GREEN EXPRESSES HIS CONCERNS

"OH MY GOD," HE SAID, AS HE JUMPED UP FROM HIS CHAIR, SURprised that it was finally going to happen. "Thank you," he responded, "I so look forward to finally meeting you, OMG!" And images of what he thought they would look like flooded his mind, images from his earlier days, but then Green heard laughter in the background.

Not quite right, Sydney, and the laughter continued. *We're making the arrangements but it's much more complicated than you think for a biological unit such as yourself to join us, even for a short time, so it'll take just a bit longer to resolve the technicalities of introducing a biological unit into our environment.*

They agreed to meet the next morning. That evening, Green went out with his friends, who were always anxious to meet with him as often as possible and hear about what was going on. They all had a great time and were glued to his every word when Green shared that he was going to actually meet the aliens, and what he thought they might look like. Green was so excited he had a restless night.

The next morning, in preparation for this special event, Green dressed up more than usual, wearing his beige dress pants, his favourite emerald green shirt, and even took out one of the few ties he had—beige with green stripes to match his shirt and blend with his pants. This was his favourite dress-up outfit. Oh, and he also had on a pair of his best running shoes. Green was ready to meet the visitors—little did he know what awaited him.

There he was in the kitchen of his apartment, just finishing breakfast and waiting for the kettle to boil for a second cup of tea. After he refreshed his tea, he went into the bedroom he had decorated with all his childhood posters. He stood in the middle of the room, sipping his tea while turning his attention to one wall at a time, looking at each poster. He was trying to focus on the one he thought would best represent the aliens when he again heard laughter in the background. He finished his tea and put the cup down.

Sydney, you don't have a winner in any of those choices either. Not even close. But it's very entertaining, thank you. Green heard more chuckling and laughter in the background.

Before we meet in person, as we mentioned yesterday, we need to discuss the issues and concerns you're thinking about to make sure we're on the same page moving forward.

Suddenly, Green found himself back in his office on the spaceship. He looked around the room and sighed as he was still thinking about actually seeing the visitors; then he noticed a glass of water suddenly appear on the small table. He went over to the table, sat in one of the chairs and, smiling, took a drink. Then, thinking about the past several years, his mood changed. He became the academic, more like the professor and teacher that he had been. He stood up as if he were getting ready to address his students in one of his seminars.

"Are you okay, Sydney? You look great, by the way. Love the running shoes, said the visitors, trying to lighten the mood. *Although you didn't need it, we thought the water would help calm you down for our meeting. But first, let's discuss the issues you're concerned about and where we're headed, if that's all right with you.*"

"Absolutely," replied Green, a little relieved. "If I could go first, that would be great as there are also a number of concerns I would like to talk about and hopefully resolve, but give me a moment or two, please." He drank the rest of the water and put the glass on the table.

Of course, you can go first. Take as much time as you need to be able to share your thoughts with us.

Green started to pace a little before taking a deep breath, then going to the table with the charts on it. He leaned against it, deep in thought and still pondering his words. Again, he closed his thoughts and his feelings to the visitors in order to get organized. He turned, looked around the room, then continued to pace back and forth with his hands clasped behind his back. He thought, *this is it—if I'm going to have an impact, I have to be strong and to the point*. He was working on how to clearly express the issues concerning him.

Green's demeanour had transformed during the years working with the visitors. He had become tenacious with criminals and abusers, unforgiving, impatient, and fully dedicated to the task at hand, regardless of what that was. His apprehension, stress, and anxiety about his involvement came not from the aliens, but from humankind. He was frustrated with the general populations' uneasiness that the fundamental changes were so complicated and life-changing that they might slip back to how things had been. Then there was the ongoing resistance to change from the remnants of the privileged classes and their influence, which was having a profound impact on continuing the progress that had been made. Green knew they remained a force to be reckoned with.

One contributing issue in Green's observations was the difficulty people were having with changing their identity from the country they were born in, their background, and their culture, to their allegiance to a *region*. This was part of the complexity. People didn't understand that they didn't have to change their identities, that they were now part of something bigger. Green was concerned about the lack of communication. He stopped pacing but continued to walk around the office as he was deep in thought.

Then he suddenly stopped, looked around the room, and opened his mind to the visitors as he exclaimed, "I don't understand," he started, "how can you accept what is going on without stepping in to fix the issues? Surely you have the technology, the power, to do that?" He paused. "I know we've had a lot of time together, and moved forward in a measured fashion, but please, these past years have been challenging, to say the least, and there's a lot of commotion."

He went back to the table with the charts and leaned in, reminiscing about the time when Michelle and Sean came to him with their discovery and how that changed his life and that of the whole world, and he wished for a simpler solution. Taking hold of the edge of the table, he looked down at the charts, weighing what to say and how to express himself to the visitors when they interrupted him ...

We understand your frustration and concern, Sydney. Please understand that, as we've tried to explain, the people of your world have to adjust, to have the time to change their behaviours, and ultimately be in control of their world. We haven't accepted anything; that's why we're meeting with you. We can't impose the solutions; we can only propose solutions. You, Sydney, and others, have to implement them ... with our support. It's a process, so take your time, and when you're ready, please continue to say what's on your mind.

After gaining the clarity he needed, Green started to walk around again, as if talking to a group of students. During the next hour or so, he shared with the visitors how he perceived the events of the past more than ten years and the many issues he faced. Then he discussed his concerns that there was confusion in the general population, concern that there were still groups trying to return the world to how it was, and how those groups were a problem because they continued influencing people. He then expressed his concern that the communications and supply chain systems were not acting quickly enough to sustain the momentum. The visitors listened patiently, and then, when he stopped talking, he went and sat at his desk as they responded.

Thank you for sharing your thoughts. We appreciate your honesty and understand where you're coming from. If we may, we'd also like to briefly share with you how we've viewed the last several years and explain why we acted as we did.

Sydney, one of the unique things we noticed about humans is your egocentric nature and your focus on those close to you or your community. We couldn't understand how so many people only cared about themselves, their desires, and how they used others without caring for their well-being. How so many people knew about the abuse, the criminality, they knew that many were addicted to drugs and alcohol, or living in poverty, but if it didn't affect them directly, then it didn't seem to matter, or it was something they had no control over.

You see, Sydney, this attitude among humans on your world is unique in the universe, and that is one of the paradigms we have to change.

Something that surprised us was the widespread acceptance that the family, the situation that you were born into, was because that was the place ordained for you. This has been a major influence on the organizational paradigms of society, of religious doctrine, and in the industrial age of the development and power of the plutocracy. These basic assumptions of status being ordained, of privilege and entitlement, have led to all types of abuses, racism, and conflicts.

Sydney, as we realized that this primitive understanding that power comes from asserting one's strength and that the religious paradigm of hierarchical supremacy was actually a flaw in your social philosophy, we were saddened by what we learned. We saw that it was responsible for a lot of ambitious people taking advantage of others because of their greed, assumed entitlement, and position in society. As a result of our early actions to make this correction, many of those issues are starting to get under control, some have ended, and there are many more people who are benefiting from the changes we've implemented.

Do you not see that people are starting to realize that the beliefs of the past are giving way to a positive transformational energy? Trust us, Sydney. That will continue.

Green got up and walked to the front of his desk. "It's okay," he replied, nodding in approval and support. "I understand that you've done a lot, that progress is being made, and I need to recognize that. It's just not easy to see the frustration in adapting to new ways, the confusion in people not knowing what they can and cannot do, and the resistance that still exists. Sorry, please continue ..."

Thank you, Sydney. As we've noted, the process relies on generational changes as the concepts have been so ingrained in society that the previous generations of people cannot see or trust in anything different. That's why we focus on the youth and bring innovation. Sydney, we're here, but the people of the blue world must be in control of your future. In this respect, education and communication protocols are key to adapting to new systems, and you, not us, must be the ones to implement those changes. So, part of the key to opening that door is the younger generation starting to take control, and as such, forging the way as we move forward. Finally, please know that we'll be discussing the frustrations you've experienced and our plans to deal with the feeling of entitlement of those that remain from the power structures of what was. We've been aware that they are causing issues. This was expected, as we were just completing the first stage of your development and will now be preparing to move forward. At the same time, we'll be helping you to deal with those concerns.

"Good, I'm looking forward to that, and I'm anxious to hear your ideas as we move forward. And let's not forget that I'm really anxious to meet you, face to face." As there was laughter in the background, Green went back to his desk and sat in his chair.

7
THE VISITORS REVIEW THEIR ACTIONS

SO, NOW, IN ORDER TO CONTINUE THE PROCESS OF EMPOWERING THE *people of your world to move into the next phase, we have to see if we've missed anything and to fill in the gaps as they present themselves. It's important, when fundamental and systemic changes are being made on such a large scale, to manage the changes and evaluate the progress by looking at what is happening. Sydney, we've been through a lot together, so much so that we need to weigh the results in order to put things into perspective, and identify if there are any gaps in our baseline. So here we go ...*

One issue, Sydney, that surprised us even before we arrived was that your world's environmental stability was deteriorating; actually, if changes were not made, it was on the verge of collapse. You have no idea how frustrating this was for us. How could a world that was technologically advancing ignore the environment that kept them alive? We've said you're a stubborn race, but this was beyond belief, and we worked to understand why, which we will get to in a minute. But as an immediate reaction to the issue, do you remember that one of our first actions was to begin reversing the impact on your climate?

"I do remember. There was a focus on developing new energy supplies."

Yes, but as we studied why this wasn't creating change, we discovered that there was much more to deal with —the current leadership— and we knew there would be some difficult times. You see, Sydney, at that time, your world was controlled by a very small group of so-called leaders, whose greed and privileged disposition controlled their actions. They were a motley band of people who had wealth and power, and asserted their entitlement to all of the best things the world had to offer. All over the world, everywhere, they lived in luxury. We knew we would have to transport many of them, and the abusive, controlling, autocratic leaders, and as a result, the criminal elements that existed, to other worlds—and with your help, we did.

This created a void in leadership, regardless of how bad the leadership was, and this was the start of the resistance of the remnants of the upper classes. The resistance was not just with the elite, but also those in the upper middle class that had benefited from the wealth and power of the elite, and the subsequent corruption in politics, business, and the entitlement they also enjoyed in their lives. We had to move quickly.

Then, as we worked to bring balance to the world by meeting some of the needs of the lower classes with new housing, infrastructure, and social and economic changes, and to fill the void in leadership with new elections, we knew there would be some confusion, and even difficult times for the general population. We were confident, however, that as the youth moved into positions of authority, there would be support for our actions as long as they saw some progress and improvements to people's lived experiences worldwide. And we were right!

Yes, we had to act quickly and with impunity, imposing new systems on your world. Sydney, during this phase of your development, the elements that we started to eliminate, with you as our emissary—such as the brutality, the economic inequality, the criminality, the control of religious extremism—have started to pave the way for a new world order that all people of your world will benefit from. As well, to fill the void that was created during these early actions, and to alleviate the confusion, that even you were experiencing, we introduced six strategic goals to work on that have been developed successfully through our interactions with other worlds:

- Step one was to work with the people, prioritize community and locally-based approaches, implement a methodology focussing on the potential in the youth, and having new elections every five years as the youth mature.
- Step two was to establish seven regional governments.
- Step three was to begin to adapt the political, economic, and social paradigms by abolishing party politics and start the process of creating a meritocracy - developing leadership skills and accountability.
- The next step was to prioritize policies and programs that work to develop a universal supply chain management system as well as communication and co-operation between the seven regions.
- Then together with you, we developed measurable goals to monitor progress in reducing gaps in social and economic inequality and to begin the development of housing and infrastructure in areas where it didn't exist, or was sub-standard.
- And finally, to begin the process of developing a non-monetary economic system that places value on human achievement – a system that recognizes the contributions of people, not the accumulation of money.

Sydney, together, we've set things in motion having created the seven regional governments, and impacting many people's lived experiences by building housing, developing infrastructure, and starting to meet their day-to-day needs. It took more than ten years, but now you're ready to implement the final steps by solidifying the control of the regional governments, completing the establishment of the supply chain management and communication systems, implementing a universal education program, and dealing with those who still feel entitled at the expense of others. Once this is done, your world will be ready to continue progressing on its own and eventually interact with other civilizations. We hope you recognize that.

"I do," said Green, "and please understand that I've always believed that what we were doing was for the greater good—the journey toward the end goal truly justified the means in this case, but, boy, it has been a tough haul for me."

Yes, we know how it's impacted you, so, as we were saying, here are some examples of the first steps, and the positive impacts of what we've achieved so far, what you've helped to achieve for the people of earth.

First, the environmental technology—the clean energy supply that has been introduced—was and is responsible for the continuing environmental recovery of your world. Second, we have achieved the advancement of technologies and the new infrastructure worldwide. Third, we have succeeded in the introduction of new social prototypes. And, fourth, we focused on local governments cleaning up and building new housing units in areas where there either were none or where, like in major cities around the world, the infrastructure was so decrepit people were living in crowded and unhealthy quarters. All this has started to lead to a new experience for many families, and has to continue, but we hope that people see the benefits and positive changes in their lives because of what is happening.

As well, Sydney, the new political, social, and economic order will, in time, solidify the premise that all people are equal, that they should have no worries about their basic needs, be safe, and therefore be able to achieve to their full potential—that all people deserve respect and to have their needs met. It's an ongoing progression of events, with the introduction of new technologies and social and economic models that layer one upon the other in order to become sustainable.

"I understand that and thank you. But, again, being your representative, feet on the ground, so to speak, has not been easy. Yes, we've made considerable progress, and the younger generations have started to adjust to a new way of thinking. But there have been, and I think still remain, significant challenges, especially among the religious and ethnic groups, and in resolving continuing social issues. Much of the general population are still confused and need direction."

You're right, but we're pleased with the progress that has been made so far, and that's why we're meeting here today, so we can pave the way for the final stages of your world's evolution. Sydney, it's time for you to meet with us and see who and what we are, how we live, and to prepare to take over. You see—and please understand, that once we implement the next phase of changes and they are firmly established—it will be time for us to leave and watch from a distance how you complete what we'll discuss with you. We'll leave one ship here to assist with the development of your world, and of course, we can return if necessary.

"What! I thought you said earlier that you weren't going to leave!" Green was surprised that they were changing their approach. "You're going to leave? When? Are we ready for you to leave? How do I deal with the current issues? What's next?" Green got up from his desk, walked to the centre of the office, and asked again, "How do we deal with all of the issues and the implementation of what's to come, without you for backup?"

Sydney, calm down. We haven't come this far and dedicated ourselves to helping your world just to leave you standing alone. First, we do have a few steps left to complete to smooth the way for you and others, so please realize that you won't be alone anymore in this endeavour.

Sydney, this is your world, not ours. We've helped to make changes, provided innovations in many areas, and the ships in each region have set up spaces on their ships, just like we have here for you, to do the training we just mentioned. We've been helping people use the new innovations and technologies, and we've been teaching individuals in many different areas, and soon it'll be up to all of you to continue to progress.

"Oh my, this is a shock, but I'll try to understand where you're coming from. I just hope we've advanced far enough to continue to mature, to move forward, and not fall back to where we were. You can't leave ... at least not yet!"

Well, we won't leave until you and others have stepped up and are ready. Sydney, you must realize that we've done this many times before coming to your world. We have experience, a plan to follow, and work as one unit. So, let's discuss the plan, the next steps, and we'll see what you think.

Green went and got himself another cup of tea and went to the fridge to see if there was anything to snack on. He suddenly noticed that there was a cake that he loved just waiting for him.

The visitors commented, as he took a piece. *We've heard that it's very popular from one of our ships and we know you like it.*

Green took the package and cut himself a generous piece, took his tea and cake, and went back to his chair at his desk and munched away as he waited for the visitors to continue.

"Oh my, this is so good. I think I can get addicted to it ... you may have to use the wave." Green heard laughter and smiled.

8
THE VISITORS OUTLINE THE REQUIREMENTS TO MOVE FORWARD

AS GREEN WAS ENJOYING HIS TEA AND CAKE, THE VISITORS BEGAN,

Sydney, before we continue, understand and accept that the primary goal in what we're doing is to partner with you, and many others, to prepare your world to enter a new era. An era within which there is nothing, nothing more important than the safety, health, education, and well-being of the general population. As such, all social and municipal organizations, as well as political, industrial, and manufacturing organizations in the supply chain systems, will prioritize the needs of, and be in the service of the people, under the leadership of the world government.

Green stopped drinking his tea and put the cup down. He stood up, put his hands on his desk, leaned forward, and in a very serious tone, he replied,

"I do understand!" He spoke emphatically, slowly, and clearly. "And I can't agree more with what you've just said. You just tell me what we have to do, and I, for one, and I am sure the others, will implement what has to be done in order for what you've just said to come true." Green sat back in his chair and waited for the visitors to start.

Thank you, Sydney ... First, we have to continue working with each regional government and the administrations, to build on the foundation of the last several years. We need to keep them organized and focused in order to continue building more housing, assist in the development of new technologies, especially in the area of energy, make all the borders within each region completely fluid, message the people to keep them informed and up to date, and continue infrastructure development. We require a global supply chain management (SCM) oversight organization to supervise the work and to report to the world government once it's established. The SCM team has, as one of its first tasks, to set up the initial communications protocols between the regions. We also need to start the implementation of the education protocols and future elections, to name a few objectives.

As well, to your previous point, Sydney, the next phase of development will finally eliminate attempts by remnants of the once-elite classes to reassert their control and their extravagant lifestyles, and the leftovers of the extreme groups

around the world will also be dealt with. In this next phase, we'll finally eliminate the power base being in the hands of people based on wealth and perceived entitlement, and will replace it with individuals in positions of management and control based on their education, training, experience, leadership, and merit. In order to establish this meritocracy, we also have to expand on accountability in government to meet all the needs of every family. And, Sydney, we're determined to work with you, and others, to achieve these goals in a just and fair manner for all regions.

"That seems like a natural evolution from where we are, but do you think we can do it? You've used your power to de-weaponize countries, to remove drug dealers, and to heal addictions. We don't have those powers, so what are we to do? For example, your ability to know what is going on everywhere in the world instantly with the communication systems between your ships, and their ability to track what is going on almost minute by minute? How can we emulate that?"

Sydney, we know that it'll be a challenge, but it's time, after we implement the plan, for your world to start standing on its own. Understand that humans on earth won't achieve anything that is sustainable unless you accept responsibility for your actions. But as we've said, you'll have our support to set it all in motion. Let's continue, and you'll see how everything fits into a pattern.

Before Green could say anything, the visitors continued, *Sydney, we've discovered that part of the uniqueness of your world is that people, everywhere, have dreams for a better life for themselves and their children. The innovations, the changes in technology, and the feeling of being safe, have started to influence people's mindsets, and now the realization that the visions of what could be may come true is setting in; therefore, to keep the momentum going, we have to implement systems to let those dreams become a reality. That was part of the potential we recognized, that when individuals don't have worries about their basic needs, they can achieve, and that there are intelligent and capable people all over the world, in all the regions, who will have the opportunity to shine. So, give people the freedom to succeed and the support to do so, and they will, and they'll be behind you all the way to the finish line.*

So, the second point comes back to your question about communication and how we know what is happening instantly. Sydney, we've been developing a communication system specifically designed for your world. The technology, as soon as people are prepared to accept it, is ready to be implemented so that every individual in all regions has the opportunity to communicate with those in government—and every person, every household, will have the technology to be up to date with what is going on and to make their voices heard. It's a communications technology that is used on many other worlds. Together, and before we go, we'll implement that technology, address the people, listen to them, give them a chance to respond to what they're experiencing, and have a tool to express their needs. Although we'll train individuals how to manage the systems, it's time for the people of earth to realize that their lives are in their hands—the future belongs to you.

"That's amazing. You know we had an American psychologist who thought that way, Abraham Maslow. He was known for creating Maslow's hierarchy of needs, a theory of stability in which the mental and physical health of individuals is grounded on fulfilling human needs, and when the day-to-day needs are fulfilled, it culminates in people being able to realize their goals. Again, it amazes me that we had that knowledge, but, typically, it remained as an academic and philosophical work, impacting a few but not making societal changes. Okay, that's great, but you do realize that we still have a significant number of people who remember what was, want it back, and their voices are loud. I am concerned that we have to deal with them."

Yes, and as we mentioned, this is a typical issue with such a transition and will be addressed in the discussions and broadcasts we organize in each region. As well, the new communications systems will give people a venue to express themselves. As the people in each region continue to experience the improvements in their lives, we feel they will stand up and not abide by any fringe interference in that progress. As well, the impact of the next generation coming into power, and the remnants of the previous generation growing older and passing on, will also help to diminish those issues. Sydney, it's all part of the process, and it takes time. What you've achieved in a decade is significant, but with the implementation of the advancements in the next couple of decades, your new world order will become how your world works.

So, let's look at the positive side of the baseline. The regional governments are established, the new energy systems are being implemented, we're very close to eliminating vehicles that use gasoline engines, and the next generation of travel is in the works. There have been many medical improvements so that the average lifespan of a person born in the last ten years will in all likelihood double. Think, Sydney. The SCM system has introduced the sharing of essential goods and services, we're ready to start implementing new communication systems, and more innovations are on the way. Not only that, but advanced technology and infrastructure innovations have been introduced, and we've started to work with a number of scientists in several different fields of study to develop even more new technologies. This all started with you, but we've been helping others step in so that the work continues unabated.

Sydney, you can feel secure that you're not alone in this endeavour anymore. There are many people coming forward to learn and help. With this election cycle the changes are just about at the point of being self-generating.

"Of course, you're right," replied Green. "So, what's next?"

That leads us to the third point: we have to help people accept that removing the barriers (borders) within and between the seven regions will promote the unification of all regions. At the same time the importance of retaining their culture and language, while learning about and talking to their neighbours, and to show that working together to resolve issues works. Part of that plan is to promote entertainment and sports competitions, to create new modern facilities, to continue to advance education and training, and to continue the development of infrastructure. As well, we'll help to create a system of transport devices in each region, where specific people, starting with experts in all fields of study, can be transported anywhere in the world as we have transported you, and we'll train scientists on how these devices work. This will be critical for the continued co-operation and sharing between the seven regions.

Fourth, in order to keep those in positions of responsibility accountable for their behaviour, we need to organize new elections as it's been just over five years since the last election. In this respect, there are three important points: one is that for this election, the only individuals eligible to stand for a position of responsibility, at any level, will have to come from the age group of people who are under fifty years old; two, to come back to your point about individuals being influenced by others trying to assert themselves, we'll be making the point that anyone running for office must provide evidence of their independence from any previous political or religious influence; and three, we will introduce other basic requirements that all candidates will have to achieve before running for office. Once the elections are done, we'll work with the new teams to start a process of sharing administrative people between regions.

Fifth, the elections every five years are part of the transition overlap from one generation to the next. As the youth get educated, especially in the new educational format we'll implement, and as they gain experience and maturity, those with leadership qualities will show themselves and become mentored. They then become eligible to move into positions of authority, starting at the municipal level and moving up the ladder as they prove themselves. After this election, branch offices representing the different regions will be set up in the other regional capitals, like the embassies of old, in order to facilitate and improve communications and travel, and to resolve issues that inevitably appear. Judging from the progress we've witnessed, it will take at least another decade, or more, before your world matures enough to begin the process required to make contact with other civilizations.

Sydney, we'll work with you, and others, on making sure the elections happen in an orderly fashion, that the regional offices are set up, that the new education and communication systems are in place and operational, and together we'll organize individual regional meetings to explain the next steps. These actions will ensure that you're not alone—that there is a team at work.

To facilitate all of this, it's time to establish the world government, which, after considerable thought, will be based at the United Nations Complex, as it is recognized globally. Sydney, we'll be there for you and the others and the world government officers at all times, even after we leave.

As you discussed, once the basic needs of all people are realized, once they feel safe in their environment, have a sense of belonging, of achievement, and realize that they can accomplish their goals in life, they'll flourish. There is another human philosopher that we referred to earlier in our discussion, Victor Frankl, who argued that humans are searching for meaning in their lives. This is also critical as it encourages people to reach out, to evaluate their circumstances, their surroundings, to challenge themselves, and how they fit in with others. When people start asking questions— "Why am I here? What is my role, my contribution to society? How do I achieve my goals?"—and they search for the answers and find they have support to do so, your world will be in a good position.

Well, Sydney, there is more to discuss, such as the SCM system, running an economy based on human capital, without the encumbrance of a currency based on money, and the details about setting up the merit-based system, but that's enough for now. Are you ready to meet with us, face to face?

Green could hear chuckling in the background and was curious that every time that was mentioned he would hear laughing. He took a deep breath and responded that he was ready.

Okay, we need to guide you to another location in our "home." Sydney, you're as ready as you will ever be. Just move to your office door, go out, and follow the hallway.

9

GREEN LEARNS ABOUT THE VISITORS

THROUGH THE YEARS, THE VISITORS HAD BEEN MAKING PROMISES to Green that soon they would meet with him, "Soon," they would say, "we'll meet face to face." He always heard laughter after they said that.

Although they weren't sure he was ready to actually meet them, it was time to take that chance to bring Green into their environment—to let him know who and what he was dealing with. By doing so, they hoped he would understand why they had to wait for the right time; it was primarily a matter of mutual trust, and of him being ready for the shock of his life. The visitors hoped that it would help to finally resolve his curiosity, that it would, in a way, explain their unlimited power and how they made things happen, and finally, that it would give him unquestionable confidence in their ability to accomplish what they said they would accomplish. It was a chance they were willing to take as they had never allowed a biological entity to enter their environment, ever.

Green turned and looked around. Suddenly, a door appeared, and he walked over to it. He stopped in front of the door, took a deep breath, opened it, and stepped out into a hallway. Normally, he would be transported directly into the office space or wherever he was going, and everything he needed would be provided for him there, so he had never seen the hallway, let alone a door. He was nervous, but the area was familiar to him as it mirrored the halls in his office building at the NASA Florida base. As he moved forward, he noticed a door appear about 20 feet in front of him.

His nerves were getting the better of him, so he paused, leaned against the wall as he did when he had to visit his director many years ago, and mustered all of his strength to continue. He approached and then stopped in front of the door, waited, and then reached out, touching it with the palm of his hand. He felt a vibration through the door, which reverberated throughout his body like touching an electrical circuit. He snapped his hand back, felt his heart beating in his chest, and his breathing became fast, short, and shallow.

Sydney, are you okay? Are you ready? Take a deep breath ... it'll calm you. You'll be okay.

"Yes, I'm ready, I think, but can you prepare me a little as to what I'll see? I felt a vibration and now hear a humming. Are you on the other side?"

Well, yes and no, we're here, but you won't see us at first. Okay, we'll go a little slower. Keep calm, Sydney. After all of this time working together, we wouldn't let anything bad happen to you. Let me explain a little about who, and what, we are. First, reach into your pocket and hold on to the small instrument for a few moments. It protected you during the past years, and we set it up especially for today. We have increased its capacity to protect you, and it will create an environment that will calm you.

"Yes, it's in my pocket. I have a hold of it."

Good, as well as calming you, we've made sure it's fully operational so it will protect you from the environment we live in, and we've added some extra faculty in the device that you'll need.

After hearing that, Green just stood there, heart pounding. Even his scientific mind and his desire to see the visitors couldn't protect him from his apprehension. He was having trouble staying in control, and yet the curiosity, the dreams of meeting aliens that he had experienced from his youth, and his visions of what aliens would look like overwhelmed him.

Don't be afraid. Listen carefully. After all this time, we wouldn't let anything happen to you. You are the first humanoid and the only biological form we have ever let in to be with us, to learn about us. This is not only a special time for you, but is unique for us as well, so, without further ado, let me explain what you'll experience and tell you something about us.

Sydney, we are the universe. We are one with the dark matter of the universe, and the dark energy that fuels us, and we are committed to and task ourselves with bringing and keeping balance in the universe. We exist in a multi-dimensional environment. The dark energy and dark matter your scientists are just discovering are us and our sustenance, and together they power us and our technology. As well, our being, our existence, is intertwined with the technology of this ship and with each other. Sydney, we are, for lack of a better definition, a form of being, an energy, that deals with sustaining ... no, maintaining is a better word, the balance in the universe. We are the caretakers—let us try to explain ...

While Green was standing there in front of the door, listening, he thought this was, of all possible places, the most unusual to learn about the universe, especially about the aliens being one with dark matter, and inter-dimensional travel, and how that is even possible. But his overwhelming need to continue, the idea that he was the first ever to be with the visitors, and how that was going to happen, scared, but intrigued him. The visitors continued.

Sydney, as an astronomer and an astrophysicist, we were pleased when we discovered you because we felt that you would understand, at the appropriate time, what we were about to do. It was your work that got our attention and ultimately made us appear and come to your world. Now, it's important, before you enter, for us to give you a perspective on your world's role in the universe. There have been so many ideas cast about that you are the centre of the universe, that you are unique, important. We will put all of that into perspective for you.

First, understand that you live and exist in a three-dimensional reality and touch on a basic understanding of time, and so there are many limitations in bringing you into our reality.

Sydney, through the centuries there has been a lot of work done, and theories presented by people such as Copernicus and his heliocentric model, Galileo, Kepler, and Tycho Brahe, of Newton, Einstein, Hubble, and in particular Fred Hoyle and his theory of stellar nucleosynthesis., These scientists have attempted to understand the origins and makeup of your world. Hoyle's theory that lighter atoms are transformed into heavier atoms within stars, and are then forced out into the universe when the star dies was brilliant. He argued that these heavy atoms form planets, water, and ultimately life on the planets, including biological forms on many worlds. Then there was the uniformity idea expressed in quantum physics, but it took Alan Guth and his inflation theory to explain the fluctuations in the universe. And now, Sydney, with the attempts to observe dark matter and dark energy, the research of quantum physicists, and so much more—such as Stephen Hawking and Leonard Mlodinow—all of this has resulted in the understanding that humanity on the little blue planet does not have any special status and is not the centre of the universe. You do not occupy a privileged position in the theme of things. You are simply part of it.

The visitors paused to give Green a chance to absorb what they were saying and be ready.

"I know most of this research as I've kept abreast of it while I was trying to determine if life existed beyond our planet. Tell me, please, was there a big bang? Is that theory correct?"

Well, yes and no. Sydney. There was a big bang. But not as your scientists think it happened. You see, in the multiple dimensions, there are other what you would call life forms. You know how your scientists are experimenting in trying to find and control dark energy by colliding electrons?

"Yes."

Well, in a similar but much larger and more complex experiment, that is what happened. You see, Sydney, in the different dimensions, we deal with levels of expansion and size—as you go through the dimensions, the complexity and size changes. So, when you get to the fifth, sixth and seventh dimensions, they are on a scale that makes your universe increasingly microscopic. So, that is what happened, there was an experiment in what you would call a lab, an explosion in a controlled space in the seventh dimension, and your universe was created—that was the "big bang," as you call it.

Sydney, again, this must seem crazy to you, but it happened and was so powerful it got out of control, and well, your universe was created, and that's why it is still expanding today.

"Oh my God, are you saying to me that our universe, and the billions of stars and planets and I assume life forms, are microscopic to these other beings in a different dimension? Are you saying that the energy—the power we see in the stars, the gravity produced by the planets—to this other dimension is like us looking through an electron microscope at small life forms like bacteria swimming around, or the cells in the blood, or our DNA?"

I am sorry, Sydney, but yes, that's a good analogy. It's really complicated, and as your world expands its knowledge, we should be able to explain more, but for now, let's get back on track ... please. You see, because of what we are, because of our ability to move through the dimensions, we were selected to watch over the expansion of this three-dimensional universe and make sure nothing happens that would affect the other dimensions—we have to contain the expansion, and make sure it remains stable.

"Okay, but I'm having trouble with the concept, the model, the explanation you just presented. You have to give me time to absorb all of this. It's so unbelievable."

We will, Sydney, but we have to get back on track now. There is life out there on other planets, and in many other galaxies, as you, and those after you, will discover. The point we're making here is that the creation of your world and the life on it is by the circumstance of cause and effect. It is evolutionary, not divine. To us, the guardians of the universe, your world in that larger scheme of things is like a flower, or a blade of grass, or a tree in a forest to you. Sydney, as we are responsible for sustaining a balance in the universe; we do that by bringing balance to the flowers, the grass, and the trees that are in the universe. And that is why we're here.

Now we want to see if a biological form such as yourself can understand our existence, our environment, and what we are. We haven't given this opportunity to anyone else, ever. You are the first.

Green just stood there, trying to understand, to cope with what he had just heard. When he regained his senses and was able to communicate, he said, "Thank you for that opportunity. I'll do my best. I have to say before I enter that in our discussions, our work together to make changes, I always thought it was because we were special, but what you've described is that we are like a broken spoke in a wheel, and you have to fix it to keep the vehicle on the road and working."

Well, I suppose that is fairly accurate. I am sorry how that makes you feel, but to be part of, and make a contribution to, and ultimately meet other civilizations in this dimension of space and time will be rewarding—and will keep the vehicle on the road, so to speak. And, Sydney, knowing that the people of your world will benefit from all of this must make you feel good.

"Alright, you make a good point. So when can I enter?"

Just a few more points to think about and keep in mind when you enter.

One, when you enter, your protective shield has to adjust to the environment. It will take a few minutes. You have to keep your eyes closed when you enter, and soon after, when your protective shield has adjusted to the environment, you'll be able to see us ... it will be a shock at first, but you will get used to it. It is through our makeup, our composition, and how we direct our energy that we can read the electrical impulses that exist in your nervous system, and this is, to simplify the process, how we can communicate with you.

Sydney, the technology, the darkness, the energy that is in our environment is what we are ... although we exist separate to the technology, we are part of it, our dark matter is what it is, and so we control and direct it by supplying the energy for it to operate. As well, the area you are going to enter is like a portal to several dimensions, like a door that we can open. Oh, Sydney, you'll have a lot of stories to tell.

Two, when you're ready, open the door and take a couple of steps straight ahead and close your eyes. As we have said, when you enter, your protective shield needs a moment to adjust to its new environment, and make the required adjustments in order to maintain an environment suitable to your needs, to sustain the space you are in, and to help you maintain balance and be safe.

Sydney, you're about to enter a weightless, multi-dimensional, and gravity-free environment. Once you enter, have a sense of balance, and have calmed down and feel safe, you can open your eyes and look around. You'll notice that you're suspended, floating, as if you're in space like when astronauts do a spacewalk. That is why your protective shield needed to adjust. You'll sense movement, but not see it. You'll look around and see mostly a very large dark space with some flickering lights in the distance. Sydney, where you are about to enter, will remind you of looking out at the sky at night during your youth, but in this case, you'll be there. As you acclimatize to the surroundings, you'll see sparks of light dancing in the area, and the space will feel like there is movement pulsating around you. Your protective shield will respond to the environment and keep you in position.

Finally, Sydney, you'll need to concentrate on your sense of balance, and when you feel ready, move forward a few steps, slowly and deliberately. It's the force field that protects you that will allow you that movement and protect your physical needs. The feeling of being suspended, of floating around, will be disorienting as you'll not have any solid objects to focus on as your three-dimensional perception requires. You'll not be able to determine where the space starts and where it ends, but once you adapt, you'll begin to see formations appear and then dissolve—Sydney, in your mind, those formations are us. Then, we'll know how you're adjusting, and once all of that has given you a sense of confidence and security in the environment, I will make myself as visible to you as possible. Are you ready?

"Are you serious?" asked Green. "You're multi-dimensional?" He touched the door again and felt the vibration. He was afraid, but his scientific curiosity, being told he was the first ever, and the fact of working with the visitors through the years gave him the trust he needed to enter. What he had heard them say took over, and he knew he had to continue. He stood just a foot away from the door, took a deep breath and then said, "Okay, I'm ready."

10

GREEN ENTERS AND MEETS THE VISITORS

COME IN, SYD. WE WELCOME YOU INTO OUR EXISTENCE.

Green reached for the handle and again felt a surge of vibration, but this time the force was making him a little dizzy. He opened the door, closed his eyes, and walked straight ahead, almost losing his balance going from the solid footing of the hallway (that he was able to feel) into the space beyond. As soon as he passed the door, he kept his eyes closed and took a couple of steps as directed. He felt as if he was floating, and he sensed that something was engulfing him and penetrating his whole being. Disoriented, he struggled with his balance. It brought back a memory of the one and only time he went scuba diving. He stretched out his arms, attempting to control and maintain his balance and then took another step, but he sensed that he wasn't walking, that it was the motion of trying to walk that moved him forward.

Sydney, the force field is controlling your environment and detected that you wanted to move forward and as such responded—you have entered a space that is accessible to seven dimensions. The force field is keeping you in the fourth dimension of space and time, and protecting you from slipping into other dimensions.

Green opened his eyes. He looked down and saw nothingness. He looked straight ahead and all around and just saw a dark open space that was endless in all directions. He thought he saw motion in the void, a ripple, like something blowing in the wind or a rock thrown onto water. Then he looked for the door, thinking he should just go back to his office, but the door was gone. He felt so alone and yet sensed a presence. He thought he was in space, but wondered how he was still breathing, still alive as he just floated around. There he was, alone, in the vastness of space, with no spacesuit protecting him, but he knew that there was a force field around him.

"Seven dimensions, this is beyond my understanding." He called out, "I don't understand what is happening. How can there be several dimensions and supposed endless space existing within the spaceship? How can I be floating around in this dark vastness and yet be within a spaceship? How am I still alive and functioning?"

Sydney, the force field is protecting you and keeping an environment suitable to your needs so you are safe. As well, it has created a space around you, like a bump in the road, that we avoid making contact with as we move through the dimensions, so you are able to remain where you are. You are safe, and nothing will harm you, so try and keep calm.

You are in an environment that sustains us. We'll explain more once you adapt and your physical readings return to as close to normal as possible. Sydney, just remember that you're absolutely safe. The force field around you is protecting you. Again, we wouldn't have spent all of the time we have working with you to cause you harm now. Try and relax. Breathe. I am coming to you. Give me a moment.

Green never expected what he was experiencing. Such vastness and seemingly empty space and so dark, and he struggled to understand what it meant when they said that they were multi-dimensional, that they were dark matter and in part dark energy. He looked, and suddenly he saw what he thought was a structure, and then the space filled with structures as far as he could see. They were all the same—rectangular in shape, seemingly smooth, with no windows or variations from one structure to another. They weren't large. They were like boxes about the size of a small car.

Then it happened. Green saw flashes of light in the distance, almost like small flashes of electricity, like a spark. The vision brought back a memory of when he was young and looking out at the myriad of stars in the sky, but in his youth, they were more like flickering lights. These lights were different, but the images were familiar to him. They were now flashing all around the space, and some, brighter than others, seemed closer to him, but he had no perception of or ability to determine distance—except for the flashes of light, the space seemed dark and endless.

Then Green noticed several of the structures that he could see more clearly seemed to be coming closer to him. From them, he saw a number of brighter flashes, like tiny bolts of lightning, but pulsating rhythmically and in what seemed to him to be a controlled motion. The rectangular structures were moving toward him and started circling around at a distance. Then as they got closer, the flashes, the bolts of energy, became clearer, more distinct, more powerful bright flashes, but controlled and pulsating. They were appearing and disappearing into the containers. As they took positions around him, Green was trying desperately to understand. *How could they exist? How do they sustain themselves?* He was speechless, in awe of what he was witnessing, but scared that something might happen.

Sydney, even with your scientific background, you're witnessing and experiencing an environment well beyond your three-dimensional capacity to understand—this must seem really strange to you. This is why we couldn't meet you sooner, face to face, so to speak.

Green heard laughter as he had many times before, but he was confused, trying to identify where it was coming from and was not amused as he tried to understand how he could even hear it. He felt so inadequate, like a kindergarten student trying to understand quantum physics.

I will make myself more visible to you in a few minutes, and I will appear in a shape you might recognize, but first, let me explain in more detail where you are. You've entered an interdimensional portal. As an astrophysicist, I'm sure you are aware of the attempts by your associates to explain, to understand, dark matter and dark energy, and I'm sure you've studied, to the best of your abilities and technology, black holes, and the mathematical theories of dimensions.

"Yes, I've read papers on the topics, but why do you mention that?"

Sydney, as you know, most of the mass of the universe is made up of dark matter. We have, for all time, used the substance, by what we call phasing, to let us travel through the universe without disruption. Your protective device is made of dark energy. Our rectangular containers are a form of dark energy and also power our, what you call ships. The dark matter is also us. When we combine with dark energy, we can travel through black holes, which are, in part, gateways to distant parts of this universe, allowing us to travel through time warps. As well, there are a few black holes located in specific regions of the universe that are gateways to other dimensions. As I just mentioned, your shield, which is protecting you right now, is composed of dark energy. The rectangular shapes you see protect us from being absorbed into other dimensions as we transition from one dimension to another ... they are also collectors that fuel us.

The world as you know it and experience has three dimensions of space—height, width, and depth—and one dimension of time. This, and gravity, is what you're accustomed to, what your perception understands, and what you experience every day. As well, the forces of gravity are an essential part of your existence and physical makeup. Now, as your scientists have tried to explain in the context of special relativity, time cannot be separated from the three dimensions of space because, in your experience, the observed rate at which time passes for an object depends on the object's velocity relative to the observer ... space and time are thus part of a fourth dimension.

But, Sydney, as you know, scientists and theorists have discussed the possibility that more dimensions exist beyond your three dimensions and time. According to your string theory, one of the leading models of physics and astrophysics of the last half century, the universe operates with many dimensions. This theory is on the right track, as there are other dimensions.

Remember when we first met and we transported you to our ship?

"Yes."

You were with us for several hours in earth time, but when we sent you back to your car, only five minutes in earth time had lapsed, and you were surprised. Remember that?

"Yes"

Well, that was because, within specific conditions, we can control what you call the space-time continuum. I know this is overwhelming for you so let me introduce myself to you in person, so to speak.

Again, there was some mild laughter in the background, and even Green had to crack a smile.

You seem to have calmed down, so here we go.

Now, look over your right shoulder ... I am coming to you, but I can only be in the form you will see for a few minutes so you can have a reference point that is familiar to you ...

Green turned his head and then moved his positioning so that he was facing in the direction over his right shoulder. One of the illuminations moved out from the others and started to approach him. Then the shape began to transform into something different. Green watched in amazement as he saw the form evolve. It was taking a shape that he seemed familiar with, almost human like, but it was pulsating, almost like the rhythm of a heartbeat. To Green the form was human like, but not, and it was semi-transparent with the lightning like flashes in rhythm within the pulsations.

As it came closer, he just saw a smooth exoskeleton that was changing shape as if vibrations were affecting it, like currents. When it got closer, it was definitely not a human shape. It seemed to be like a balloon being affected by its surroundings and constantly changing shape. The flashes inside the shell were pulsating rhythmically, but as the minutes passed, they became more rapid. To Green, they were like electrical impulses going throughout the shape.

"Is this you?" Green asked. "How do you breathe, or do you breathe, or hear, or eat, or see?"

Sydney, we do not eat, breathe, or have vision and hearing that you would understand. We are from a different dimension, and as I have tried to explain, we are not anything like a biological form. We are, to try to simplify the terminology, like an electromagnetic field. The flashes you see are like electric emanations. They are the us, and the shape you noticed is a protective layer of energy that we use, as I just explained.

The space you're in, our environment, contains access to seven dimensions, and that is why the visions you see come into view and disappear. We keep moving from dimension to dimension. Sorry, but I cannot sustain this form any longer, so I will revert to our current status and then continue.

With that, the vision disappeared, the rectangular shape returned, and then the lightning-like form went back to where it had emerged from—the rectangular "box."

"So, have I entered an area that is actually another dimension in a weightless, gravity-free environment, composed of dark matter and serviced by dark energy, and I'm being protected by the force field?"

Yes, that's close enough ...

"This I didn't expect. Do you have a name? Do you need any other type of energy to sustain yourself?"

We are visitors. We do not have individual names as we are one. As I've mentioned, we are energy. We are the bolts of energy you notice. Although we use dark energy, our technology is also fuelled by our energy, which is stored in the rectangular shapes you see. Things appear and fade away because there are several dimensions at work here. The movement from one dimension to another creates the energy that we store in the rectangular shapes you see, which creates the vibrations you feel. We're protected by the rectangular shapes, and those shapes are also how we are joined with each other. We are one system. When I communicate with you, all of the others are with us. And when you respond, you are talking to all of us. And that is why we need to communicate with you telepathically and why you've been taking the pills. We have also, through the pills, given you the ability to hear other people's thoughts, but that is only temporary. Do you have any other questions?

"I do, but I am getting dizzy, headachy, and disoriented. I think the shield might be starting to wear down, or something is going on, so perhaps I should go back, and perhaps we could continue later. Is that possible?"

Absolutely, your physical form is not strong enough to sustain being in this environment, even with the force field, so we'll send you back to your office on the ship. Then, once you recover, we can discuss the next steps and answer more questions that you may have about this space and us. Just one last thing to mention: because you exist in the three dimensions, our technology is specifically created so you can see it, and we can use it for our intervention.

With that, Green found himself back in his office, where he leaned against the wall just inside the door for a few minutes to recover his senses. When he felt ready and able, he went straight to the chair behind his desk, dropping into it, holding on to the arms, as he still felt dizzy and unbalanced. He looked over to where the door was, but it had disappeared.

He was trying to comprehend the immense significance of what he had just experienced, the powers of the visitors, how they communicated, and how they controlled and used their powers to do all of the things he had witnessed during the past several years. He tried to understand, but there were so many questions ... and this was certainly not what he had imagined, what he had dreamed about when he was thinking about meeting an alien race.

II
BACK TO REALITY - THE FIRST ACTIONS

IT TOOK ABOUT TWENTY MINUTES FOR GREEN TO GET OVER THE shock of what he had just experienced and start to feel normal. Then he tried to cope with and understand what had just happened. All he could think of, to visualize, was that the aliens were the bolts of energy, like lightning, and that they were able to move between dimensions and assume shapes that he was able to see. And he wondered, *How is it possible for a bolt of energy to communicate with us—to be our visitors?* The whole experience was so beyond what he had expected, the immensity of their powers and the idea that they were the "caretakers of the universe." He just sat there, lost in his thoughts, and thinking about so many other questions—*Are they the creators? Were they the ones responsible for the Big Bang?*

He knew he had to be ready for the visitors, and he would never "see" them in the same manner again. He loosened his tie, took it off and placed it on the desk before getting up to make himself some tea and have another piece of that wonderful cake, just to get back to reality, and to try to come to terms with, to cope with what he just experienced. He stood there, waiting for the kettle to boil.

After he made the tea and cut a piece of the cake, he went over to the table where he kept the original charts showing the discovery of the aliens' ship. He looked down at the dot that represented what became six ships, and he shook his head as he stood there, remembering the first time the visitors had contacted him. Taking a sip of the tea, he started to feel more in control and went back to the chair behind his desk—he took a bite of the cake, had some more tea, and he felt a little better.

Sydney, we'll come back to what you've just taken part in and answer your questions, but are you ready to have a discussion about the next steps? We're not sure if we'll be able to bring you back here, but we'll see if that is workable later on. I hope you now understand why we had to work through you these past years and couldn't make ourselves physically present.

"Yes, I understand academically, but I have no idea how to understand the science behind your existence. It's overwhelming trying to comprehend how you function in multiple dimensions and are able to do what you do. And your explanation of how we came into existence—the big bang—well, that's just beyond being believable. Was that you? Nonetheless, having experienced the space where you live, and actually, well, sort of 'seeing' you, raises so many questions, so I am anxious to further that discussion after I've had some time to try to absorb what I've experienced and heard. Just one question, though: if you can travel using interdimensional means and can control time, why were we able to track your approach to earth?"

We did that to give you the time you needed to adjust. We knew that because you existed in three dimensions you would need to have a physical representation to track, and to deal with the idea of extraterrestrials coming to earth. It's that simple. Doing so also gave us a lot of additional information about your world and how it operates. And by doing so it also gave us the capacity to adjust the time distortion in order to research your history, go over our past exposure to your world through our probes, and create our initial plan.

"I think I get it, and I must say that now I understand and appreciate your rationale for working through me. Actually, I've learned so much from the experience, oh, and yes, I'm ready." Green pulled himself closer to the desk and sat up straight, "I'm ready," he repeated as he took the last sip of his tea and finished the cake. "Okay, I'm ready. All of this is really beyond my comprehension, so if we can focus on the circumstances here on earth and develop the plan in three dimensions," Green heard some laughter, "that would be better, and it would help me calm down."

Good, here we go. The first thing we have to do is to deal with the people you've said are speaking out, causing issues, and trying to go back to what was. Sydney, we mean them no harm, but we've followed them during the past several years and have found that they have something in common. They're all egocentric, condescending to others, feel entitled, are power hungry, and greedy, all of them, everywhere, the same.

They have no empathy for others and will do anything to regain their previous status in life. But, Sydney, it's primarily the older ones, those over 50 years, who believe so strongly in what was, that it was the right way for society, and therefore they argue that your world must return to the way it was. This attitude is so antithetical to what we're working to establish in order to prepare your world for the future.

They paused just for a minute, then continued. *Therefore ... the first step ... is that we have to go region by region, gathering these groups together one region at a time and discuss their options with them. We'll give special attention to the younger ones in their midst. We'll study the responses of the group before taking any action. As you know, they can't hide their true feelings and thoughts from us, and we would much rather that they become part of the solution rather than fight it, but we'll see how that goes.*

"What will you say to them ... well, I mean, what will I say to them?"

Okay, so what we're proposing is that we'll gather the players as we go to each of the regions. As you talk with them, we'll be evaluating how they respond. We don't want to send those who are resisting and extreme in their responses to another planet. Enough of that. What we want to do is establish a community in each region where we can send them and treat them with respect and dignity while they live out their lives together with like-minded people, but separated from the general population. They'll have access to everything everyone else enjoys, and, hopefully, they'll see the benefits and change their mindset as they interact with each other—we'll see.

Green interrupted. "So, we'll go to each region separately, and you'll bring together the people who are causing issues. Then we'll explain what has happened and what is planned, and tell them that they can have a positive role in supporting the changes as they occur, for the benefit of others. And then I'll ask them for their co-operation. Am I correct so far?"

Well, for the most part, yes.

"Then you'll be watching the reaction of the group, and those that are obstinate, disbelieving, and determined to keep acting as they have will be sent to that community. Correct? Oh, have you established the community in each region already?"

Yes, and, as well, we've discovered that there are a number of people who were in the inner circle of the way things used to be who have been quietly working to influence others who are younger and prone to suggestion. So, those influencers are the ones we need to send away and any youth who have bought into their stories. But the rest can go back and join their families. It's like the young boys who were forced into the military in the Middle East. Remember when you freed them from that negative and forced behaviour? They ran back to their families, apologized, asked for forgiveness, and then re-acclimated within their families and communities and became active in supporting the activities of the moderates.

"I do remember. It seems to be our pattern that so many of us, under the stress of threats and the pressure, just go with what is happening and not stand up and make our voices heard when we see something that isn't right."

But it's the same age disparity at play that we're dealing with. It's the older group that's trying to assert their influence on the younger generation, similar to what you've just mentioned, and they're causing issues.

And on another level, in dealing with the remnants of the religious factions, with fundamentalist ideology, Sydney, we're afraid you have to be stronger. Throughout your history, religion has been the root of many conflicts, wars, prejudice, and even the justification for things like slavery. It's been used to control the masses and impose segregation and class structures, and even to try and acclimate aboriginal cultures all over the globe. Sydney, religion has created a sad history for your world. You can't imagine our confusion when we reviewed your history, wondering how this could be, and then our disappointment, even disgust, at witnessing its continuation through the generations when we studied your current social tendencies and the existence of extreme groups.

So, you have to point out to this group that they're wrong in their conviction that their beliefs are the only way, that they are sanctioned by God to lead their "flocks," and that their actions toward secular individuals and those of other religions have been responsible, as they have, for unconscionable brutality, death, and starvation. You have to explain to them that their time is up, that their radicalism and intolerance are the problem, and it's their demeaning behaviour toward others that diminishes them. As we did in the US Congress, we'll monitor their thoughts and reactions, but we're afraid that many from this group will have to be sent to live with the others in the regional communities. The universal philosophy of religion to "Do unto others as you would have them do unto you" seems to have been lost by many believers.

"Okay, I just want to be clear. Once we've sent the older, more stubborn, and extreme groups in the regions to the 'communities,' the others will return to where they live. Oh, and the more stubborn element from the different groups will be sent to the same community in each region? Well, that should be an interesting mix if they can survive each other. Are we not doing to them just what they have done to others?"

Sydney, the areas they'll live in will be remote, but they're an open concept. They're not ghettos or concentration camps. And after a time, they can come and go as they please. They're not in jail—just in a remote area, and any contact with communities outside is strictly controlled. We hope that being together, having to live and deal with each other every day, will help them come to their senses. In the beginning, they'll be supplied and visited by government people, who are trained social workers and who'll listen to, engage with, and discuss their concerns. We'll watch how things progress.

"Well, I'm ready, so we can start whenever you're ready."

During the next few weeks, Green went to the seven regions and met with each of the groups. Once the more belligerent members tried to make themselves heard and to control the discussions by interrupting, yelling insults, and telling Green he would go to hell—they were sent away. The visitors probed the others that were left, and a few more had to be sent away as well. Then Green met with those who remained and explained that they were going back to their communities and he hoped they would become part of the community, be a positive influence, be helpful to others, and enjoy what was to come. He impressed on them the importance of everyone working together to prepare themselves to meet other civilizations. He also discussed and answered questions about where the others went and what was to happen to them. Once he was finished, they were sent back to their families.

All right, Sydney, the most difficult part is over. Now we can concentrate on starting the next steps of the plan, and if you can be patient, we'll try to arrange another in-person visit with us, or a time to answer your follow-up questions from your first visit. Then, once we've had the elections and have implemented the other parts of the plan, such as establishing the world governmental offices, we'll leave, following up with you often ... remember, Sydney, we're leaving one of our ships here to continue the training and to help you if you need it. As well, that ship will be your direct contact to us.

Green stood up and walked away from his desk concerned.

Sydney, there are many planets that operate successfully under what we're about to review with you. But before we start, please get the glass of water on the table and drink it all up.

Green went over to the table, drank the water, then he went and made himself another cup of tea, and got another piece of that wonderful cake he enjoyed, before returning to his chair at his desk. When he was settled in, the visitors began to explain.

Sydney, as you know, we've worked together during the past years to build the foundation for moving forward, and that foundation has been established, but it's not complete. Therefore, there are a number of actions that have to take place to build on that foundation, so we've developed the following objectives:

1. *The Blue World Government has to be established.*
2. *The universal education system that experts around the globe are working on has to be fully established and running smoothly in all seven regions.*
3. *The regional systems of communication and the SCM program have to be operating effectively and showing results. As well, communications with the world government have to be active, and in an ongoing dialogue with the regions to resolve issues as they arise.*
4. *The housing developments and infrastructure need to be close to completion, and people settled in to their new surroundings and comfortable with their lived experiences.*
5. *At least one more election, after the one we are about to have, has to happen for the changes to become self-fulfilling. By this time, the idea of electing people with leadership skills, experience, education, and proven management resumes will be well established and the idea of "promote from within" understood.*
6. *The individual identification, communication technology, has to be operational and all data receptors in place so that all people are treated equally in all sectors of life—such as education, healthcare, housing, food, and infrastructure systems—and meeting all the needs of individuals and families.*
7. *A series of regional broadcasts, using the new communication systems, has to be implemented, and used on an ongoing basis, to keep the general population up to date and sessions organized to make sure everyone knows how to use the system.*
8. *Money as the prevalent form of currency, of one's value, must finally be eliminated.*

The visitors continued by answering Green's questions, and they didn't stop until Green was confident with his role in the coming events.

One last thing, Sydney. We were thinking it would be good for you to visit a number of locations to see how things are going and get some feedback, to talk to real people, on the street, so to speak, and find out what they're thinking and what they would like to see happen next, and compare the results of the visits with our baseline analysis and projected plan. Remember, even after more than ten years, your world is still at the beginning, and there is a lot left to do to fulfill the objectives we just outlined. Also, keep in mind that as soon as the universal education protocols and the communication systems and procedures are fully established, we'll be able to identify potential leadership at an early stage in life. These two protocols will play a significant part in developing a true balance in society and equal opportunity for everyone, but this does take time.

"Thank you for the clarification, and what a great idea to visit areas to see what people think on how we're doing. I've been travelling from region to region implementing tasks, but not talking to the general populations and seeking input from them." This time Green went and opened a bottle of wine and filled a glass right to the brim. He then went to the fridge, took a piece of Swiss cheese, and went to sit in one of the chairs by the coffee table. He enjoyed some quiet time, thinking about actually going to each of the regions and talking to people.

12
PREPARING TO GET FEEDBACK

"I'M EXCITED," HE SAID, "TO SEE FIRST-HAND HOW THINGS ARE progressing." It was one thing, he thought, to speak with the visitors and hear what they understood was happening. It was a whole other matter to go to the different regions, talk to the elected leadership, and, most importantly, walk the streets and talk to the people—to hear what the people have to say. He imagined that getting first-hand experience would be quite another story, but hoped that what the visitors had discussed would be accurate.

He wanted his first trip to be a visit to his sister Joy, who by this time was in her last year of teaching before retiring. Green had returned to Whitehorse several times, keeping in touch with Joy, and had gotten superficial but exciting reports about what was happening. Now it was time to learn more, not only about the First Nations in Yukon, and Aboriginal groups in other regions around the world, but also how living conditions had changed during the past ten-plus years.

"I first want to go to a place where I know the results have been positive. I don't want to start with taking a chance of hearing and seeing issues. So, if I'm correct, I can form a reference of what the results of our work looks like from visiting Yukon, then I'll have some comparisons, perhaps some ideas for people, when I hear the problems." Green knew he would hear about some difficulties from the general population.

That's a good idea, Sydney, especially to get a picture from the people on the street of where we are, what they may recommend, and how that fits in with what we're planning to establish as we move forward—so let's get started. Remember that the Yukon is a microcosm and they're distant from the major populations, so it would have been easier for them to implement the changes—they're ahead of just about any other jurisdiction.

The visitors stopped and just observed Green for a few moments.

Wait, Sydney, are you okay? You look a little different.

"It's the wine. I don't really drink much, so one glass, especially this size," Green held up the glass, "does have an impact and makes me feel really good. I'm fine. It'll wear off soon. So, let's get organized." With that Green smiled, finished his glass of wine, then he picked up and ate the last of the cheese. He was enjoying feeling a little dizzy.

The visitors gave him some time to recover, then, together, they set out a preliminary visitation schedule and once that was done, they transported Green to the front entrance of Joy's house.

13

VISITING JOY AND THE YUKON

IT WAS A BEAUTIFUL SUNNY DAY IN WHITEHORSE ON A FRIDAY IN late May. Green walked around to the back of the house, enjoying the area that was surrounded by greenbelt. It was probably his most desirable place to be, so peaceful and yet so active with nature. Joy had created a small bird sanctuary with about a dozen bird feeders, and she even had a couple of birdbath fixtures that were quite elaborate with a circulating water flow like a small fountain. As Green approached the back deck, he enjoyed watching a few birds splashing in the water.

As he stood on the back deck, watching the different types of birds enjoying the feeders and the birdbaths, he was trying, not very successfully, to identify the different species. Then he saw squirrels and even thought he got a glimpse of a fox. It was exciting to see all of that activity, to hear the birds chirping, and see the squirrels jumping through the trees that were just starting to bloom. *Here is Mother Nature in her glory*, he thought, *the ultimate example of the power of regeneration, a new season. All will be well*, he concluded.

Then he went back to the front, feeling reassured, and waited in a chair that Joy kept in the covered area by the front door. Shortly after 4 p.m., Green heard the garage door open as a car pulled into the driveway. Green got up, waved to Joy, and headed to the garage to meet her. She was really excited to see him, jumped out of her car, ran up to Green, and gave him an extended hug and a kiss on his cheek.

"Oh my, the most famous person in the world is right here in front of me, and he's my brother, fancy that!" They both laughed. "Come on in, and I'll make you a tea, and I can really use a coffee. You know I'm about to retire at the end of this school year, Syd, and it's only three weeks away." She was obviously thrilled about her retirement and seeing Green. As they went into the house and got settled in the kitchen, Joy couldn't stop reminiscing about when Green suddenly appeared in Whitehorse all those years ago, and how after that event, her career as a teacher had been impacted and now, how that phase of her life was about to end.

"What are you planning to do?" asked Green.

"Well, I was thinking of moving to Florida to be with you." They both laughed. "No, I love Whitehorse. I love my house. I have so many friends here, so I'll stay, do some travelling, do some volunteering at the school, and visit my brother from time to time. And Syd, the changes in the Yukon have been amazing. I'm so proud to have been a small part of that. Well, enough about me, why are you here?"

"Well, I was just with the visitors, Joy. I actually met them. I was with them face to face." He smiled. "I was actually in their environment, which was unbelievable and nowhere near my expectations. Then we discussed the final steps in our development and in preparing us to meet with other civilizations."

"Wait ... You actually met the visitors? What did they look like? Tell me everything. This is so exciting ... I know you've dreamed of that your whole life, and now it's happened. Tell me, tell me."

"Joy, it wasn't what I expected or anywhere near what I dreamed it would be like. It's so complicated, but I will try to describe it later, okay?" a little disappointed Joy responded,

"I don't know if I can wait, that's not fair Syd, why can't you tell me now? Then why are you here?"

"I'm here because the visitors suggested, and I agreed wholeheartedly, that I should talk with people in different areas around the world to find out how people feel things are progressing, and what they've experienced over the past decade or so. You know, before we go forward are there any shortfalls, gaps, and most importantly if people have any ideas, suggestions, or needs going forward. This is important, to make sure all the regions are on the same page and to evaluate the level of achievement so far. I wanted to start here in the Yukon."

"Okay, I guess I can wait for dinner to hear about the aliens. Do you need me to do anything on the other matter?"

"I don't think so. First, I'll go to meet with the chief, whoever that is, and then I was hoping to try to meet with Elijah and Mary, if they're still around. You know, during those early days, I saw and heard them speak, but I never formally met them. Then, over the years, you spoke about them every once in a while, so I thought they would be perfect to talk to, as well as others, of course."

"Oh, they're still here, and as I think you know, they married. But did you know that they have two kids now?"

"No, you didn't tell me that." Green made a face at Joy.

"Sorry, they—"

Green interrupted her before she could continue. "Wait," he said, "it's wonderful they had kids, but don't tell me anymore as I want to meet them, if possible, and get their story, their impressions of what is happening with them, and their thoughts, so I can see the expressions on their faces."

"I think I can arrange that tomorrow; I'm sure they'll want to meet you, the most famous person in the world," replied Joy as they laughed.

With that, they went to get comfortable in the living room, smiling at the familiar surroundings as they entered. They talked for about an hour, getting caught up, and then made reservations at a restaurant Joy frequented. Joy went upstairs to her bedroom and got changed, and out they went.

When they arrived at the restaurant, they had to park about a block away. As they approached the restaurant, they noticed there was quite a commotion and that the media were outside of the main entrance.

"Well, I guess the restaurant let them know you're in town and coming for dinner," said Joy as she poked him.

The reporters blocked their way, and in expectation of some announcement, their cameras were flashing.

"Ladies and gentlemen of the media," started Green, "I am here as a follow-up just to visit my sister and to see how things are going. There is nothing new to report right now. Thank you." With that, they posed for some pictures before working their way past the media and entering the restaurant. They had a nice dinner, responded to people asking to take some selfies, and finally were able to leave.

The next morning, Joy contacted Elijah and Mary, who were thrilled to be able to meet with Green at their house later that day. Green borrowed Joy's car and drove into the village. He met with the new chief and council, who took him on a tour of the village. He was amazed at how well kept it was—what a difference from when he first visited. The landscaping at the entrance was full of trees, shrubs, and flowers, and there was signage giving directions to the different buildings and areas. As the tour continued, Green noticed how each house was landscaped like they were show homes.

When they returned to the chief's office, he got an update on how all levels of government and the communities in the territory were working together. The chief and council members had arranged for a light lunch, during which

Green expressed his congratulations and admiration for the wonderful results of their work. After the lunch, Green took his leave, and with instructions from the chief, headed out to meet with Elijah and Mary.

As Green pulled up to the house, he saw a child playing on the front lawn and who he assumed was Mary standing by watching, holding a baby. When she saw the car pull into the laneway, she asked her four-year-old son to go inside. Then she turned to greet Green, who had stepped out and was standing, waiting for her.

As she approached, he noticed how attractive she was. It was like she had just returned from being at a salon. Her demeanour and the confidence in the way she carried herself and held the baby fascinated Green, as he remembered when he had first seen her, which had left a very different image in his mind.

"Good afternoon, Dr. Green. It's a pleasure and an honour to meet you," said Mary, giving him a polite but friendly hug as she held tight to the baby.

"Thank you," replied Green, "and I'm pleased to finally meet you as well."

"Come in, please. Elijah is inside."

Green followed Mary into the house, where he saw Elijah waiting just inside the front door. Green was anxious to hear their story. He stopped and smiled, then reached out to shake Elijah's hand.

Elijah responded by pulling Green closer and giving him a hug.

"Oh my," said Elijah pausing for a moment. "Sorry, I was about to use a four-letter word." He paused again, just looking at Green, "Wow!" he yelled. "Dr. Sydney Green is in our house. I can hardly believe this. Please, before we sit down and chat, we must get a selfie, a picture of this. Let's go in the living room."

Green followed Mary into the living room and got settled on the sofa while she handed the baby to him to hold. Mary picked up their four-year-old son, positioning him on her lap, while Elijah set up the phone for the pictures. He then ran over, sitting beside Green, who was now in between Mary and Elijah, awkwardly holding the baby.

"Thank you," said Mary after the phone snapped their photo, getting up and taking the baby from Green. "I'll get the kids settled in and be back in a minute."

While Mary was doing that, Elijah asked Green, "Why are you here? Why do you want to talk to us?"

"Elijah, I never forgot your stories and how you and Mary responded to the actions of the visitors more than ten years ago. Oh my, and just look at the two of you now."

Elijah smiled politely as Green continued, "Although I've kept up a little with reports from my sister through the years, both myself and the visitors thought I should get first-hand information on how things are progressing. So here I am, and after chatting with the chief and council, this is my first stop. I'm travelling to all of the world's regions to follow up with people on what has happened and what individuals feel would be appropriate as we move forward. Because I was here in Yukon when the visitors arrived, I wanted to come here first and well, to be truthful, you two were the first who came to mind."

"So, what specifically is it you want to discuss?" As Elijah was asking this question, Mary came back into the room.

"What did I miss?" she asked, and Elijah responded, telling her what he and Green had discussed.

"Mary, Elijah, I just want to hear how things changed for you both and what you've done during the past ten years. Of course, I can see the kids, the house, and you both."

They all smiled as Elijah looked at Mary and asked her to begin. She positioned herself facing Green.

"Dr. Green—" she started, but was interrupted by Green.

"Please, just call me Sydney, or Syd, or Green."

"Okay, Sydney, as you know, as a young girl, I loved school and did really well until I was about thirteen years old when my life changed. I couldn't cope with what happened and turned to alcohol, drugs, and very bad behaviour to try to compensate for what I had lost—to cope with my feelings of guilt. Then, with the effects of the 'wave' that night, everything changed. During the immediate aftermath and the following days when the First Nation supported us, gave us a new look, new clothing, and a chance to renew our lives, I was overwhelmed, rejuvenated, and became determined to make something of myself. I felt young again, alive, and determined. I also met a new Elijah, a person that I didn't know existed before that day."

Mary leaned over and gave Elijah a kiss before continuing. "We went shopping together, and we became friends because we recognized that we both wanted the same thing—to help each other by returning to school and making something of ourselves. We both wanted to make a difference." Mary turned away as she became emotional and started to cry.

Elijah took her hand and kissed it, then gave her a hug while she calmed down. He stayed by her side.

"I'm sorry," she said as she gathered herself together. "It's just that the memory is so emotional, and the results of that week so impactful."

"I understand," replied Green. "We've all been through quite a big change in our lives. Please, are you okay to continue?"

"Yes." Mary stood up and started to walk around the room. "After those eventful days, I was determined to complete my high school equivalence, and Elijah, who already had his equivalence, decided to stay with me and do some extra courses to get back into learning. All of this took more than a year, and then we decided on two things: one, that we had to continue our education if we were to make a difference; and two, that we made a great team and couldn't be without each other. We just stood there one day, looking at each other, and realized that this must be what love is ... and so we got married."

The three of them laughed. "But this is an important point because until then, most of us in the community just thought about surviving each day and 'using,' because doing so, we would feel better and forget our circumstances for a while. The changes in those circumstances, in our lives, and the opportunity presented to us was the incentive, the intervention we needed. We just existed day to day before that, but now there was a feeling that we were in control of our future – that someone was there to help and support us.

"Just look around the village now and see its beauty, how everyone is looking after it; and I tell you, people are working together. We feel a part of a community, a responsibility to contribute—we've found meaning, a clear focus in our lives. All of this is indicative of your impact."

Elijah interrupted. "Do you want some tea or coffee?"

"I would love a cup of tea," responded Green, "Black tea with some sugar and milk please."

"Thanks Elijah, you know what I like."

Elijah went off to make tea for Green and Mary and some coffee for himself while Mary continued, "I decided to study education, with a minor in sociology. Elijah decided to study organizational management. I went on to get a master's degree in education, focusing on early childhood developmental incentives, and Elijah got a master's degree, studying the principles of ethical leadership. When we finished our studies, we came back here as I was pregnant with our first child, Max, and Elijah got a position with the Yukon government." Mary got up and gave Max, who had wondered into the room, a hug, smiled, and checked on Maddi before continuing.

"After a year on maternity leave, I went to work, helping to set up an early childhood education facility in the village, focusing on creating cognitive incentives for early childhood learning. I had some help and mentorship from Ms. Taller, Joy. Late last year, I got pregnant again and gave birth to our daughter Madison. We call her Maddi. Well, that's our story."

Just as Mary was finishing, Elijah came back with the tea and some pastries.

"While I was making our treats," Elijah said, "I heard most of what Mary was saying." He paused as he put down the tray and Mary and Green took their drinks. "I want to add something to the discussion." He sat down, took a drink of his coffee and started.

"In my position in the Yukon government, I've been able to participate in developing the principles of leadership, change management, and accountability at all levels. In this role, I've been fortunate to participate and assist with the continuing transformations taking place in the Yukon. While we were away studying at university, we returned during the summer months. The First Nation—in supporting training and the implementation of substantial renovations to housing, the development and upgrading of infrastructure, and considerable innovation in social renewal—worked to focus attention on participation, recognition, and cultural awareness." He paused for a moment to have some more coffee.

"As well, the territory's concentration on reversing the damage to the environment is impressive, while at the same time positioning the Yukon as a supplier of essential products from the mining sector such as gold, copper, and lead, to name a few. And our tourism sector is thriving. These past few years have improved the lifestyles of all of us. And the First Nations, well, what can I say, we've regained our culture and traditions. More of us are learning our language, regaining our pride in who we are, and our membership is thriving beyond all of our wildest dreams. Finally, the partnerships and communications that have been developed between the Yukon and the North American regional government have put us on the map. Sydney, the territory is flourishing, and people are involved in their families, their community, and beyond."

Mary interrupted Elijah. "I agree with everything that Elijah has just said, but I want to ask a question. I remember, in the beginning, you kept on talking about how the younger generation will be responsible for implementing the 'changes' and that they had to study hard and be ready."

"Yes, I remember that," replied Green. There was silence in the room for a few moments as the three of them seemed to be reflecting on what it was like in those days and that it seemed like ages ago.

"So, the question, Dr. Green," Mary said, "one that has bothered me for years, is that I have felt that we could have done all of this on our own. Why did it take an intervention from aliens—what was wrong with us?" She took a deep breath. "What do you think?"

"I have asked that question of the visitors many times as I've travelled throughout the world. The visitors explained to me that how we developed socially, politically, and economically—how our relative modern history evolved—moved us in a different direction. They explained that it all started with the age of the 'Enlightenment,' with its scientific discoveries, the Renaissance, then religious philosophical and social domination, and control. Then there was the greed that developed because of the Industrial Revolution and urbanization, which brought the rise of capitalism, nationalism, and the amassing of wealth and power in a small minority of society. All of this interfered with the normal evolution of society, and created class disparity." Green went on to explain. "The visitors said that our systems were so ingrained into our social structures, so weaved into who we were, that it would have taken decades to change ... and the will of the people."

"I agree," said Elijah. "I think it still would have been possible, but the need to preserve the power of negative leadership, the entitlement that produces, and the general acceptance of the state of affairs in the people generally, were standing in the way, we needed an intervention. And thank God it came!"

"I understand now, and I agree," responded Mary. "We were so embedded in the status quo as it developed, it would have taken a massive and co-ordinated effort, and we just weren't ready or able to do that. The coming of the aliens was momentous for all of us, and I just want to say that today the children are so different—Sydney, they're happy. All of the elements that held us back are gone, and what a difference that has made in giving us the power to make change. And I want to thank you—and I know that Ms. Taller, Joy, was very involved as well—I want to thank both of you for all of the work you've done. I am sure it hasn't been easy, but Dr. Green, look at us, our success, our family, and we're typical of our community, not unique."

"I totally agree!" said Elijah.

"I'm almost speechless, and that is very unusual," said Green, and everybody started to laugh. "This is just what I was hoping to hear. Thank you both ... what a way for me to start finding out what actually happened after the arrival of the visitors. I hope I hear more stories like this."

Green stayed a little longer with Elijah and Mary and tried to play with the kids. They took some more pictures, and then he took his leave and went back to be with Joy. He stayed a couple of more days, told Joy about his face-to-face meeting with the visitors as best he could and he heard more wonderful stories, from others, before returning to be with the visitors to set up his next meeting.

Sydney, remember that the Yukon is a microcosm and an example of what is to come, but it is not typical of the rest of the regions, so please be open-minded.

In response to Mary's question about your world resolving your own issues—Sydney, we were laughing at how naive that question was, and it really emphasized why you needed the intervention. To be honest with you, we have to say that if your world leaders were strong enough, responsible, and caring about others, and had a communication program in place, they could have been the intervention ... it didn't have to be us.

Sydney, the rest of your visits will help you understand the need for us to move quickly to the next level, implementing all that we have discussed. So, let's get back to it.

14

GREEN CONTINUES HIS TRAVELS

AFTER HIS EXPERIENCE IN THE YUKON AND LISTENING TO THE visitors' response, Green was anxious to visit large population centres in all the regions to see what the visitors were referring to. He knew there were still issues, so he wanted to visit cities that had problems with the inequality between the wealthy and the homeless. He also knew that all the regions, and the centres of population, had started to work to improve housing, infrastructure, and opportunities, but he needed to see what progress had been made and to what degree the changes had been implemented.

So, in preparation, the visitors took the time to show him archived files of the conditions in major cities when they arrived. They showed Green visions of communities that had areas in their city with issues. The conditions that people were experiencing in these communities were desperate and showed many similarities in most large cities all over the world. This had been the lived experience of millions and millions of people. Then the visitors showed Green visuals of the extravagance of the wealthy classes during the same time period, which in many cases were close to the homeless and the shanty towns and the slums. The contrast was unfathomable.

Then they asked Green ... *Sydney, think about it. How could these people, the powerful and wealthy, living in luxury and entitlement, even consider changing their lifestyle in order to work together to improve the conditions of those in need? Not a chance. You saw the greed, the entitlement, the resistance to giving up their privileged lifestyle. No, the only way was for us, with your help, and now many others, to intervene and bring change. So, are you ready to visit some of these cities, actually talk to people to see if there's been some progress in their lives, and find out what's happening? Are you open to hearing the recommendations they may have?*

"Yes," replied Green.

So, we'll start by sending you to New York City, then different areas in the Middle East, Africa, the Philippines, China, India, and other places from the schedule. After all of that, we'll talk, learn what you've discovered, and get to work.

"Please, and I hope we've made some progress." With that, Green visited two areas of New York City, the South Bronx and the most eastern part of the lower east side of Manhattan. In both areas, he saw some new structures but also considerable vacant land. He spent a bit of time in the Bronx area, where he saw a family in a park outside a new housing complex. He noticed the landscaping, and kids playing in the park area, which had swings, a skate park, a basketball court, and other sports activities. He also focused on a number of vacant properties. As he walked around the park, he was trying to calculate how many families lived in the new housing units.

Then he slowly approached the family sitting on one of the park benches. "Hi, my name is Dr. Sydney Green and I was wondering if we could have a chat?"

"Wait," replied the mom, "are you the one who has been working with the aliens all these years? Oh my God, you are! Bill, do you know who this is?"

"I do now," replied her husband, smiling.

"Well, yes, I am that person," answered Green. "I was wondering, if you don't mind, can we talk a bit? I just want to get an idea of what you think about what has happened in the past few years, and if you think there's been an improvement in your lives and those of the kids? As well, if you could honestly share your thoughts about what should happen as we move forward."

"Yes, of course," replied the woman. "How could we not? My name is Laura, and this is my partner, my husband, Bill."

Her husband stood and shook hands with Green. "So, what would you like to know?" Bill asked.

"Well, if you don't mind, could you explain your circumstances before the arrival of the aliens, how their arrival impacted your lives, then describe your circumstances today, and finally if you could share any thoughts you may have on what you would like to see as we move forward." Green paused to let all of that sink in as Bill returned to his seat.

"Oh my," said Laura. "Well, if you really want to know and have the time, we should gather up the kids and move over to that picnic table on the other side of the park so you can sit down."

With that, she called the kids while Bill packed up what they had and off they all went, with Green trailing behind. Laura made sure the kids were okay, explained what was happening, gave them a treat, and got them playing. Green was impressed with how co-operative the kids were. There was a food truck close by, and after checking with Bill and Green, Laura went over to get everyone tea, coffee, and a treat

Bill looked at Green and asked, "You're sure you want to hear this?"

"Absolutely," replied Green as he looked at Bill. "You and Laura could have an impact on what is going to happen as we move forward ... I really need to hear what you both think." He paused for a second, and then said, "please."

Bill looked at Green as Laura returned.

She noticed how serious they were. "Oh my, is everything alright?"

"Yes," replied Bill. "Dr. Green—"

Green interrupted Bill. "Please, just call me Green, or Sydney, or Syd."

"Okay, well, Syd," replied Bill, looking over to Laura to see if she wanted to start the discussion.

"No," replied Laura, taking a deep breath, "you have much more to say, so go ahead."

"Thanks." With that, Bill stood up and started to walk around the table, deep in thought, as both Green and Laura followed his movements.

Green sensed what he was about to share.

"I want to paint a picture for you as it was for me when I grew up. Syd, as a Black man, in this area of New York City, it was difficult. There was racism, guns, gangs, and poverty. Our schools were underfunded, and there were many other social issues, such as addictions." Bill stopped walking and sat down across from Green, and took a drink from his coffee before continuing.

"Somehow ... I managed to make it through school and graduate. Then I went to college to study and apprentice to become an electrician. I got my ticket, and I thought the world was mine, but I couldn't break out of this community. Nobody would hire me when they saw I was Black, and where I lived. They would set up an interview on the phone, but when I went to the other side of New York and showed up for the interview, nine times out of ten, they said, 'Thank you,' and I never heard back. A few times, I got a part-time position, but the others on the job, well, weren't very supportive, to say the least."

Bill stopped, took a breath to compose himself, had some coffee and took a bite from one of the donuts that Laura got from the food truck—he was obviously overcome with emotion and had to take a break.

Laura got up and came over to him, put her arm around Bill, whispered in his ear, and gave him a kiss.

"I'm so sorry to hear that," said Green, "please continue when you can."

Bill composed himself. "I couldn't understand what was going on, and it made me really angry. Although I didn't join any of the gangs, I did know them, and some of the members were friends. I even spent some time in jail for assault. That happened when I was with some friends at a bar and a white guy would say something stupid to me or one of my friends. That kind of bigotry, the racist remarks, I just couldn't ... I wouldn't back down from and usually it ended up in a fight, and even though I didn't start it, I was always blamed."

He took another drink, got up, and walked around the table. "One time when I just got out of jail, I saw Laura, who I had met while in college. She was so beautiful and such a good listener and so supportive. I opened up to her, and we started dating, mostly with her money, as I was broke."

Laura blushed, smiled, and gave Bill a kiss on the cheek.

"Thanks," responded Bill, then he continued. "After a couple of months dating, she introduced me to her dad, who, ironically, had a small construction company, and he needed an electrician—he hired me, and my life started to change. Laura was really special and was the office manager in her father's business. We were getting really close when the aliens, and you, came on the scene." Bill stopped walking around and sat down again.

Laura noticed that both men had both finished their drinks and that Green was deeply committed to what Bill was saying, so she went off to check on the kids and get some more tea and coffee.

Bill continued, "Syd, at first, we were frightened about what was going to happen. Then, as we watched the actions that were being implemented, like removing the guns from the streets, getting rid of the drug dealers and criminals, then helping people with addictions, and how that impacted our community, we started to pay attention. It was confusing at first, I must admit—I mean, it was unusual for us, being safe to walk the streets. Also, the political actions, such as getting rid of the political parties, was puzzling at first, but then after the broadcasts, it started to make sense." He smiled and paused for a moment. "Imagine voting for the right person for the right job?"

Both Bill and Green laughed.

"Then you had the nerve to remove interest rates on loans and with credit cards, you froze prices, took control of big businesses like the pharmaceuticals, the banks, and then, through your broadcasts, announced that you were implementing free education, and free medical coverage for everyone, and that all jobs would continue as they were as the changes were implemented. Generally speaking, we couldn't understand how all of that would be possible, but as time passed, we started to experience the impact, and it made a huge difference for all of us."

Bill paused again for a moment and stood up, and leaned against the table as he continued. "All of these things were great, but it took time and effort for the streets to start to change. There were still homeless people on the streets. There were no guns, but that didn't stop the violence in the rundown districts and the old infrastructure that was falling apart. The living conditions in the apartments got worse, if that was even possible, because the landlords did nothing, not knowing what was ahead for them, and blame and racism and abuse were rampant."

Green could see the strain on Bill's face. He paused when Laura brought back fresh coffee, and tea. He was obviously emotional and turned it over to Laura after explaining to her what he had discussed so far.

There was a short break as Bill took his coffee and sat beside Green so that he was looking at Laura across the table. As he got settled, he leaned in, watching as Laura was getting her thoughts together.

"Now the good part begins," he whispered into Green's ear as Laura started.

"Well, the most important part of the story, and what made things happen, was threefold: one was, as Bill already outlined, getting rid of the guns; two was getting rid of the gang leaders and the violent criminal elements like the drug dealers and gang leaders. Then somehow the recovery of people, getting rid of the addictions—people started to change, to calm down, to be positive about their future and to look for something to do. Three was when you addressed the Congress—that was the moment that I, and many others, felt that our hope for the future was realistic. It was amazing to see someone stand up to those in power, speak the truth, and hold those people, at all levels, responsible, accountable." Laura looked to Green and mouthed a thank you. "And you got rid of the president ..."

They had a good laugh before she continued.

"It was amazing to learn that most of the politicians that were standing in the way of progress, that were abusing their privilege, their power, their responsibility to the people, were also sent away. We didn't then and still don't understand what that meant and what actually happened to them, but it didn't ... doesn't matter. Then almost immediately after your national broadcast, our newly elected state officials, and those who were left from before and re-elected, came on the news and announced what they were working on."

Laura paused, looking over to the kids to make sure they were okay. "Dr. Green, oh sorry, Syd, it's just hard for me, knowing what you've done, to be so informal and use your first name ..."

Green acknowledged her respect, "I understand, Laura, but please, just say Syd, or Sydney, if you can. You see, what we're trying to do is to bring balance to our social structures, to respect each other, to acknowledge each other's contribution, but not to set someone over and above others as it used to be."

"Thank you," responded Laura, "so, after the new elections, we learned that the municipal priorities were to tear down old and dilapidated structures and replace them with new housing, to clean up and restore the areas of the city that had been ignored. Also, the new people in power said that they would also be creating parks and landscaping, and all of this activity would focus on creating training and providing jobs. It took a couple of years to get organized, and during that time, there was a lot of confusion and anxiety, but the new leaders, the management, pulled the people together and insisted that they be included in the design of the architecture, the community, and have majority input on final decision making of the facilities—it was amazing. As well as the cleanup and construction, we made some progress on upgrading our schools." Laura paused again to have some tea.

"Syd, it happened slowly, but my dad's business got to do a lot of the work in our part of the city. Also, Bill was able to become a certified journeyman electrician, and as such, he took a lot of young people under his wing and did a lot of training. His students loved him almost as much as I did. We got married six years ago, and as you've noticed, we have two children, a boy Justin, who is five, and a girl, Alestine, who is four. The housing development you see over there ..." Laura pointed to her left to a building that was six stories high, had a very large footprint, and some wonderful landscaping all around it. "My dad's company built that unit and has started another development just beside it."

She paused for a minute. "The main reason is that the huge construction companies were working overseas, in the other regions, and so the local smaller companies got the work here. It has 100 units in it, made up of two and three-bedroom apartments, underground parking, and all of the modern amenities, such as an indoor swimming pool, a fully equipped gym, and meeting rooms.

As well, we immediately built a preschool facility, as we were informed and got professional help from the committees that were established about developing schools. They were close to home, just a short walk through the park, with staff from our residents that got special training. We also organized an M&R committee, a landscaping committee, an IT committee, and an office to assist families as needed. We are a self-contained community and a model for other similar developments being proposed and designed. We've been asked to duplicate our model right over there on that bare land."

Laura stopped as she stood up, looking for the kids and calling them to come over to the park table. She introduced them to Green and asked if they could take a picture. She saw a friend walking by and called her over to meet Green and take some pictures. After that was done, she said, "We're running out of time as we have to get the kids home and prepare for supper." She invited Green, but he said he had to get back to the visitors.

"Is this enough?" asked Bill. "Or do you have more questions?"

"Thank you, if I'm reading you correctly, you've made some significant strides, the new housing with more in development, government officials that are supportive, but there is still more to do in organizing the communities and in the management and accountability of elected officials."

"Yes," replied Bill, "you know, when we experienced the changes in big business, such as the insurance industry, and we realized how much we had being paying to insure our apartment, our car, our life insurance, health insurance, and so on, and that we never actually made a claim, we were shocked! And now no one needs insurance, there are no interest rates on loans, and we have heard about changes in industry controlling the wages and benefits for CEOs and recognizing the importance of the managers and workers—one's contribution is what counts now. Syd, all of this is bringing balance to the working world. People want to go to work, to be recognized for their efforts... thank you for that."

"Yes," replied Laura, "but, Sydney, we also need to be clear with you that the social issues, like the remnants of the racism and entitlement of the privileged group, who are still living in luxury and feeling that they deserve more, must be a priority as you move forward. We don't yet share in the access to the benefits of that lifestyle. Although it's changing, it's slow to happen. It would be nice to completely get rid of money as a currency of one's value, and emphasize the importance of sharing, of caring for each other ... that would bring the rich and powerful to their knees, to understand what it has been like for us!"

Laura stopped as Bill was clapping and yelling, "YES!"

"We need to keep getting our kids improved school facilities," she said, "more highly educated and experienced teachers, and full access into all universities. We're better off now than we were, there is no doubt about that, but we don't yet have all the promised opportunities that you've talked about in your addresses to the nation."

"Understood," said Green. "Let me be clear that you and your children will benefit from everything that we'll be implementing in the next few years. You'll witness and benefit from the changes, such as in education, infrastructure, communication systems, technology, and your standard of living—sharing, developing effective and responsive dialogue, and participation in decision making. You and your kids will experience a whole new era. And you'll be able to watch your kids achieve their dreams—I promise you; the future is just around the corner. There is no turning back—you'll have your voices heard as we introduce a new innovative communications program, a revamped education system, and socio-economic programs."

Green stood up, went to Bill and then to Laura and gave them each a hug. "Thank you so much for your honesty," Green said, "and your story. What you've said we've heard loud and clear, and it will make a difference. We're about to implement some of the changes you've mentioned, and so I thank you for emphasizing the importance of fixing those issues. Thank you again, and thank you for your time today."

"It was an experience meeting you and being able to tell our story, thank you," said Bill.

"Absolutely, and I hope we've been helpful," said Laura as she went over and gave Green another hug. She whispered in his ear, "Thank you on behalf of our children. We're moving in the right direction," she repeated, "but just a little too slowly."

Then Bill finished, saying, "Dr. Green, there is more to do. From our perspective, we need to progress, and soon, and we're waiting to hear from you, and the aliens, what those instructions are, and we're anxious to get going."

"Yes, thank you, we got the message loud and clear, and really that was very important, so again, I thank you for that. Have a good evening, and as I just said, you'll see more good things happening as we move forward, and sooner than later." With that, Green stood, shook hands with Bill, waved goodbye to Laura and the kids, and disappeared.

Green visited several other areas in the US, such as the Southern states, which were known for their social disparities and racist laws. Green experienced similar responses in the other areas he visited. He also heard about, in more detail, the lack of communication, questions about the financial changes, and concerns that money still played an important role. Then he found himself back in his office on the ship.

Well, that was quite an eye-opener. People were honest and straightforward and made a lot of excellent points. They're anxious for things to happen. We think the new elections and the implementation of the new communication systems will help resolve some of the issues they raised. We have to make sure that the communication devices get provided and explained as soon as possible. Then the discussions we had with the specific groups and the establishment of the "communities" in each region will also help resolve part of the entitlement issue.

"I hope so," said Green. "We'll have to keep a close eye on that progress. One last thing that came out was that the general public were confused with what they should be doing and what they can do. It seems we've been concentrating on the technology side, the infrastructure and political side, more than focusing attention on informing the general population and keeping them up to date."

This is something we had considered early on. We thought the general broadcasts would be sufficient, but it seems we may have been wrong. Then again, Sydney, you were talking to people in the United States, so let's see how other areas are doing. The Yukon seems to be getting along just fine. But we have to admit that we got so involved with the political issues—in establishing the regional governments, developing infrastructure, and getting rid of the abusers—that we may have lost track of the concerns you've discovered. So, this is a really important exercise. Sydney, you should visit more regions and see what you find in those locations while we work out a proper response to this. Is that reasonable?

"I think so. You were right about the Yukon being a microcosm and not the norm. It'll be interesting to see what's going on in the other regions. I would like to visit Africa first. Then we can revisit the schedule to the Middle East, Asia, the European Union, and other areas as we proceed—that should be interesting."

Okay, Sydney, here you go ... but first a little background about Africa that most people don't know.

15
VISITING THE AFRICAN REGION

SYDNEY, AFRICA HAS FIFTY-TWO COUNTRIES, AND THERE ARE MORE than 1.1 billion people there. Our ship responsible for the region has divided it into three sectors: the twenty countries with a population base below 10 million, the twenty-five countries with a population between 11 million and 45 million, and the seven countries between 50 million and 200 million.

The visitors suggested that over a couple of weeks, or more if required, they send him on a tour of each of the three sectors, visiting and getting an overview of as many of the countries as possible. They also targeted the largest cities and the areas where they'd witnessed difficulties in implementation. They then suggested starting with the countries with less than 10 million people and working up from there.

This way, you can evaluate the progress. Of course, you should chat with people, perhaps in focus groups as well as individually, whatever you see that works best for an area. Are you ready to start?

"Yes, but can you set up an office space like this one on the ship responsible for the African region? That way, I can communicate with the visitors who are there and have first-hand knowledge of the region. Then they can transport me around."

With that request, Green found himself still in his office, but a strange voice greeted him.

Yes, we can, Sydney. He heard some laughing in the background. *But please understand that when you discuss something with us in your office, or if you are on any of our ships, you are also talking to all of the ships and all of us at the same time. As we explained when you visited us, we're one, so welcome to the African region Dr. Green. We're pleased to host you.*

"Sorry, it's still something I'm working on trying to understand, but thank you. If you're agreeable, I would like to know your perceptions of the progress made in each of the three sectors you've established in the region. And then I would like to visit a few areas just to see, and hopefully talk to some of the people to get their feedback. Does that work for you?"

Absolutely. So, as we agreed, we'll start with the sector that has countries with a population base below 10M? And then we can go to the other sectors when you're ready.

"Thank you, let's get started."

Over the next few weeks, Green visited the three sectors identified by the visitors' spacecraft hovering over Africa. In the areas with a smaller population base, there were towns and villages rather than large cities, and it seemed that a lot had been accomplished. In the villages, new housing units had been constructed, power was supplied, treated fresh water was in place, basic septic sewage systems had been developed, and preschool systems were set up, as well as schools at the elementary and high school level. He noticed that the classrooms were full of both boys and girls. In many of these smaller areas, agriculture was the primary activity, followed by precious metal mining operations (e.g., gold and diamonds), which had new operating guidelines, eliminating child labour and implementing safety regulations.

The new SCM systems for goods and services provided the sector with more supplies than they had ever experienced. In general, there was a positive response to the changes in the focus groups that Green had arranged, but there were some concerns that needed to be addressed.

The concerns expressed were fourfold. First, the people were concerned that the changes in technology, infrastructure, and communications with other areas, will negatively impact their culture and language. Second, they needed to have a stronger voice and representation in the regional government so they could participate in the decision making for what is coming. Third, as the changes continued, they needed to have visitations from expertise in the government to help with the implementation, and prepare their people. Finally, they were also concerned about the impact of their youth travelling to other larger communities and cities for college and/or university. They worried that their children, having experienced other regions and after completing their post-secondary education, would not return to their communities. Green assured the representatives that he heard their concerns and would share them with the appropriate sources.

In the sector where the countries had a population base between 11 million and 45 million people, it was a little different. There was typically a large capital city and several other smaller cities. Undesirable elements still existed in these cities, such as religious/ethnic tribal bigotry, racism, abuse, and gangs that wandered through the countries, agitating against the changes. The visitors, through Green, acted immediately and targeted the troublemakers, the remnants of the radical groups, and removed them from the general populations to the community established for the African region. Then they organized general broadcasts to inform the people of what they had done and held meetings with the elected officials. Green discovered that these countries had the potential to be more successful, better organized, and have safer infrastructure in the mining sector, which was not implemented yet. They were also able to contribute to other regions, but SCM had not yet been effective, so they were not contributing equitably.

What Green discovered was that when the visitors had arrived and he'd gone throughout the African region eliminating the Boko Haram and other religious zealots, freeing children who'd been forced to join rebel groups, the women who had been kidnapped and held to be sold into servitude, that the general population celebrated, but lacked the capacity to implement and make the required social and foundational changes. He also found that the elections were still influenced by the remnants of the elite, religious zealots, and gangs.

It was a slow process, as the alien ship had to continue eliminating many of the leaders of the resurging radical and tribal groups, and keep working with the new local government to control those groups' remnants to get a semblance of peace and security. It would take more time to show the people they were safe. Then, after the visitors worked with Green and instructed the local and regional governments, they promised to start having them organize projects: cleaning up cities, empowering individuals to participate, and developing housing, infrastructure, schools, hospitals, and other essential items that had been overlooked. They told the leaders to begin to make the lives of the people in their general populations, better.

In the focus groups for this region, Green made sure he had representatives from both the rural communities and the cities. He heard different stories, but the baseline was that they needed to see more progress being made. When he asked what they hoped for in the future, everyone said that they wanted to see results more quickly, more support, security, peace, active communication, and participation.

Green wanted to pause for a day or so to contemplate what he was hearing from the two sectors he had visited before going to the third sector, which had the major populations such as Nigeria, with over 200M people, and South Africa not far behind.

Back in his office on the ship responsible for Africa, Green made himself a cup of tea before discussing the situation with the visitors.

"So, what do you think?" he asked

What you've heard parallels what we've reported to our mother ship. Because of the rural and the tribal nature in these two sectors, we knew it would be more challenging, primarily because of the historical lack of education and the subsequent lack of capacity among the people. There was also significant distrust of outsiders. The traditions, culture, and the historical role of women are other factors affecting how long it will take for people to accept change. Education is also a key to making a difference, and the fact that we've built schools, upgraded schools, and brought teachers from other regions is having an impact, but it's slower than in other areas because of the concerns you've heard. Finally, our plan to provide technology—like computers and laptops, and do training on how to use the technology, especially with kids in school—is slow in being executed because even the kids had not been exposed to any technology, especially computers.

"All right, you have plans, but do you have the right people to deal with this situation? People who are trained to handle the gap in dealing with technology, who can work with the people to implement the plans? I remember being told that you'll be leaving soon?"

Actually, we're doing the training as we speak. We're developing people who can respond to and deal with the locals on these issues. As well, much of the training is being done on-site by experts we have transferred from other, more advanced regions. The next election will be instrumental in finding the right local youth to assume leadership, and work with the elders in the communities.

"It's reassuring to hear that you've got the procedures in place. Change takes time to permeate the old social structures, but these areas are unique and require added attention.

"Well, I think I'm as ready as I will be to visit Nigeria. I remember that it was the seat of the Boko Haram, as well as extreme Islamic and Muslim radicals in the north of the country."

Sydney, it will happen. In certain areas, such as Africa and the Middle East, where the social paradigms are so deeply ingrained, we all have to be patient. That is why it takes longer in some areas. Reliance on the new generations that will grow

GREEN'S DISCOVERY 2: CREATING A FAIR AND JUST SOCIETY | 87

up in a new environment that is supportive to their well-being, and their ambitions, is important. As you know, the younger generations are the key to the future.

So, Sydney, after you dismantled the religious extremists in Northeast Nigeria, Northern Cameroon, Niger, Chad, Mali, and other areas, such as Egypt, we looked after the remnants that started to show up and tried to re-organize in the months that followed.

You see, Sydney, when people have nothing, when they have to rely on those in power for their sustenance, their lives, and the safety of their children and families, they look to find something that gives them a rationale to follow. That is what the extremists thrive on. So, in removing the extreme elements in the region, and indeed in the world, we had to respond to the need to be part of something—we needed to replace what they had with the knowledge that now they're safe, and are able achieve their goals. We had to provide a new lived experience for people and their families—to have meaning in their lives.

It's just a slower movement than in other regions. Now, go see what life is like now.

"All right, I'm ready to go to Nigeria and then South Africa and Egypt."

Green found himself in Abuja, the current capital of Nigeria. He also visited Lagos, which historically had a reputation as being one of the most dangerous cities in the world, and the northern regions of Nigeria, which were the base for the radical Muslim groups.

Abuja was a beautiful city in a picturesque area of the country. The people there were mostly government workers, with support services provided by businesses. It was peaceful.

When Green set up a focus group, the participants discussed how hard it was, in the beginning, to let people know that they were safe, to conduct elections, to clean up the slum areas, to get the schools up and running with both boys and girls welcome, and to construct new housing and infrastructure. They were proud of the advancements they'd made and were looking forward to what was to come.

Green, listening to their thoughts, sensed the pride of accomplishment and the gratitude for the support. They said that it had taken several years, but once the people saw and trusted what was happening, and realized they could travel to visit family without fear, they slowly but surely came on side.

South Africa, however, was a different story because of latent racism and fear. Apartheid had ended decades before, but it didn't disappear. Since that time, the country had experienced constant emigration in the white communities. The relationship between the Black and white communities didn't change even as the Black majority took power in government. There were problems; the slums and horrible living conditions remained. When the visitors arrived, the legacy of Nelson Mandela had come into question, the economy was in decline, and areas of the country were dangerous with gangs, poverty, and friction between the races.

When Green arrived in South Africa, in Cape Town, he sensed that there was tension in the air. He was cautioned not to go into the Cape Flats area or the city's poor areas. Concerned, he reached into his pocket to make sure his force field was still there and operative.

He walked through the downtown area of the city and saw a clean business section, high-rise buildings, and people walking around, mostly white. It looked like any city in the US. Then he went to the suburbs and noticed that the white areas were clean, had well-kept lawns, flowers, and tree-lined streets. The opposite was true for the Black suburbs. They were unkept, dirty, very few front areas had lawns with grass, there were very few trees, and garbage was strewn along the sides and fronts of the houses.

Then he visited Cape Flats. It was frightening, and he witnessed abysmal living conditions—no running water, no sewage facilities, and no other infrastructure such as roads or garbage collection had been built. The homes he saw were shacks. He was shocked and outraged that with the history of the area, nothing had happened—no cleanup, no infrastructure, no housing!

Green wandered about and asked a few people to join him for a coffee and have a talk. The people he approached were hesitant even to greet him, but the few who did agree suggested a place to meet. A crowd followed him as he walked about the area—again, he reached into his pocket. When Green approached the agreed-upon location, he noticed there was a large group waiting for him. He was concerned, but two people came forward to greet him, shook his hand, and smiled.

"Welcome, Dr. Green. We recognized you wandering about the city earlier this afternoon, so we wanted to have a representative group to talk to you. Please follow us into this building. We have some coffee ready, and the kettle is boiling for tea as we heard you are addicted to it." The group laughed. "We also have some treats."

"Thank you," said Green as he reached into his pocket and calmed down. There was an open space inside with a table on a riser and chairs set for the three of them at the table. Once they got settled, the two men who had greeted Green sat at the table and pointed to the chair in the middle for Green. The two men stood up, introduced themselves to Green, and then one asked, "Why are you here?"

Green didn't know how to address the group, but he explained, "I'm visiting areas to see what progress has been made."

There was rumbling among the crowd, fists were thrown in the air, and people yelled, "What about us?"

At that point, the two men calmed the crowd down and asked members of the audience to discuss their experiences since the arrival of the alien ships and the general broadcasts.

Green listened carefully as one after another got up and told horrific stories. He listened for more than an hour before the two men stopped the discussion. After they were finished, Green stood up, lowered his head, covered his face, and then moved closer to the crowd and responded.

"First, let me say that I am outraged at what I have just heard. I am so sorry you've experienced such a difficult time and that literally nothing has happened here."

He raised his voice. "I promise you ..." He paused for a moment as he looked around the assembly and then faced the two men. "I promise you that I will make this area a top priority as soon as I leave, and changes will happen immediately. I promise you that you will see a difference, and quickly. The visitors have been listening to your comments, and I will make sure that the issues, the treatment you've experienced, the horrible conditions I have witnessed here today will be fixed."

He paused for a moment and sensed disbelief among the people, so he repeated his promise.

"I promise you that you will see changes, and in the next few days, there will be meetings." He paused again. "I have to visit other regions in the next two weeks, but I will discuss your circumstances with our visitors as soon as I get back to the spaceship this evening and will follow up in the next week or so."

Green walked off the stage area and stood before the front row of people. He approached each one reassuring them, and shook hands. A few of the women in the group shook his hand and then gave him a hug. He then walked among the group as they got up and approached him. He apologized to each and every one before going back to the raised area.

"Again, I'm so sorry for what you have experienced—it is not acceptable, and I repeat that it will change, and now. I have to go now to discuss what I've learned from you with our visitors, and to make arrangements for you to get the help you need to clean up the area, bring in food services, and get immediate help in the areas of housing, infrastructure, schools, education, and medical care, and to make sure you're in charge of it all. As in other areas, we will have a power shift to make sure these things happen!"

Everyone started clapping and cheering as Green moved off to the side, waved goodbye, pointed to the two men in a reassuring way, and disappeared.

16

BACK WITH THE VISITORS, TAKING A BREAK.

BACK IN HIS OFFICE ON THE SHIP, GREEN WAS SO UPSET WITH what he had just heard and witnessed, and he angrily voiced his opinion to the visitors, with obvious urgency to resolve the issue.

"How could this be he asked the visitors ... we must do something – NOW!" he walked around the office shaking his head and raising his arms in disbelief.

"You heard what they described. I don't know how this district of South Africa could have slipped through the cracks. How could we have missed such an important area, especially with their history? We had better get on it immediately. We have to get them what they need, bring in expertise from other regions, and start planning and talking to them, like tomorrow. Can you do it? As well, we must look at the other areas of South Africa and see if this is repeated anywhere else in the country." Green's tone wasn't asking as he stood in the middle of the room.

Okay, we'll focus on the country and see if this is repeated anywhere else. And yes, we'll get started tomorrow, plan to bring in the expertise to work with the residents, and start making the arrangements. Sydney, not to shift the blame, but we feel that this is a function of the continuing racial problems in that area, and well, we have to admit that no one, not even us, with all of our systems and tracking, is perfect. And we apologize for that!

"Understood, accepting responsibility is important. The people, however, need to see that something is happening, that their lives will improve. So, we had better set up a meeting right away, as we've done for the rest of the African region, with the white community represented as well, and during the meeting get rid of the people who are causing the problems. We've already set up the African 'community,' and we can send them there; otherwise, they'll interfere with the proposed developments. Some of the more extreme elements, and for sure they still exist, just have to go elsewhere—perhaps to other planets.

"Also, if there are other communities with similar issues—and with the history of South Africa, I'm sure there are—we should set up meetings, expose the racists, and deal with them in front of the residents of that area. Then we must include those affected areas in the planning to get them housing, infrastructure, schools, and everything else. We must bring South Africa in line with the rest of the region. I tell you again that we need to have a power shift." Green was furious. He knew this had to be done immediately to have any credibility, and set it all into motion before he went anywhere else.

The visitors, to their credit, surveyed the rest of the country and found three other areas that had the same issues, to varying degrees. The next day, in an open field in Cape Flats, the meeting was set up, and officials from Johannesburg, Durban, and Port Elizabeth were transported to the meeting. These cities remained divided and had issues with the implementation of the guidelines provided by the visitors at the regional meeting.

Many of the participants who were confronted for their racism had to be sent away to the "community" to join the other remnants of previous dominant groups in the African Region that were trying to influence others. Once that was done, the guidelines were reviewed again. The visitors, through Green, initiated the preparations and dialogue to have new elections run, with a racial balance at all management levels, and like in all other areas, anyone running for office had to be under fifty. The visitors met with Green, and together they determined it was necessary for this area to run the election before the rest of the world. They couldn't wait.

Expertise was brought in from other regions to organize and train the locals in preparation to run the elections in each affected area. During the next few weeks, the elections were organized, and the results were shared with the residents. Then meetings were held to organize and plan for developing the areas and bringing them into line with other jurisdictions in South Africa. Green advised everyone that the visitors would be paying particular attention, and that he would be following up on the progress being made.

Relieved, Green then continued his visits and ended his trip to Africa by going to Egypt. There he was pleased to see the results of their work. They had achieved considerable and impressive progress in all areas.

Before travelling to the Middle East, Green got an update on the situation in South Africa, which was positive. He was then transported back to his office on the main ship.

There the visitors noticed the strain he was experiencing. *Sydney, you look exhausted. Why not go back to your apartment, have some fun with your friends, rest, and we'll bring you back in a few days.*

Green really liked that idea and found himself back in his apartment. The first thing he did was to go to the room full of posters of the visions of what the aliens would look like. As he looked at each one, he started to laugh.

A few days later, a refreshed Green was contacted by the visitors and asked if he was ready to come back. Green was anxious to get back to work, thinking that if there were other hot spots like the one in South Africa, he had better find them as soon as possible.

Back on the ship, the visitors updated Green. *Welcome back, Sydney. Seems that you had a good time, especially at the party they held in your honour. Anyway, we'll give you a quick update on South Africa before discussing sending you to other regions.*

The visitors discussed the positive news from South Africa and then mentioned they would send Green to the Israeli Knesset, where they would bring all of the representatives from the region to discuss their progress. They reminded Green about the difficulties he'd experienced when he visited the region. This area was the most problematic to deal with because of the religious diversity, the abuses of the leadership, the ongoing conflicts, and the need to pull many of the countries out of medieval social and religious practices. Finally, they reminded Green that they had to send many, many people away, to demilitarize the area, and help the moderates take control. With that, Green found himself just outside of the Knesset. He was happy to be back in the area and just looked around at the historic sites of Jerusalem before entering the building.

17

GREEN IN THE MIDDLE EAST

WHEN HE DID ENTER, HE WAS SURPRISED BEING GREETED BY TWO guards. However, they were unarmed, very friendly, asked if they could take a couple of pictures with him, and casually had some small talk until their phones pinged.

"Dr. Green, please follow us." They took Green to the entrance of the main chambers, opened the door, and escorted him to the stage area at the front while the representatives stood up and gave him a standing ovation. As he walked up the few steps to the stage he received a very warm greeting by the Head representative of the Arab delegations, and the President of Israel. Both men shook hands, embraced him, and then the three of them raised their hands together to the cheers of the assembly. Then the President of Israel went to the podium, and got the attention of the assembly.

"Ladies and gentlemen," he began, "I know we were here just last week, so thank you for being understanding as the visitors have brought us back together. Dr. Green and our visitors have requested an update on how we're progressing as they consider if we're ready to implement the next stage in our development."

"So, if we may, Salman and I will give a general update about the regional government and how it's working. Then if we can hear from the delegates from each province as to how you're doing in the areas of education, training, the role of women, housing projects, infrastructure development, and anything else you may want to say, that would be great."

He paused for a moment. "Is everyone in favour? Does anyone have any questions or additions?"

Again, the men, standing side by side, waited a few moments. "Excellent," he said. "Hearing no objections, we'll start with an overview, and then, after a short break, we'll hear from each of you, in alphabetical order." The president then introduced Salman Abd Al-Rashid, the leader of the Arab delegation, who switched places with the president at the podium and began.

"Dr. Green, Nathaniel," he paused and took a deep breath, "As you know it wasn't easy at first, after so many years of conflict, to trust each other. But after the visitors, and Dr. Green of course, eliminated the extreme leaders, their militant followers and the weapons," both Salman and Green turned to each other and embraced - there was thunderous applause - then, after everyone calmed down Salman continued, "... we were able to slowly take control, meet, and got to work to make change. So, our first challenge was to get to know each other and learn to trust that our motivation to act was mutually beneficial. We had to learn to be patient, listen, and give each other a chance to express ourselves. Not only that, but we needed to bring that practice of listening and sharing with us when we went home. As well, because most of us were coming from the moderate opposition movements, our mindset was to be a little disruptive."

Salman had to stop as there was considerable laughter and applause, then, after everyone calmed down, he continued, "And so we had to develop our leadership and communication skills, both with each other and with our people. It actually took a few years to convert the people from the fear, apprehension, hatred, and misunderstanding of others in the region, to realize that they were safe, that they have become partners in change, and that their children will benefit from this new age."

Then he turned the podium over to the president, Nathaniel Levi, who took the mike and moved away from the podium before continuing.

"On top of the challenges," Nathaniel said, "our general populations in each of the countries were so used to military enforcement, to seeing guns and weapons on the streets, and to the pervasive radical religious preaching and hatred of others; that there was confusion and fear that something bad was about to happen, that there would be repercussions if they spoke out. So, we had to listen to the people, to give everyone a chance to be heard. It was slow going in those first stages and difficult to develop trust. But with your help, Dr. Green, and that of the visitors, it started to happen.

"And the children"—both men repeated "the children" — "one of our most important steps was to make sure our teachers stopped preaching hatred, as they were previously directed, and start to discuss and teach the value of our neighbours. We also began arranging field trips so our kids could experience other areas and people of the region, and learn that they were safe, and could enjoy themselves. This continues today, and they have been very helpful—no, not helpful; productive is the right word—in changing attitudes and bringing peace and co-operation to the region." The president paused again as there was resounding applause from the delegates—then he turned the mic back to Salman.

"Dr. Green, those early-stage meetings and broadcasts were very helpful, but we had issues to deal with, even though the visitors had eliminated the most serious and fanatical religious groups, the weapons, and the autocratic governments. We had to get control of the remnants of the religious fanaticism that remained in our respective countries, our resultant negative views of each other, and the role of women that had been rammed into our minds from childhood. The structure of family life, of equality, of opportunity, had to come into the twenty-first century." He paused as he moved back to the podium.

"The first elections were helpful, but it took several years of working together—showing people that they could be themselves, that they could hold their heads high, that they had no threats, or even worries about military intervention, or war, and that the militaries had been de-weaponized. A big part of that was the reunification of families. Then, when people started to see that we were partnering to build infrastructure, housing, schools, hospitals, rebuilding destroyed communities the attitudes started to change. They realized there were jobs and training, especially for women, and experts from other regions helping—that made the difference." Salman turned the mic back to Nathaniel.

"What started to develop was a sense of believing that something good was happening, and, therefore, there was a renewed desire to get to know more about our neighbours, to learn about others and to share. Then, after the second election, and with the kids in school and women in positions of power, communications developed, and the sense of unity in the whole region spread." There was applause, so he had to stop momentarily.

"Now, after ten years of commitment and dedication to task, and with the help of the visitors, we're working as one unit. We're together. After ten years, our borders are fluid; we move from one area to another, helping each other grow and prosper, building infrastructure, sharing expertise, and teaching our children about our cultures, about valuing all people, and about sharing what we have with other regions. After ten years of developing our friendship and support for each other, we're ready, Dr. Green, visitors, to go to the next level."

Nathaniel and Salman embraced and then raised their hands to a standing ovation and yells of support.

Then, one by one, each representative got up and discussed what they'd learned and achieved, and how their people were prospering and were now fulfilling their desires to participate—to have meaning and purpose in their lives. They also discussed that the exchange between regions—students from the Middle East being able to go to other regions to study at university, the active communications between the regions, and the products and services that were brought in through the SCM systems and communications—were all very supportive and contributed to the sustainability of the transformations in the region. It took several breaks through the day and into the early evening before the delegates were finished.

They had one last break and returned to their seats as they noticed Green approach the podium. Green waited for everyone to be seated.

"I never dreamed," he started, "that the Middle-East Region, with your history, would progress as you have ... my sincere congratulations. When I arrived, I must say I was nervous about what I might see and hear, but this is amazing. Thank you for all of your hard work and dedication. I am sure this region will have a lot to offer as we move forward."

Green paused as he looked around the room. He took a couple of steps away from the podium, then raised his hands in the air as if the team had scored a touchdown and yelled, "Yes!" An enthusiastic response to his comments accompanied him back to the podium. He took hold of the mic and walked to the centre of the stage.

"Just before coming here, I met with the visitors, and they shared with me the next steps for our world. The first stage, as you and the other regions will participate in, is to have another election. So those who remained as managers or have risen into new positions, and those who are new to the system, will have new work to do—new priorities and objectives as we move into this current phase of development."

Green dropped the mic and looked around the room, sensing the mood. "You have a big responsibility to make sure the amazing progress you've made is sustained and continues to evolve. The start for the Middle East in the first phase, which you've completed, was to get organized and to act as one. The visitors have expressed to me, and I agree 100%, how proud they are of the work you've accomplished. Congratulations."

With a big smile, Green pumped his hand into the air as he went back to the podium—there was enthusiastic applause. He replaced the mic and took hold of the podium with both hands as he leaned forward and repeated what he had said in the North American and African regions, and he would say as he visited other areas.

"Ladies and gentlemen, we're moving into the most exciting time in the history of our world. As you are now acting with one voice, so will we all be part of one world—the visitors call us the 'little blue world.' This is our continuing challenge—to become one world, speaking with one voice, with all of the seven regions contributing, partnering, sharing resources, and equally valuing all the people of earth."

With that Green, explained a little about what was to come, the priorities and objectives, and hinted at preparing their world for interstellar travel. He then discussed the establishment of the Blue World Government. He finished by once again congratulating the representatives as he moved back to the centre of the stage, thanked everyone for their attention, said he had to take his leave, then disappeared.

Green found himself back in his office on the visitors' main ship. He was briefed on the Eurasian and the Asian regions.

18

VISITING ASIAN AND EURASIAN COUNTRIES AND MEXICO

AFTER A RESTFUL WEEKEND IN HIS APARTMENT, GREEN WAS SET to go. He contacted the visitors and found himself back in his office on the main ship.

Sydney, before you go to these last few regions, we need you to know that when we arrived, and saw the disparity that existed globally, we investigated and found the ten most impoverished districts where millions upon millions of people were crammed into slums with up to triple the actual capacity of the areas. These hot zones had shacks that had been built over rooftops. People were crammed into fragile, substandard housing that was usually along rivers, near garbage dumps, along railroad tracks, under bridges, or beside industrial establishments. There was no or very little infrastructure, and the areas were very dangerous—full of criminals, gangs, drugs, and weapons.

Among many others we could mention we started with these ten areas: Khayelitsha in Cape Town (South Africa), Kibera in (Kenya), Dharavi in Mumbai (India), Neza (Mexico City), Orangi Town in Karachi (Pakistan), Conakry, (Guinea), Cite-Soleil, an area of Port au Prince, (Haiti), Tondo, Manila, (Philippines), Dharavi, (Mumbai) and Addis Ababa, (Ethiopia). The social and economic problems, the living conditions in these cities, were problematic to say the least, and we knew it would take time to resolve. But for your world to move forward the living conditions of the people in these cities, and the many others we identified, had to be fixed.

We found it sadly ironic that there was such attention, even in these areas, drawn to who the "richest," most powerful people were ... and the attention they were given when millions of people lived in squalor. So, as we continued to find the cities we just mentioned, and the state of the people living in those areas, we became determined to equalize the lived circumstances for the people. Of all of the progress we've made in the last ten years, the one that showed the real potential to impact your world as we moved forward was the reclaiming of these slum areas.

We now realize that the Cape Flats in South Africa didn't respond well. But bringing infrastructure, housing, schools, educational opportunities, and medical care, and making the others new and vibrant urban centres has produced results. Of course, we're now bringing the South African communities that we identified up-to-date and on side, thanks to your observations.

All right, here you go. The visitors reminded Green of what the areas looked like at the beginning of their investigations by showing him pictures and videos of the ten areas. Then, during the next two weeks, he was sent to all ten locations. To say he was impressed with what he saw happening would be quite an understatement.

Green talked with the leadership in each centre, and he met with his counterparts that the visitors had brought to the ship in their region to train and become their representatives. During the meetings Green had with his counterparts, they mentioned that there were still a few acceptance issues within the affluent groups in the other parts of the city, but generally speaking, the contributions being made by the new urban centres were recognized and appreciated by the majority of the people, and they were dealing with the entitlement issues. Green explained to the leadership in these areas that the next phase would end that issue by getting rid of money completely.

After his discussions in each community, Green realized there was a lot of catching up that had to happen, especially in education, training, and developing pride and sense of belonging in the communities he visited. When he went to some of the schools, he noticed that many of the teachers were from other regions and that the students in early education and elementary facilities were adapting much more quickly and showing confidence, pride, and commitment to their studies. Green would return to the ship and report on what he saw after each visit. Then, after all was said and done, he had a follow-up conversation with the visitors.

"Impressive. One can see the transformation from slum to community, from struggling to survive to having their basic needs being met, from degradation and bigotry to pride, confidence and having a voice. Congratulations ... what about the regions of South Africa that were overlooked? Have they completed the required actions? And what about the South American region?"

Thank you, Sydney. We know that there is more to do, but we are off to a good start in many parts of the world. The South American region parallels the achievements you saw in the North American region. We have other initiatives to work on now so we can pass on visiting the South American region. In the areas in South Africa that slipped through the cracks, we've implemented the same process, and they're starting to do well. It'll take time, but they'll catch up.

Sydney, did you know that in China, there were no slums to be found? China has been slum-free since the founding of the People's Republic of China decades ago. As well, there were no slums in the US and Canada. There were still poor people in these countries, and people living on the streets, but that's another issue.

Green was standing in his office looking at the charts and the dot that represented the aliens so many years ago. He had turned on the kettle. When the kettle started to whistle, he went over and made some tea, then sat in his favourite chair and slid closer to his desk. He leaned forward on his elbows with his hands clasped together, covering his mouth, and he closed his eyes.

Sydney, is something bothering you? You seem pensive and sad and are hiding your thoughts.

Green sat back, took a sip of his tea and then, strained and tired, he said, "The process seems to be developing smoothly and becoming self-generating, and you're attracting many other people to keep the work progressing. Are we at the point where it's time for me to stand down? To retire? You're incorporating many others to implement the changes going forward. Do you still need me?"

He sighed.

Sydney, how can you even think that? You're not retiring, unless that is your choice. From our perspective, we need your role to evolve, not end. We need others to step in and work on the daily issues for consistency and sustainability, which we're doing of necessity. You know that with the chapter we're entering, it'll take many people, and the support of the people in each region, for it to be successful. And because we'll only have one ship here, it's about time to start preparing to set up the Blue World Government. Sydney, that's where you come in. That's what we see in store for you, if you want it.

What we were hoping for, and planning to implement, is that while all of this work is proceeding, your task will be to get a 30 000-foot view of what's going on, and follow up with each of the regions to see how they're doing, and start developing the authority and influence of the Blue World Government.

Sydney, we need you to become the president and chair of this world government. Ultimately, once your world is ready, we hope you will be the person to start, to create the format, to engage in discussions and to make contact with other worlds. We thought you would have recognized that we need you now more than ever. Please, Sydney, you're more important for your world now than you know.

To give himself a chance to think about what he had just heard, Green said, "Of course, I know why you call it the blue world, because of the abundance of water, but why the Blue World Government, right here on earth?"

Sydney, there are many worlds and civilizations out there, but very few with as much water as you have here on your world. As you know, from a distance, it presents as a blue world. We have always called it the little blue world, and that's how it's known among other civilizations. So, down the road, when your world is ready, you, and each of the other representatives from the regions, will be introduced as representing the "Blue World Government," as that is what will distinguish you from other worlds. It just seems appropriate to call it here on earth the same as when you meet others.

Surprised, Green just looked straight ahead thinking about that ... and what he'd just heard.

After a few moments, he got up from his chair and leaned forward, putting his hands on the desk. He lowered his head and closed his eyes, remaining still for a moment. Then, taking a breath, he reached for his cup of tea and emptied the cup. He moved out from the desk, stood up straight, and took another deep breath, standing there in silence, contemplating everything that he had just heard. He was thinking about his legacy.

He started to walk around the room, and as he responded to the visitors, he moved with vigour and renewed energy. It was his dream to be there for first contact, to meet other civilizations, and so there was no choice for him.

"Okay," he started. "I'll be honoured to continue with my work as you see fit." He paused for a minute, smiled, and then continued, "But, in order to give this new position the status it deserves, I should move my office from Florida to the United Nations Building in New York. And it better be a nicer office ..."

Everyone, including Green, had a good laugh, then he got serious.

"If she is willing, I would like to have Joy come to work in the office with me, and we'll obviously need staff to help organize meetings, assuming you'll not be here."

Actually, that's a great idea, and to be honest, we've been working on that. As well, we'll work on making an announcement to all of the regions about your new role and that you'll begin the work to develop the Blue World Government and establish its role. And yes, we think Joy would be a wonderful addition. She proved her value with the work she did in Yukon. Would you like to visit Joy to talk to her about joining you?

"Yes, please," and with that, Green found himself at the front door to Joy's house. It was a Saturday, the middle of November, and late in the afternoon. Green rang the doorbell and waited. Soon after, the door opened, and Joy stood there, surprised, and just looked at Green.

19

GREEN TALKS TO JOY

"WOW, WHY ARE YOU HERE?" SHE ASKED.

"Can I come in? I have a question or two for you."

"Oh no, should I be afraid?" She just stood there, making Green wait outside.

"It's a little cold out here. Can I come in?" he asked again, and they laughed.

"Of course, I just can't believe you're here, come in … come in." Joy stepped out, gave Green a hug, and then they entered the house.

Joy led the way to the kitchen, put the kettle on, and just happened to have a coconut vanilla cake on the counter that she was about to enjoy. "Want a piece?" she asked.

"Of course, it looks great. It's my all-time favourite. I think I'm addicted to it." They both laughed, but then Joy got straight to the point.

"Okay, Syd, I know you're here for a reason. The last time you surprised me like this was more than ten years ago, and it changed my life. I know that you know I'm retired now, so what's up?" They both smiled, and then, before Green could respond, the kettle started to whistle.

Joy, smirking, turned to make Green some tea, herself a coffee, and cut two pieces of the cake before coming back to stand beside Green. Concerned about what he wanted she didn't sit down and just looked straight at him. A little nervous she took a sip of coffee, expecting a surprise … Green started to explain.

"Joy, first let me say that you look great … retirement seems to have been good for you."

"Thank you, to be honest, I've been having a great time, and I feel great."

"Wonderful, I'm so glad to see you. So, let me explain. I've just come from spending some time with the visitors, and I have travelled to many places around the world to see how we're progressing."

"Oh my, you have to tell me all about it! How are we doing? I know the Yukon is great!" Joy was excited to get an update about other regions of the world and calmed down.

"I will." Green paused and took a sip of his tea. "Let me explain a few things to you first. The visitors brought me up to date with their plans. We discussed where we are right now and then what we have to do to move forward, and that's why I'm here.

"Joy, they've been training many people around the world not only to keep the progress going, but to be prepared to implement the next phase of the plan. And they said they really like what's been achieved in the Yukon and have actually been replicating your successes in other regions."

"Fantastic, wait until I tell everyone." Responded Joy, obviously excited.

Green continued after having some cake and more tea. "When the next elections are completed, the new generation will really start to step up so the work can proceed, unimpeded, in completing our tasks to bring the world into the future. The visitors discussed the youth, explaining that as a new generation, they have different perceptions of the world than their parents and the older generation, and they're more adaptable and therefore have to lead the way as we implement new programs. Remember they had me say this the first time I was here at your school, that the future would be in the hands of the youth?"

Joy acknowledged what Green was talking about. "I do remember that. Through the years when I was teaching, I would see the kids at school focus on, understand, and appreciate new and different music, new technology, new ways to deal with each other, and even create new words to express their feelings. And we just shook our heads when we saw them dance, or heard the music they liked, or how they quickly adapted to the new technology like their cell phones, and caught on so easily to computers, new innovations, and how they interacted with each other."

"Exactly, Joy. There's so much to say about that, but one of the key priorities the visitors talked about I think you will like. It deals with education. The visitors brought together experts, academics from each region, in order to dialogue in establishing a universal education protocol that will be implemented. After more than a year, they have a draft proposal, and now there is going to be a type of 'peer review' of their work with classroom educators and management in each region."

Green stopped and took a sip of his tea and another bite of the cake. He sensed that Joy was happy to hear that education was a priority, but anxious as she knew he was there for a reason. "Oh, this is so good, thank you."

Joy was listening patiently, but she knew he was putting off the reason he was there, so she sat down while she had some coffee and gestured to Green.

"Okay, Syd. I know you're here for a reason, not just to visit, not just to update me. So, out with it. Where do I come in? Why are you here?"

Green took another drink from his tea and another piece of the cake, then he stood. "Joy, please be patient. I'm getting there."

"Okay, but don't take the whole night." Making a face, she said, "By the way, I knew about the education piece, and even helped Mary establish an early childhood program, before any of this started ... so what do you want from me? Tell me, and then Sydney, you owe me a nice dinner."

"Alright, well, here we go. Joy, there are a couple of things I have to share and a request to make. You see, I thought my work was done, that I'm not needed anymore, and that like you, I was to retire."

Green paused as he took the last sip of his tea before continuing, "But that wasn't the case. Quite the opposite!" he said emphatically. "Joy, the visitors told me that now we must set up, and organize, what they call the Blue World Government—"

Joy interrupted him. "Blue World Government?"

"Yes, blue because of the amount of water on the planet, and I'll explain more in a minute.

The visitors said that now we have to set up a world government headquarters to supervise the work being done in the regions. This world government will lead the regions in completing the priorities and objectives that are set out to get us to the next level. Each regional government will have one representative on the world government, who will be responsible for their region."

Green stopped, sipped on a fresh cup of tea that Joy handed him, finished his cake, and then continued.

"Thank you, Joy, that was really good ... anyway, the visitors want me to establish the offices at the United Nations Building that will ultimately become the seat of the Blue World Government."

Green paused, closed his eyes, took a deep breath, then he looked straight at Joy. "They want me to be the CEO, the chair, of this world government and when we're ready, to be the one to actually make contact with and represent our world to other civilizations."

"Oh my God," yelled Joy. "That's fantastic, congratulations!! I am so proud of you." She could hardly contain her excitement. She walked around the kitchen and then returned to Green, looking at him and taking hold of his shoulders. "I am so proud of you," she repeated. "I can't believe it. My brother, the kid I had to protect in school."

They both laughed.

'Sydney," she said with a determined tone, "this all sounds fantastic and all of that, and really I'm so happy for you, but why are you here? I know you want something from me."

Joy stood up and went to the other side of the counter and looked at Green. "Get to the point," she demanded.

"O.K," Green said, "there is something important that I would like you to take on."

"What?" Joy was surprised, assuming he was asking her to help him set up the new offices. "You want me to give up everything I have here, to move to New York to help with the world government? Oh my God, Sydney."

Joy walked away, relocating in the living room, and sat down on the sofa, then stood back up right away and started to pace.

Green followed her, slowly, to let what he had just said sink in. Then, before she had a chance to continue, he said, "No, Joy. Please, just listen. I'll have a team for setting up the offices, and representatives from each region to take part. But the two of us have made a great team in the past, and you've accomplished so much here in the Yukon, both working with the First Nations and with your teaching. And like I said, the visitors have used what was accomplished here, what you did, and how that all happened. Now I need you to help."

He went up to her and stopped her pacing by taking hold of her hands, and then he continued. "Joy, the real reason I'm here is because of the work currently being completed on the education plan." He paused just for a second. "I would like you to review the documents and respond with any changes, suggestions, or new ideas you may have. And to be part of the team working on the education piece. To be honest, with your background and expertise, that's the main reason I'm here, and well, to visit with you, of course. Would you do that?"

"That's it? Of course, I will because I can do that right here in Whitehorse ... Syd, enough for now. You have to take me out to dinner and be ready to be molested by people." With that Joy, went and made reservations and then went to freshen up.

By the time they arrived at the restaurant, just like the last time, there was a crowd waiting for them and the local media had set up. As Green went to the front of the crowd, they started to applaud. He called Joy to his side, addressed the group, telling them some of the plans they could expect. He answered their questions, and then said that he and Joy were hungry and had to go in before the restaurant gave away their reservations. The group laughed and started to disperse. A few people came up and requested to take a picture, which Green agreed to do.

Inside, Joy and Green had a nice meal and again greeted people as they asked for selfies and autographs. After dinner, they went home, chatted for a while, and then agreed that Green had to make breakfast in the morning.

The smell of freshly brewed coffee and bacon woke Joy up, and she worked her way to the kitchen, where Green was busy setting up the counter and finishing the breakfast.

"Good morning," started Joy, "I wasn't serious about you making breakfast, you know."

"It's my complete pleasure," responded Green. "The least I can do." And as he served breakfast Joy asked ...

"So, what are the next steps, other than the education piece?"

"Well, so far, as it's been explained to me," Green said, "we'll continue to develop the housing and infrastructure upgrades and construction, as that's a work in progress. We'll develop the universal education system that you'll be helping with, and at the same time, the visitors will continue to train people and introduce new technologies, such as communication systems and transport technologies for each region to share expertise.

"As well, and most important, is to set up and staff the world government offices. The world government leadership and staff from each region will work with local offices to keep the visitors' plans, our plans and priorities, on the right trajectory, to mentor and track the youth as they move into positions of leadership, and to work with the leadership from the other regions. This work will be ongoing well into the foreseeable future." They took a little break to finish breakfast, clean the dishes and put them away. Then Green continued ...

"To facilitate all of this, the world government offices and staff, once they're in place, and operating efficiently, will be available 24/7 to make sure everything goes smoothly." Green discussed several other priorities with Joy, such as some details about the communications system, more about the new governance and economic models, and he tried to explain more about his experience with the visitors.

"Well, it sounds good," Joy said. "We'll see how it evolves. So, you're going to go back to the United Nations Building to work to set up the offices for the world government?"

"Yes, I'll work with the visitors to set the offices up and get the spaces staffed after the elections. It would be great for you to visit once the offices are in place and I have an idea of how things will work. Then you can see it for yourself and let me know if you have any ideas. I think we're looking at a few weeks for all of this to happen, then we can transport you to New York for a visit. How does that sound?" Green waited for Joy to respond.

"It sounds okay," she said.

Green detected that she wasn't fully convinced, thinking that he had something else in mind for her. So he continued, "Fine, but Joy, think about what we've discussed, read through the education papers I'll leave with you, and look around you to see what's been achieved here. You see, Joy, the visitors and I have watched you work. You have an energy that radiates. When you're in a room, you exude confidence and have an impact on others, and we need that. People respect and listen to you. You, Joy, brought that energy to the First Nations, and you were the impetus that resulted in the changes here. The visitors told me that they've targeted others that have that same kind of impact and exude that energy."

Joy just looked at Green, speechless. "Sydney, thank you for saying that. I just did what I thought I had to do." She turned and looked out the window to the backyard, the greenbelt, the birds, and she sighed.

"Joy, please understand, be aware that this is the start of our future—of a new era for our world. I have to go now, but I'll be in touch as soon as we're ready. Thank you, I enjoyed seeing you again. If this whole thing produced something, it was that we've been able to work together and enjoy some time together."

He went over to Joy, who had turned to face him, and they embraced. Then Green stepped aside and disappeared.

He found himself back in his office on the visitors' ship and was greeted with a surprise offer.

Good, now, Sydney, before we begin all of this, do you want to try another visit to our home? We can attempt to answer the questions you have about us, and try to explain things in more detail?

"Yes, please, I've dreamed of this my whole life, and I do have a number of follow-up questions from my last visit."

Good, so once again, go to the hall and move to the door as you did last time. Also, make sure you have the force field tool with you, as we've increased its power so you can stay longer.

Green made sure he had it in his pocket and headed out down the hall. As he approached the door, he felt the vibration, but this time he was more interested in experiencing the environment of the visitors and trying to get some answers to his questions. To Green, it was more of a scientific experiment now, so without hesitation, he opened the door and entered.

20
LEARNING MORE ABOUT THE VISITORS

AS GREEN MOVED INTO THE SPACE, THERE WAS, AGAIN, A MOMENtary feeling of disorientation as he worked to maintain his balance and adjust to the area. With the modifications to the force field, Green found that he had more control over his movements and a clearer vision of the area. He looked around and thought he now understood how the astronauts working in space, or walking on the moon, must have felt. He looked around and again saw the rectangular shapes fading in and out of view, and periodically, inside the rectangular shapes, he noticed the bolts of energy. Some of the shapes seemed very distant and moving in all directions. Again, he sensed motion around him even though he didn't see anything. Then he felt that the motion was penetrating the force field that was protecting him, like the wind brushing on a person's face.

Sydney, we're here with you and ready to answer your questions as best we can.

"How many of you are there?"

On this ship, we number just over, in your numerology, 150,000 energies. The other five ships have between 50,000 and 75,000. So, altogether, there are just over 500,000 of us, but we are not like humans, we are one, and that oneness gives us increased power and ability.

"You are one. I don't fully understand how you can be 500,000 and yet be one. During my last visit, I saw that you're not biological beings, so what you are still escapes me. I don't understand the rectangular shapes. Are the lightning bolts really you? If so, what are you? How do you communicate with each other, with me and others when you're comprised of energy? What kind of sustenance do you need to sustain yourselves? Can you explain the dimensions that you experience?"

Good questions. As we've explained, we live here and are sustained by dark energy, which, by moving between different dimensions, produces the power we need, and that we store in the rectangular shapes you see. That movement you sense as a wave action is our sustenance. Sydney, because you live in and understand three dimensions, as well as a fourth dimension which you call time, it's difficult for us to explain and put into words how the seven dimensions that we experience work; however, let me try and explain it in a way you might understand.

Sydney, we are energy, but we are one, like a hive, and work together to sustain our existence. I suppose it's easier for you to understand that the rectangular shapes you see fading in and out are collectors of energy. It's like a battery getting charged. And think of us as a house that has a supply of energy to power the lights and the appliances, which all operate separately but get their energy from one source. As well, we adapt dimensionality to create our tools, our equipment.

Again, let me try to explain. We live within the equipment we have by providing that equipment with the power to operate. That power comes from us. We have the capacity to create and transform existing technology to manufacture other systems, tools, and devices, like what you call 3-D printers, but obviously our technology is a bit more advanced than that.

Green heard laughter.

That ability provides us with what we need and when we need it at any specific time and place. The communication and transportation capacity you are asking about are examples of that technology and innovation. Another example of the technology and our capacity is how we can probe your mind and talk to you; it's how we can absorb all of the information we need from the other ships positioned above the regions around your world. It's how we know what is going on in your world at all times. The technology allows us to store memory and do all of the other things like transporting you. Sydney, we live in multiple dimensions all at the same time. But understand that as you exist in a three-dimensional reality, we have to adjust ourselves, and our technology, to that reality. Do you understand?

"I understand a bit of what you've explained – bits and pieces - but the ideas are way above my comprehension of how any of it is even possible, but thank you for trying. One thing I don't understand is this space, what is it? Is this really part of your ship, as it seems endless? It seems to me to actually be like we're in outer space? Is it contained in the physical shapes that showed up on the scans? And here I am floating around, I know I have a protective shield, but I don't see it … I'm just floating in space."

The short answer is yes, it's part of our ship; and yes, it is space as you understand it; and yes, your technology perceives us as physical shapes in your scans. Sydney, it depends on the dimension from which you're experiencing, witnessing, and probing us. If you're probing with your equipment, which is basically in the four-dimensional space-time continuum, you'll see us as a physical object, but if you're able to view us in other dimensions, then we appear different and much more complex. Sydney, again, as we've tried to explain, you're in a multi-dimensional space right now, and that's why we needed you to have the shield—to protect you, as your physical nature could not exist in this space. It must be quite an experience for you, and remember, no biological being has ever experienced this, ever.

Well, enough for now, let's get you back to your office, and we can discuss the next steps.

Green was back in his office, and after a few minutes to recover, he again went and opened a bottle of wine and filled a glass right to the brim. He needed to have a drink, and he took a large piece of Swiss cheese and went to sit in one of the chairs by the coffee table.

After actually being with the visitors again in their environment and learning more about them, Green understood the need to continue the work on the "roadmap" to prepare the world for the future. He knew that they were much more than he could imagine, and the idea that they were the protectors of the universe was overwhelming. Whether humans wanted it or not, Green knew that the future was going to come to them, so they had better get ready and be in control. He drank his wine, munched on the cheese, and started to feel the effects as he discussed with the visitors the timeline for implementation. As well, he thought that the idea of introducing interstellar travel and meeting other civilizations would be the incentive for humans to really commit to moving forward, even after the visitors left.

Green sat there, enjoying the wine and the cheese. He loved the smell of the Swiss cheese and the unique taste as he took a big bite, and then he took another swig of the wine—he was feeling really good.

21

IMPLEMENTATION BEGINS—ELECTIONS

SYDNEY, THE VISITORS BEGAN, *WE HAVE TO BE CLEAR WITH YOU about something. As we told you, you were the first biological being ever to visit us. It was an experience, a test for us as well, to see if there was any significance, or reason to bring others to be with us—an experiment. We've come to the conclusion that there was no added benefit, and therefore made the decision that you will be the one and only biological, ever, to visit with us. Now, let's get back on track.*

The visitors paused as Green was drinking and munching on his cheese, trying to cope with what had happened and what he had just heard.

Sydney, you O.K?

"Yes, I'm just shocked and amazed at what you've just said, and I think that it's sad that others won't experience visiting you. I'm just trying to understand the decision, but we have work to do … I'm ready. Let's get this done."

Good, the next step now is to organize new elections. If you recall, between the first and second elections, we eliminated political parties, the influence of the industrial sector and people of wealth in positions of power trying to control governmental elections—the kingmakers, so to speak. It's taken the last two elections before people started to really understand that rationale and see the benefits of eliminating outside controls, political parties, and those with big money being involved in elections.

After those two elections, people started learning about identifying the right people to be in positions of leadership and management. Now it's been several years, so the youth who were in high school during your first press conference at Joy's school are now adults. People are starting to understand the true significance of accepting responsibility, accountability, empathy, and having significant management skills. Elections are meant to identify and promote leadership and put into positions of authority those people who have shown their leadership and management skills.

Sydney, identifying, training, and developing leadership skillsets is fostered by actually honing those skills from an early age and placing people, as they develop, into positions of authority—it's a lifelong learning curve. Then those who show their leadership acquire experience in municipal, then provincial, and ultimately regional governmental levels. It's critically important now, in this election process, that the "right" people assume management positions. Sydney, we're not sure if you've ever heard of Dr. Robert Greenleaf?

"No, I've never heard of him."

In the 1970s, he formulated something called "Servant Leadership." We found his work while we were researching your history and found it to be germane to what we were looking for in managers and leaders.

"What is it that he was proposing as a leadership model"?

Sydney, the phrase "servant leadership" refers to the premise that the leader is servant first. This conscious choice brings one to aspire to a leadership model that mentors others, that is aware of and cares about the needs of one's staff and works to meet their needs—he/she serves them. Sydney, a servant-leader focuses primarily on the growth and well-being of people and the communities within which they belong. During your history, traditional leadership generally involved the accumulation and exercise of power by the one at the "top of the pyramid," often ignoring the needs of others.

This work by Greenleaf was exactly what we were searching for as a model to guide future leaders and managers. It was part of the potential we saw in humanity, but it's been a challenge to get the general population in each region to know that elections are not a popularity contest and how important it is to target the right people. It's just starting to take root as people are beginning to hold those in power accountable.

All right, Sydney. Here we go—elections. We start by having announcements in each region that elections will be held, reinforcing the details we just discussed. As we did in the previous election, we have to explain, in detail, the requirements to be eligible to run for office, such as the age limitation, education, and the required experience for each level of office. It's a system based on merit, so if someone in a position, at a municipal level, wishes to run at a higher level, their proven leadership is on the line. That's the purpose of the system, to promote from within those with experience, as long as they have proven their management and organizational skills—their leadership.

"You know, this system of government, of lifelong training, of accountability, of sharing, of how people must have the education, experience, and leadership skills to hold office, the idea of servant leadership, is impressive! And I must say that what you propose about how elections should be run is right on the mark! No longer does wealth buy elections or influence and control the ideas, the priorities, of those running for office, nor does it label a person as better than others. I really believe that if we had the sense to implement this, without needing your intervention, well, I'm sure our world would have been a very different place."

Thank you, Sydney. Well, let's get on with it ...

Over the next couple of months, Green and the visitors organized each of the regions, sent out specific broadcasts with the details reminding people how the elections would work and how to vote, supplied the list of qualified people running for office, and responded to the many questions that were raised. As Green was the lead speaker, each region had a number of others who appeared with him and were charged with supervising the election process. After everything was ready, the elections were held, starting with municipal elections and ending with the establishment of the regional governments.

Right after the elections in each region were completed, with the new government officials in place, meetings were held to explain the next steps. Among several other important issues, Green discussed the setting up of offices from each region, like the embassies of the past, and the sharing of elected officials between each region.

Now that all of the people are in place, that the "embassies" are set up and selected officials from each region have been transferred to other regions, we're set for the next steps in the plan.

The visitors brought senior administrators and managers from each region to the United Nations Building in New York City, where the Blue World Government would ultimately be located. During the three-day session, there were many procedural questions about the SCM system, the sharing of expertise, and the need for an ongoing dialogue between the regions to be established. It was a very positive and reinforcing experience for the participants. Finally, before the session concluded, the visitors had Green discuss the importance of the proposed changes to the education protocols and the implementation of the new communication technologies that would be introduced in the next few months.

22
CONTINUING TO GET ORGANIZED

DURING THE MONTHS OF WORKING WITH THE VISITORS AND local managers in organizing and running the elections, Green used his office on the ship as his main location. He would be transported to each region for meetings, organize general announcements for the region he was in, and observe how the elections and those responsible for managing the elections were progressing.

From time to time, he would go to his apartment to get a short break, and a couple of times, he visited Joy to see how she was doing and how she was interacting with other experts about the draft education plan. The whole process seemed to go smoothly using news broadcasts, all the available social media, and the visitors' use of the communication systems they still controlled. It all seemed to be well received by each region.

After the elections and the follow-up meetings were completed, Green went back to his apartment to relax for a while. He was there for just over a week when the visitors contacted him.

Sydney, are you ready to get back to work? We have to start with a discussion about education, then we'll get into technology, innovation, and most importantly the economy.

"Yes, I've had a good time back here, reconnected with friends, attended a couple of welcome back parties, and just relaxed—I'm ready." And with that, Green found himself back in his office on the ship.

Okay, Sydney, now that the elections are completed and everyone is in place, we have to deal with the upgrades to the education system and apply those universally. You see, early on what we found was a huge gap in educational opportunities for children getting a proper education in different sectors and regions and a lack of opportunities to succeed in life. We need to do a lot of work to balance the system, especially at the preschool and the K–12 levels.

Standing in the middle of the room, Green lowered his head, silently acknowledging what the visitors were saying. Then he added, "I lost track of this problem, not as an excuse, but there was so much to do I never thought of how we were overlooking the educational needs of our kids. I feel so guilty. I told the students in my first presentation that they were the key, but we failed to follow up on that."

Sydney, we didn't fail the kids. We had to prepare for what is to happen now. You see, when we arrived, we saw areas of the world where people were labelled and viewed as not having the intellectual capacity to learn, even in communities within cities, and we saw the rampant disparity in education between those who had money and power, and those who didn't. And we saw that your economic and political systems supported this disparity. Sydney, whether it was a capitalist, socialist, or autocratic system, or a system based on religious beliefs, it was all the same. Those families in positions of power, those families of the wealthy elite class, they were able to provide educational opportunities for their children while the poor were ignored and degraded. The economic and political systems that were in place supported what was going on. So, we knew what we had to do, and that it would take time to implement. We had to make the systemic societal changes first, which we've been doing with you and others and now, with the new leadership we've been focusing the attention on education.

While he was listening, Green started to pace, and then interrupted the visitors. "Now it's starting to make sense. We had to purge the power of the plutocracy, get rid of the corrupt political leaders and the extreme groups around the world. Then we could fill the gap, the void that was created, and work on the disparity that was widespread." He stopped pacing, went over to his desk, and sat in the chair. "I knew we were headed in the right direction; I just didn't see the implications for education, for our youth."

That's okay, Sydney, we didn't completely neglect education as part of the infrastructure development included schools. Everything was happening quickly, then there was the confusion with what was happening that we had to deal with, and the remnants of the previous plutocracy working to sustain their position of power and prestige, and the political issues, and the elections, and the list goes on—you are a complex race.

Green heard laughing.

But now, we're in a position to continue with the next phase of the plan. Together we've completed the most recent election; we're establishing new communication systems, and we've been sharing elected officials between the regions to promote dialogue and fully establish the SCM system. Now, as we continue that work, we can begin establishing a universal education policy that will give lasting recognition to people.

"You know, when I created SORT, it was a highlight of my career." Green stood up proudly. "I had recognition. I was listened to, sought out for participating in research projects. I thought the world was mine, but it didn't last very long. It was a flash in the pan, as those in power started to take ownership, and I was sidelined." Greene sat back down in the chair. "But this—I can see how well organized you are—the plan, like a puzzle, is fitting together and creating an aura of what is to come ... so what do we do now? I'm all in!"

Thank you, Sydney. As you know, experts from all the regions have been working on creating a new universal educational protocol. We have to let them do their work, and Joy has gotten fully involved as she has been talking, and meeting, with the group.

"Okay, so where do I fit in with this plan?"

Sydney, this is where we'll continue to build the team—we have other plans for you. We started more than a year ago when we brought experts together to review what is happening and focus on education at all grades and the curricula in each region. They gathered in New York at the United Nations Building, and each group of experts at each educational level conferenced for as long as it took to review the current guidelines and develop new procedures and instructions for classroom teachers in all the regions. The experts worked in teams and periodically over the year came together to present their concepts and develop a draft report. That is the report you provided to Joy to review. We have watched her as she reviewed the documents. As we just mentioned, she has even contacted, and met with the others with her questions and recommendations to finalize the report.

Now we need Joy and the experts to organize meetings in each region. First, the early childhood educators will go over the intention to implement the draft plan and get feedback from the teachers before finalizing the document. After that is completed, we'll do the same for the elementary panel and the secondary panel. Once the final document is completed, it will be a guideline, and teachers will be trained and then responsible for its implementation. It's time, Sydney, to promote dialogue, to work together, to get input from professionals and, at the appropriate time, to phase in the final outline and see how it works, tweaking it as is required for the uniqueness in different sections of the regions. The experts in a specific area can be shared between all regions and transported where they're needed. Joy will be a critical leader in all of this as it moves from the academic to the practical application.

"Where do I fit in with this process?" Green asked again as he stood up and walked around the room.

Sydney, you've done a great job during the past years, thank you, and please be aware that we, and the people of your world, are indebted to you. Now it's time for others, experts in their particular fields of study—in this case, educators—to come to the table in implementing the specified work. We will get to your role in all of this shortly.

Green noticed a glass of water on the small table. He went over, sat down, and drank some of the water as he listened to the visitors.

So, this is how it works ... First, in the new work environment, when a couple has a child, they're not only entitled to, but will be encouraged to be home with the child until he/she is at least 12–18 months. Then the preschool system kicks in. All preschool staff will be trained and specialize in early childhood education. In the preschools, the kids are observed, evaluating how they interact with others and what activities interest them. The team will use the appropriate testing that has been established, through controlled events and activities, in order to identify the early-stage talents of the children. In these formative years, the children will enjoy activities, learn language, and interact with each other, which will also bring out any leadership qualities and/or specific talents. The program is full of fun activities for the kids—for the kids—and challenges that will stimulate their curiosity, their innate need to learn.

The education and intellectual growth of the children is a priority in which the system has to expend a considerable amount of energy. By the time a child is ready to start their elementary school education, we should have a basic idea as to their potential and what areas they'll excel in. As they enter the formal school system, they'll have the opportunity to be exposed to several areas of study, either to reinforce what was identified early on, or, if other interests emerge, to change the direction and focus of their education. At every grade level, there are always basic general education lessons to keep the students on track. To facilitate the universality of the process, the early childhood education teachers, from preschool situations to the first few years of elementary school, will be able to work in an active exchange program between the regions. As well, with the new communication technology we're implementing, classes in one region will be able to interact with classes in other regions—to learn about each other. Of course, parents will play a considerable role in all of this.

In elementary school, the basic coursework will be in the core areas of general knowledge such as language, history, math, science, the merit system, and social studies. As well, students will have extra-curricular studies and activities in the recognized areas of interest that they've shown ability—such as the various trades, or the sciences (physics, biology, environmental sciences, or research, etc.), or leadership, teaching, music, the arts, entertainment, sports, or athletic activities, to name a few. Sydney, also, as part of the required study, there will be discussions, explanations, and sessions, to help children develop a basic understanding of the key elements of the new society (responsibility, accountability, commitment, respect for others etc.), as well as learn the history of each of the regions, and the basic working concepts of the SCM system.

Once students enter high school, other than the core programs, they will join advanced classes in the areas of specialty they have started to develop. They'll prepare to advance to college or university and begin to pursue the potential career opportunities ahead of them. Learning will become a lifelong endeavour. Finally, it's in high school that what started earlier to be developed for those with leadership qualities and abilities will be put to the test. Those students with leadership qualities will be tasked with leading school councils, school newspapers, clubs, and other activities such as helping teachers by peer teaching with students who need help. Let us be clear: if a student becomes interested in a different field of study, at any level, they will be supported. We will be developing an open and supportive system.

Sydney, this is lifelong learning whether one goes to college, university, or gains work experience. After school, some may not want to proceed to post-secondary education and want to enter the work force, and that is just fine as you'll need support workers in all areas. Others may enter a college to become a trades person and enter an apprenticeship program to study to be an electrician, plumber, carpenter, or a technician to deal with the new technologies, or other fields that are best taught at the college level. Still others will go to university to continue to specialize academically in their chosen field. One of the key elements in all of this is the need for flexibility. As individuals advance in their educational career, we must recognize the possibility that they may specialize or change their focus, and we must emphasize, again, at that point, it is up to the system to adjust—not the student. The average person will attend school until their early to mid-twenties, or in the academic areas—such as engineering, medicine, different areas of research, physics, mathematics, or electronics, to name a few—they could continue their education, which includes on the job training, well into their thirties.

Education is more than just studies. It's also gaining experience, learning how to interact with others, becoming good listeners and problem solvers. Teachers are obviously a critical part of all of this—they are the servant leaders developing the potential in others. They must be proficient at creating a positive group social mentality of working together, sharing, and supporting each other. At this level, teachers will develop concepts of social capital and racial solidarity. Finally, teachers get to know their students at a very early age and can recognize, over and above testing, the qualities in their students and even their potential. We have to use this unique expertise for the long-term benefit of the students.

Okay, there's obviously a lot more detail, but that'll be developed as the experts, and Joy, meet with the teachers. So, what do you think?

"Actually, it sounds amazing." Green stood up and walked over to the table that had the charts on it, and he looked down at the small dot that represented the alien ships. Then, after a short pause, he continued, "When that is applied worldwide, in all regions, I can see a very bright future for our youth to achieve their full potential and experience a rewarding and fruitful life. You know, we've talked about balance, equal opportunity, and a fair and just society ... well, in terms of education and career, this seems to be a great example of that. I wonder what Joy is thinking right now."

Sydney, as people will begin to realize that when their kids have questions, are curious about something, they are supported to find answers, they will be thankful. When the students show interest and skill in a specific area and are given the opportunity to excel, their parents will see the benefits of a real education. When the students come home and are excited and don't stop talking about what they're learning, and want to share, then we're on the right track. Sydney, the parents will learn from their kids.

Now let's turn to other important issues.

23
THE CHANGING ROLE OF MONEY, TECHNOLOGY, AND INNOVATION

GREEN WENT OVER TO HIS DESK AND SAT DOWN.

Sydney, now let's briefly turn our attention to technology, innovation, and the economy. We have to ensure that we're on track with implementing our priorities. So, here we go ...

By establishing the new education protocols, the SCM, the communications systems, and as we continue implementing new technologies, innovations, and infrastructure, we're establishing a fair and balanced society. These actions are really important, but the most critical change that will have the most impact is the transition we have to implement in the economy.

Sydney, remember how it was when we arrived? We've discussed how everything was tied to money as a currency of exchange. From food to housing, to education, medical care, insurance, to banking, borrowing, clothing, having a vehicle, trying to go on a vacation, or even out to dinner and a movie—everything, everything was based on having money. Do you remember credit cards, interest rates, banking charges, mortgages, taxes? Anywhere you wanted to go, or what you wanted to do, cost money. From restaurants to pubs, theatres, sporting events—everything. Even communication devices like mobile phones, computers, the internet, and then there were the charges to use those devices by the telecommunications companies and service providers. Having money determined the essence of one's lived experience, all over the world.

As we've said many times, we noticed almost immediately that your economic systems were broken, being based primarily on a model of capitalism—of profit and the accumulation of wealth and power. And all levels of society just accepted this as though it was meant to be. To be blunt, this economic model is predisposed to support the lifestyles of a very small group in society, disengaging the vast majority of people. Sydney, the greed of those in power, the lust for financial acquisition, the control of the plutocracy, and the resulting exploitation at all levels, was rampant. It became apparent that there was a belief that getting as much money as possible, by any means, would lead to the realization of one's goals – and happiness.

This contrived expectation, was, and is, the false narrative of capitalism. Sydney, regrettably, we also identified that the general populations bought into the ideas presented, and were apathetic to doing anything about it.

Therefore, we needed to address the social and economic dependence on money as a primary form of currency, and as an assessment of one's status in society, as it stood in the way of making progress. And we knew to do this we would need a step-by-step effort. During the first phase, and with your help, we started to resolve the issues. Money in the economy has become less of a burden during these past few years, and in a short time, there'll be no more money in circulation. As we move forward, human capital is what will count—people, Sydney, people count—and that will become the primary exchange in goods and services.

Green got up from his desk and walked about with his hands clasped together behind his back, and then he started to pace, and in a concerned voice, he asked, "How can that possibly work? I know there have been changes already, but they've caused a lot of confusion. Now you're talking about a fundamental change in how our society operates – how we live." Green paused to collect his thoughts, but continued pacing.

"What about all of the jobs that are involved in the economy? Jobs like the bankers, the accountants, and the jobs in the government agencies that are meant to supervise and track economic activity? What about the lawyers, the courts, businesses? What about the day-to-day workers? It's a complex system that in our estimation, works. If there'll no longer be money as a currency, how will anyone purchase goods and services like food and accommodations? Where will the incentives be to work hard, to be challenged?"

Green was taken aback as he heard laughter, so he stopped pacing, waiting for an answer. "What's so funny?" he asked.

Excellent questions, Sydney. The laughter continued a little longer before stopping. *You talk about supervising economic activity—the courts, lawyers, business, buying goods and services. Sydney, that's where all the problems exist, but all of that becomes moot, as money has led to corruption, criminality, and people taking advantage of others. Sydney, all of that disappears as money is eliminated from society. Just listen for a few minutes ...*

Has a day gone by that you haven't reached into your pocket to see how much cash you have, do you have enough? Do millions of people not dream about winning a lottery and what they would do with all of that money? What about the various "costs" of insurance, financing a car, getting a mortgage to buy a house, like your sister saving for years just to have a down payment to qualify to get that mortgage, or the rent you've been paying for years, to line someone else's pocket? Sydney, the lusting for wealth, for power and possessions, has been a serious distraction and has led to a corrupt system that deprives most people in your world the ability to experience a comfortable, worry-free existence – and has created a class structure that labels people as poor, middle class, upper-class and the entitled – we don't need to go further with what impact that has had on society.

Government, you say? What about all of the political leaders in government you had to send away because they were abusing their privileges, getting money from big business to support the agenda of the plutocracy? Oh Sydney, the abuses we could list such as the pharmaceuticals, the banking system, interest rates, business gauging, taxes, insurance, and we could go on and on. Sydney, your economic structures were a mess, and you bet they were complicated – on purpose. We'll now make the final changes that will bring simplicity and balance to the system so that everyone has equal opportunity. And not to worry Sydney, because all those positions you referred to will have the opportunity to make a contribution to society and be rewarded.

You see, you heard laughter before because on more advanced planets, people have access to everything they need. They have no concerns about housing, food, healthcare, education, entertainment, vacations, family, and career – and there is no money in circulation. Sydney, eliminating money as a form of currency, providing for the day-to-day needs of everyone, with the new education and communication protocols coming into play, and all of the other lifestyle improvements, people will have opportunities that they have never experienced before.

Sydney, as we've said, this is a process—change happens over time. This new economic prototype becomes a two-way street, as one provides goods and/or services, so one receives goods and/or services, meeting one's day-to-day needs and desires without any conditions – as it is on other far more advanced worlds, people live, people participate, people are provided for.

Also, please be aware that the new innovations and technologies we've introduced are initiating new opportunities for training, new job opportunities, and for people to have a sense of ownership and control in their lives. As well, making these economic changes increases the importance of education and training - to prepare people to learn about and participate in these new systems and technologies. Also, the development of infrastructure and housing has created new positions in several areas of engineering, architecture, construction management, support services, SCM, and jobs in all other aspects of infrastructure development.

The accountants you've mentioned, the government workers, the lawyers, and businesses all have work to do. Yes, they may be moving into different sectors, or new branches of government, but they're still fully engaged, their expertise needed, and there are many, many opportunities to be filled. There are jobs and training for everyone! As individuals are part of the system, the system supports their ambitions, rewards their accomplishments, and provides for them.

"I didn't mean to be critical," responded Green. "I was just asking questions that I'm sure are on, or will be on, the minds of many people." He went back to his desk and sat down in his chair, leaning forward, giving the visitors his complete attention.

So, how will all of this new lifestyle impact people? Sydney, people will be safe, their day-to-day needs will be met, they will be free to determine their future, be supported, and they will have meaning in their lives, like it is on other more advanced planets. Sydney, would you rather we just leave things as they are? The corruption, greed, the disparity in lived experience, the entitlement, the abuses and criminality, and all the other problems you have now?

"No, I understand what you're saying, so what is the process?"

In each region, people are now seeing an improvement in their lifestyles. Together, Sydney, we've ended poverty. We made a start on ridding the world of greed, of autocrats, brutality, criminals, weapons, dependencies—people now are beginning to experience the satisfaction, the freedom that comes with knowing they're safe, no matter where they live. Together, we've continued that process by responding to issues as they've surfaced through the years. Now, with our baseline evaluation of your current global situation, we'll finish our work. Again, Sydney, understand that as your world advances, there will be no need for jails, prisons, courts, police, or the military ... imagine that.

We're now in the process of developing, and soon implementing, the universal education program and consequently restoring the dignity and potential of the individual. So, the educational impact on people in all regions will be that children will grow up in an atmosphere of equal opportunity, free of obstacles to their learning, as their innate skills and potential will be identified, supported, mentored, and developed to their full potential. Finally, Sydney, all people around the world, in all regions, will learn about each other. Universality means understanding the world, not one small area of the world—but being one world. Universality means everyone has the same opportunities, no matter who they are, what they look like, or where they're born. In this system, there is no need for any other currency, especially one like money, because people are what brings the stability, the equilibrium, to society.

We sense you're asking ... what will the world look like in such a system?

Well, the first observation will be that all areas of the world are clean and the environment has recovered and is as it should be. No matter where one goes in the world, one will see organized communities and people walking about, content and free of worries—and friendly, welcoming. So, the first impression, as you've already experienced when we showed you an earth-like planet, is one of being awestruck, and looking forward to your future. But where does all of this come from? Why are people content, fulfilled, and so willing to be contributing members of society?

Part of the answer is that everyone is looked after from birth to old age. This is where the new communication systems come into play. At birth, everyone gets an identification card. The so-called card, which is embedded as a type of small tattoo on one's shoulder, is a link to personal communications, such as your smart phones of today, and all governmental systems at all levels. It also tracks the individual's education, their skillset, and the courses they take; it's also their connection to regional management teams. The identification system grants access when shopping, when one goes to sporting events, arts, theatre, when they go on vacations, and when they vote—it's the key that opens all of the doors.

It's a communication tool used to dialogue with friends, family, teachers, and local authorities, especially if there are any questions or issues. It also tracks one's health and detects issues before they become serious. And before you ask the obvious question, this technology, like what we've done with you using the water and the pills, can be private when required. It gives access to all levels of government, just like when you want to talk to us, or not.

Again, Green heard some laughter.

Sydney, it is not intrusive or controlling, quite the opposite, but you and others will learn more about it as we progress, and again, let us be clear, this system is used successfully on many other planets. You saw it in action on the planets we showed you.

But, after hearing this, Green couldn't get beyond the idea that if everyone is watched, are they really free? If there is constant communication that is tracked, do they really have any privacy? And then he thought, *There doesn't seem to be any incentive, or reward, for excellence.* If everyone is provided for, it seemed to Green that people would just live without any excitement, without achievement or reward, and just exist, day to day.

Oh, Sydney, the opposite is true. Think about it, Sydney. Think back to your uncle's influence on you as a youth—was that not challenging you as an individual? Think about it Sydney, as one grows up without fear, not worried about day-to-day living, and able to be the best they can be, is that not challenging and rewarding once one starts to achieve one's goals? And think about it. As a person starts to engage in work that he/she has trained for, work in which one has chosen to be engaged, is that not rewarding to be able to work in a field that you've chosen and to be recognized for the contributions you make – instead of just getting a job so you can make money to buy things? And then, to add on to that, to be able to have your voice heard, to hold elected officials accountable, to be part of something important. And to be able to enjoy going to sporting events, or live music performances, or theatre, or out to dinner, or enjoy vacations anywhere in the world, simply by the use of the communications ID people will get when they were born, is that not reward enough?

Sydney, people will work hard from childhood to adulthood. They'll be supported and mentored. They'll work, participate with people of like mind, be part of a team, contribute, and enjoy each other's company, and have fun – unencumbered. They'll be able to enjoy life. Sydney, the fulfillment that one feels in achieving a goal, being free, participating, and being recognized for one's contributions gives meaning to their life. Compared to the way your world was, this new world will be like living in a paradise. There is so much more we can say, but that will come out later.

Green got a glass of wine and some cheese to munch on.

Are you sure you want wine? The visitors were a little concerned.

"I need it right now," replied Green, "Anyway, one or two glasses is no problem. It's almost like a toast to the future, a celebration of what you've explained."

Okay, sounds good, so, as you sip on your wine and have some cheese, let's talk a bit about technology and innovation.

The visitors paused for a moment as Green had some wine and cheese, then they began …

As you know, we've introduced new technologies—some that have reversed the impact on your environment, such as renewable energy systems—and we'll continue to train scientists and tradespeople on the usage and maintenance of that technology. In several areas around the world, Sydney, people can see the blue sky again, and they don't have to wear masks as the pollution has dissipated and the world's environment is recovering. As well, we've introduced new farming and production technologies, so that food products support healthy living. We've also just about completed the process of getting rid of internal combustion cars, vehicles like trucks and large equipment, and heating or cooling systems in homes and buildings that use fossil fuels.

Sydney, once the new communications systems are in place, all regions will be connected and will be able to fix any technological issues that present themselves. As well, with the communications we're implementing, the regions will be able to share expertise as the new technologies are introduced. The transportation technology that we've used with you to send you all over the world will be installed in many areas, and then needed expertise can go anywhere instantly.

The education and communication systems that are being introduced promote dialogue, the sharing of research and innovation, partnership, and leadership as well as cherishing the value of the contributions of people—of experts. There will be opportunities, incentives, and recognition for individual expertise and partnerships. As we move forward there will be many new opportunities for training and jobs in new areas of study, and research and development, such as interstellar travel. As well, in a meritocracy, men and women, and people of all races in all of the regions will have equal opportunity to get involved.

Finally, Sydney, remember, even after we completed the first stage, your world was still in the beginning of the transition, and there is a lot left to fulfill the objectives we outlined earlier. Also, keep in mind that your world will have a true social balance and equal opportunity for everyone, but this does take time. And to make this all come to fruition, the most important item now is to establish the world government.

"Thank you for the clarification ... I feel confident now that with the training you've been doing, with many others having specific expertise coming on line, we'll see the changes gain impetus and become the norm. I do feel, however, that I'll need more information on the operation of the new communication protocols to be able to explain them, and sell them, to the community."

Of course, Sydney, we understand, but now let's get the Blue World Government set up.

24

PREPARING FOR THE BLUE WORLD GOVERNMENT

GREEN, SITTING BEHIND HIS DESK IN HIS OFFICE ON THE SHIP, got up, refilled his glass of wine, and then went back to his desk and sat down. He was enjoying his wine when Joy came into his mind.

"Do you think Joy will join me at the world government offices in New York?" asked Green.

Not if you keep drinking...

Even Green had a good laugh.

"I know. It's just that so much information, especially about the money and the communication thing, is a little overwhelming." Smiling, he took another sip of wine.

Well, Sydney, trust us, all will be well, you'll see. Now, about Joy, we think the chances are really good. So, we better get on track with setting up the offices. Finish your drink, and then we'll discuss it.

Green got up and walked around the office, taking a drink every so often, and thinking about Joy and wishing she was there with him. After a few minutes, he rinsed out the glass and then the visitors began discussing the process of setting up the world government.

Sydney, this last election has brought in a number of younger managers with education, experience, and managerial reputation. They've come into senior positions, and they're eager and ready to embrace the responsibilities of leadership. So, we're finally getting the right people coming into positions of authority at all levels. As well, as we just mentioned, there are many individuals in each region who have moved up the ranks of government, who are gaining experience and leadership skills to be candidates for assuming senior positions in the future—like a feeder school. That is what you need to follow up with the implementation of the new education systems, the continued developments in housing and infrastructure, the communication protocols, the SCM systems, and explaining and comforting people on the elimination of money. This will help you set the future agenda for the regional governments.

This is it, Sydney. The next few years will be the most exciting time in your history—this is your legacy. Imagine having schools named after you.

Everybody was laughing, including Green.

"Ha, ha, very funny. Seriously, though, I understand the plan. I really do. Everything is starting to make sense now," he said, "And I see where this is all headed. To be honest, I do want to be part of it all, schools or no schools." Then, after some more laughter, he sat down again and anxiously waited for the visitors to continue.

Sydney, the first step for us was to set up an office area, and we've been focussed on implementing that design while you were busy with the elections. During the past few months, we've been restructuring the interior design of the United Nations Building, directing local contractors. Just before starting the reconstruction, and preparing the office space, we moved the North American Regional Government headquarters out of the building, to an area just outside of Pierre, South Dakota.

Green interrupted. "Pierre, South Dakota? What?" He was surprised, to say the least, "I've never heard of it. How did you find Pierre, South Dakota, and of all places, why South Dakota?"

Very funny, Sydney. We searched for the best place for a while. We determined it should be in the US because it's between Canada and Central America. There were three reasons we settled on Pierre: one, it's a small community distanced from traditional centres of government; two, Pierre is located in an area of the US between Canada and the countries in Central America and, geographically, it's easy to get to, especially with the transportation technology we've implemented; and three, it's a small rural town. We developed an open area just south of the town by constructing an office building using locals as much as possible, creating housing complexes, support facilities, a technology centre, and then moving everyone in. Of course, we had discussions with the North American Regional Government representatives first and ended up having to include several perks before we got full support from all of the delegates.

"Perks?" queried Green. "That sounds good. When can we discuss perks?"

Again, there was laughter.

We like the humour that humans use. It's not something we had experienced before we came here, but it's something we're learning to use and enjoy. Thanks, Sydney. Anyway, we'll get back to the perks later.

Again, there were a few chuckles before the visitors continued. Green got up and started to wander around the office as he listened.

So, the ultimate task of locating the world government at what was the United Nations, has been, for the past few months, a work in progress. We needed to have eight specific areas—one is for the chair and CEO of the world government. Then we needed space for each regional government, which has a small conference area, a main office, and an area for support staff. As you can imagine this set-up, with all of the offices and other facilities, requires a large space, so, we put the chair and CEO's office, your office, in the centre of the space, with the regional offices in a semi-circle facing the entrance hallway to your office. We like the design and the atmosphere of the space.

As people enter the area, they'll see an information wall with updates, videos of the activities from each of the regions, and a Q&A section. This wall is actually the back of your office. Along the hallway and at the entranceway to the CEO's office is a snack bar, a coffee shop, public washrooms, and areas where people can just sit and talk. Your office will be quite elaborate, with a fully equipped conference room used for meetings with the world government delegates, offices for staff, a communications area that will give the expert staff access to all the regions, and a transportation facility that can be used by all the delegates to go directly to their regions, or other locations around the world. There is another transportation device in the general offices for large groups to use. Sydney, as you'll see, the regional offices are just a few steps from each other, the coffee/snack bar area, and the entrance to your office.

So, Sydney, we've already prepared the space, but of course, right now, it's empty—no people. Your task—after touring the area to become familiar with it and suggesting any changes or upgrades—will be to go to each of the regional governments in your role as chair, explain that you're setting up the Blue World Government, answer any questions they may have, and then ask them to appoint a leader for the region and support staff to become part of that organization.

We will, as we've done all these years, help with those travel arrangements and the meetings. At the end of all of this, each region will have representatives at the "embassies" set up in each region, at their home office area, and of course, several staff representatives at the Blue World Government offices. There will be eight delegates on the world government: you and one representative from each region. Oh, and one last thing, in your office where the technology is located, and one of the transportation devices, and because of the global time zones, will have to be available 24/7, so we'll train a number of people on its operation and maintenance. What do you think?

Green had stopped walking around the office and was leaning against his desk as the visitors finished. He was thinking about the responsibilities they had placed on him and wondering if he was capable of fulfilling the tasks ahead of him and actually representing the world to other civilizations.

"Are you sure I'm the right person for this job?" he voiced his concern. "I know it's been my lifelong dream to meet representatives from other worlds, but I'm not a politician, and without you being here in the future, and my age, and —".

Before he could finish, the visitors interrupted him. *Sydney, there's no doubt that you're the right person. We've known that from the beginning when we recruited you, and have worked with you during these formative years. As you've experienced, there have been a lot of tests that you've responded to that proved to us that you're the right person for the job. So, put that aside and, by the way, we've made sure that one of the side effects of the water you've been drinking, and the pills, is an anti-aging formula. You've been too important to us to let you grow old ... at least not yet.*

Green could hear considerable laughter in the background.

You see, we're getting into this humour thing ... but seriously, Sydney, you're much more capable of fulfilling the position and bringing others on side than you give yourself credit for. Trust us, as you have all this time. As we've discussed earlier, you'll be able to reach us at will because when we do leave, as we have said, one of our ships will remain here until your world is completely proficient, standing on its own, and doesn't need us anymore.

"Thank you once again. That's reassuring. Okay, I'd like to visit the space you've designed. Once I've had a chance to look around and get familiar with it, perhaps we can contact Joy and bring her here."

Good, then let's get started.

And with that, Green found himself at the entrance to the world government offices. There were elaborate wooden doors with signage above them saying "Blue World Government Headquarters," but what got his attention right away was the white marble floor—beautiful and welcoming in its simplicity, strength, and the atmosphere it created. As Green entered the space, he noticed a multi-coloured carpet along the middle of the hallway, and then he couldn't miss what the visitors had called the information wall. It was parallel to the circular shape of the space, at least 20 feet long and about 10 feet high; it had a section for each region, and at the top of the wall, there was a bright sign that read 'Look How Each Region is Doing'—it was a sight to behold. As he walked along the hallway, he noticed the offices were set up to allow each region to decorate the space as they wanted. The snack bar and the coffee shop were still being worked on. As he stood there, Green noticed that the way they were being constructed created a passageway that pointed the way to the entrance to the chair of the Blue World Government's office—his office.

Green walked down the short distance to the entrance to what would be his office. The visitors mentioned the short hallway's walls would be decorated with pictures, videos, and audio updates for each region, similar to the wall at the entrance to the area, but in more of a decorative manner. As Green entered the office, he noticed there was a conference room on the left-hand side and an open space to his right with a few desks. Looking around, he saw a door at the back right-hand side with a sign that read "Communications." On the left side at the back of the office was a large door with "Technology and Transportation" written on it. In the centre of the space was the large glass door to his office.

He entered and was impressed. It was similar to what he had on the visitors' ship, but much larger. The desk was beautiful and ornate, and the office felt welcoming as there was a counter with a sink, facilities for making tea and coffee, a fridge, and closets. He saw an area with a sofa, two chairs, carpeting, and a coffee table. With a little jump in his step and a big smile on his face, he left his office area and went back to the main entrance. On his way out of the general offices, he had one last look at the space when he noticed another door in the far corner with a sign that read " Regional Communications Centre."

The visitors explained that this space would be available for each of the regions, when necessary, to communicate in private with their representatives "back home." They explained that inside the space was a small room for each of the regional offices. The whole area—the regional offices, the snack bars, the information wall, and even the flooring—felt very welcoming and created a warm environment.

"Impressive," he said, "I have no suggestions. You've done a wonderful job."

Over the next several days, the visitors arranged for Green to visit each of the seven regional head offices to discuss setting up the world government and to request that each region appoint someone to represent them. He brought videos of the area. He also discussed setting up their office space, having support staff, and that they just had a few weeks to get everything organized and in place.

Once Green completed the last of his appointments with the regions and he was back on the main ship in his office, the visitors discussed that now was also the time for him to move to New York, to be close to his office and stop having to be transported to the visitors' ship.

On that matter, he was transported back to New York and found himself in a new apartment the visitors had set up for him. It was right in the United Nations Building and close to the world government offices. It was similar to his apartment in Florida, but much more spacious, more modern, and it was set up for him to be able to host receptions. Green was overwhelmed with the space.

It was mid-morning, and Green went over to the glass doors to the deck, which opened when he approached. He went out to see the morning sun and the amazing view of New York City. Then the visitors continued, explaining that he had to keep his apartment in Florida as in his new position, he'd be visiting NASA and several other research facilities to keep an eye on the progress of the work being done in developing capacity for interstellar travel. The visitors explained that because the Florida campus was in a much less populated area, it was more appropriate for the developmental work for which the researchers in the North American region would be responsible.

"So, our work in the North American region, in Florida, is just part of a larger project?"

Absolutely ... each region will be responsible for some aspect of the development. Sydney, as you'll learn, it's much more complicated than any of your associates can possibly understand at this time. As well, the platform for interstellar travel starts with the development of a new space station and training centre that will be in orbit around the earth and house thousands of people. Also, in the early stages, launching to other worlds will take place from the facilities established on the moon. Anyway, we'll discuss this more at a later date; let's get back on track.

"Thank you, the apartment is beautiful, and thank you for setting up the world government offices and establishing the specific priorities and goals for us to have a clear focus as we implement our move forward. Our world is forever indebted to you ... I need Joy. Can you bring her here now?"

Yes, Sydney, and thank you for all of your work and commitment. We couldn't have done it without you. So, let's talk about Joy. For your information, we did bring her to the ship, had a very detailed discussion, and after agreeing to her conditions, she agreed to join you. She'll be here momentarily.

"Wait," Sydney was curious. "Conditions? What conditions?"

Don't worry. It wasn't anything too burdensome, but we'll let her tell you the details.

With that, Joy appeared in the living room of Green's new apartment. He was happy, and relieved, to see her. Green knew that he needed to have her close as she gave him confidence, support, and a sense of being protected, as she had when he was young.

25

GREEN WELCOMES JOY TO NEW YORK

"WOW," WAS ALL SHE COULD SAY AS SHE LOOKED AROUND. "THIS IS gorgeous." Then, walking over to the sliding glass doors, which opened for her as she approached, she turned and looked at Green as she went out onto the spacious deck, "and what a view! I'm going to enjoy my time here." The doors to the deck closed as Joy came back into the living room. She looked around some more, surveying the rest of the apartment, then she returned and sat on the sofa.

"Boy, did you ever get a great perk." They both laughed. "The technology—I enter a room, and the lights go on; I open a closet, and it lights up, and a voice asks me if I need any help, would I like some music, dim the lights, adjust the air conditioning—my God, Sydney, this is amazing. And it's so comfortable, welcoming, and spacious. I hope they do the same for me in my apartment. Oh, Syd," she said, smiling, "who decorated this for you? I'm sure it wasn't you."

They both could hear laughing in the background.

You know, you two, we're beginning to really like this humour thing, but we'll leave you to talk, go out to dinner, and we'll get together tomorrow morning. Oh, and Joy, by the time you get back after viewing the Blue World Government offices, we'll have completed one of your conditions that we're sure you'll like.

Green walked to the back of the sofa, tapped Joy's shoulders, and then walked over to one of the chairs opposite her and sat down with a curious look, almost a jealous frown on his face.

"Oh right, the visitors told me that you had some conditions, some perks. What's that all about?"

Joy stood up and walked to the kitchen. "I'll make us some coffee and tea. Come to the kitchen, and we'll see if the visitors thought to do some shopping for you. Then I'll tell you everything."

Green got up and followed her to the kitchen. Once in the kitchen, the first thing Joy did was to look around. "They really did a good job in here. It looks great ..." She searched through the cupboards and fridge to see what supplies were available. There was a kettle on the counter, a microwave, a variety of teas, coffee, sugar, some utensils, dishes, a package of cinnamon rolls, muffins, a vanilla/coconut cake, and milk in the refrigerator.

"Well, the visitors know what you like." She paused for a moment. "But, Syd, you'll have to do shopping for some real food, or give the visitors a list."

Both Green and Joy laughed as she put the kettle on and opened the package of cinnamon rolls. Then, while waiting for the kettle to boil, Joy held on to the counter and got serious. She started to explain ...

"Syd, I've been so content in my retirement. I drop in to the school to help out if one of the teachers is sick. I have my friends that I get together with, but most importantly, I'm free. My time is my time to do what I want when I want. It's hard to give that up. The most rewarding time I have is when I can meet with students and work with them ... challenge them."

The kettle was boiling, so she stopped to make the tea and coffee. As she was serving Green his tea and rolls, she continued, and then sat opposite him.

"The visitors promised me two things that made me agree to continue to be involved. One was that I would have a nice apartment here, close to you, which they said would be down the hall. I'd just have to spend a few months helping with something they said you would explain, and I would be here on-site for that. And, two, once we're up and running, I could operate out of my home in Whitehorse. With the transportation and communication technology in the world government offices, I could do meetings from Whitehorse, or they could transport me here for meetings whenever necessary. How does that sound to you?"

Green was elated with the news, and as they were enjoying their tea, coffee, and pastries, he approached Joy and gave her a hug.

"As long as you're comfortable with the conditions, that's great with me. I really wanted you to participate, and I think we'll be doing some exciting projects and missions, so thanks for agreeing. Why don't we go downstairs, and I'll show you how the offices are set up and the décor. Then we can make arrangements to go out for dinner."

"Wonderful, I'm anxious to see what it all looks like. Then, depending on the time, I'll go to my apartment to see what they've done there, get changed, and then we can go out. But wait, Sydney. Tell me what the visitors said you, and what they have planned for me?"

"It's just an extension of what you're already doing, the implementation of the education priority. I know you'll like it, but we don't have the time now to discuss it, so let's go and see the space downstairs ..."

"Okay, but don't make me wait too long."

"I promise you, Joy, that we'll get into that, a little intro at dinner, but probably first thing tomorrow morning when we're fresh and have time, okay?"

Joy nodded in approval, and with that, Green led the way down to the world government offices. At first sight, Joy was impressed by the organization, the initial décor of the space, and the information wall that would greet visitors. As they were walking around, they saw the Middle-East and the Eurasian contingents setting up their offices. Green greeted the delegates and introduced Joy. Then he invited the principal delegates, the leaders of the two regional governments, to join them for a nice tour of the city and dinner. Both of them agreed, and they made a time to meet at Green's apartment later that afternoon.

Joy was surprised and impressed by Green's ability to hear, and seem to understand, and then respond in their native language. She was politely quiet as this exchange happened. Green translated what they were saying and mentioned to Joy that from then on, they would speak English.

While they were still in the area and studying the set-up, the visitors interrupted them. *Joy, Sydney ... we've booked reservations at a nice restaurant downtown, and we've arranged for you to have a car and a driver. When it's time to go, you'll find the car in the parking garage on the first floor in the basement parkade, stall number three. As well, Sydney, one set of keys is on the table at the entrance to your apartment just in case you need the vehicle.*

Again, there was some laughter in the background.

Also, just to let you know, the other regional governments will be setting up their office space, and they should all be in place in the next few days, a week at the most. Once they're all settled in, we'll help you arrange the first meeting of the Blue World Government. Finally, Joy, please take a drink from the glass of water on the table in front of you, and you'll also see a small container with some pills in it. These are so you can develop the language skills we've given Sydney, to be able to be heard in the language of the people being addressed. Also, when they speak to you in their language, you'll hear the English translation.

To say Joy was excited would be a gross understatement. She grabbed the water, drank some, took out one of the pills, and swallowed it with the rest of the water.

Good, well done, Joy. Now, finish your tour. It's still early, so you can enjoy some time together. Then, when everyone is ready, take a drive around the city, see how it looks, and have a nice meal with each other and your guests—the manager at the restaurant will be ready when you arrive.

Joy was still so excited about trying out her new skill, but the visitors did say it would take a day or two to become effective.

"Syd, how do they do all of that? What does their living space look like? Even more, importantly, what do they look like?"

The visitors interrupted him before he could respond.

Go ahead, Sydney. Try again to explain who and what we are, and what you experienced when you visited us.

Green heard some chuckling in the background and started to laugh himself.

"What's so funny," asked Joy.

"The visitors are learning about humour, and I guess they don't think I can explain any better who and what they are, how they live and how they do what they do." *We'll see,* he thought. "So, let's get back upstairs, and before you get ready, I'll try to explain more about the visitors, about what's happening, and try to answer your questions."

"I remember that you tried to explain about them, but that just didn't work. Okay, well, I think they did a great job on the offices." Joy was just standing and looking around as she felt the need to repeat herself. "I really like the hallway, the carpet, the way the regional office areas have some space between them, and such a welcoming front area. It just seems like a wonderful, friendly, open concept that will support dialogue, sharing, and working as a team. And Syd, I like the space where we'll be working while I'm here. But the best part is the wall at the entrance. It's amazing. It has such huge potential to welcome and relax guests coming to the Blue World Governmental Headquarters." She stopped and then said, "Syd, I'm glad to work with you, and the visitors, of course."

"Thank you for that, and I agree with you on the set-up of the offices," said Green.

It was early afternoon, so Green and Joy had a few hours to relax, talk, and sort things out. Back in Green's apartment, Joy found some wine and some cheeses to celebrate. They settled into the living room, and started sipping on the wine, and having some cheese, as Green organized his thoughts to try to explain his experience meeting the visitors.

She wanted to hear about them and prodded Green to get going as she waited for him to start.

Green, finishing his first glass of wine, started to feel good – he was ready. He got up, filled his glass, then walked around, thinking of how to start. Finally, he plunked himself into a chair opposite Joy. Leaning forward, he took a deep breath and drank some wine.

"Oh my, this wine is so good," he smiled and took another drink. "Okay here we go …" Green explained as best he could about the whole experience.

Joy still had trouble understanding what he was saying, continuously stopping him to ask questions.

Green tried to clarify, to explain everything in more basic terms, but got frustrated and eventually just looked at Joy and threw his hands in the air. At that point, both Green and Joy agreed that he should stop, but he heard considerable laughter in the background.

Good try, Sydney. Take another sip of wine and try again, but just focus on a few key points. Good luck …

Green took another sip of wine as he heard more laughter. Then he began, "Joy, the visitors are pure energy. When we talk to them, we're talking to all of them. They're in one place, and all places at the same time. And as you've seen with my apartment, and probably will with yours, and the offices, and transporting us anywhere at any time, they have unlimited powers."

He got up but was a little shaky from the wine, so he sat back down. "When I was with them, it was unbelievable—like I was doing a spacewalk, and when I saw them, it was like seeing small bolts of lightning. Joy, there is so much more to explain about the visitors, but it's so complicated that I don't even understand it," He paused for a minute, "Can we move to other topics now?"

"Of course, but that was much better," replied Joy. "I think I understand a bit about them. I understand that they have powers beyond our understanding, and that we just have to trust them and go along with their plans."

"Oh, good for you, absolutely on the mark."

And then Joy continued, "Well, it must have been quite an experience, and I'm sure you had a lot of questions … you've finished your wine, and I think, just looking at you, that you've had enough. Do you want some tea now?"

"No, thank you, I think I'll save my appetite for dinner." Joy went into the kitchen to make herself a cup of coffee. Green followed her there and again thanked her for listening and for agreeing to help with the education file.

Once Joy had her coffee, they went back into the living room, and Green, feeling better from the wine, started to explain. "Joy, the visitors talked about a new quality of life for everyone in the world. What's to come, what we'll be working on, is establishing a society within which people can achieve their dreams and find meaning in their lives. Joy, in this new age, it won't matter what you do or where you live. People all over the world, in all regions, will be equal—and recognized.

"As the visitors have explained to me, all jobs are equal in the makeup of this new age. Those working with the new technologies, in education, in support services, in all areas, will do as significant a service for society as everyone else. And so it goes, Joy. Whether you're a scientist, a doctor, a musician, a maintenance person, a teacher, or a government worker, a restaurant server, storyteller, an athlete, or whatever you excel in—we all contribute, we all support each other in making a balanced global society." Green paused for a moment.

"And as such, *we* are the new currency, and that is where the identification technology—the new communication systems that we get at birth—come into play. That technology opens all the doors for us."

He walked around the room and then said, "Joy, as we continue our work, we'll bring dignity, respect and opportunity equally to all regions and people—people will have meaning in their lives. There will be no need to worry about if you have enough money. No more taxes, no more banks, loans, debts, no more worries about being able to afford anything ... Joy, as the visitors have been working hard preparing for this transition, we'll be partnering with many others around the world to keep us on the right track. Our future looks so bright, like the light at the end of the tunnel." Green then sat in the chair across from Joy. His passion was obvious.

She put up her hand to stop him, smiled, and suggested, "Let's stop on that positive note as I have to get ready for dinner. If it's all right, you can continue tomorrow and let me know the specifics of the role you see me playing. Now I'm ready to have a nice dinner with our friends."

"Good plan, but one last point before we leave this." Green stood to emphasize his point. "The visitors have recognized that we must now deal with the issues from the bottom up. To establish the regional governments, they were dealing from the top down, implementing massive changes. Now we have to work from the bottom up, developing leadership, management, and communication skills, and the SCM system in all areas. This is why the new education systems are so important."

Green looked at Joy to see if she heard what he was saying, but he sensed she was distracted, so he dropped the discussion for the time being. "Just come back here when you're ready and make sure you tell me about your apartment, then we'll go."

As she left to get ready, she commented, "Syd, I know you're excited and committed to what is happening, and I want to hear more, but I need to know what I've agreed to in all of this. See you soon."

"Sure," replied Green.

About an hour later, there was a knock on Green's door. As he opened it, he saw Joy and the two representatives they met in the offices. Down in the parking garage, they found the vehicle and saw someone waiting for them.

"Welcome," he said. "My name is Andy. I'll be your driver and tour guide for this evening. Please get in and make yourselves comfortable." As the driver negotiated traffic, he discussed the different boroughs in New York. He drove through the different areas, pointing out Broadway and famous buildings like the Empire State Building and what they were known for. As well, he discussed the advances in cleaning up the city and the work being done to eliminate homelessness, pointing out a few of the new housing complexes and the new schools. Most importantly, he mentioned several times the impact of ridding the city of weapons and healing the addictions that had been causing so many problems.

Just as they arrived at the restaurant and parked the vehicle at the entrance, Andy looked at each of them. In a very serious tone, he said, "I hope you have a nice dinner; I'll be here when you're finished to take you back to the UN, but please, there is one last point I would like to make. I have to say that as things look good in the city, my friends and I want you all to know that there is a lot more to do, on the ground, so to speak. Thank you and see you soon."

With that, they all thanked him as they stepped out of the vehicle to be greeted by the restaurant's manager.

As the manager led the four of them into the restaurant, cameras were flashing from the media that had gathered. The four of them posed but didn't answer any questions. Once inside, the manager brought them to a special table that had been set up for them. As they approached, the people in the restaurant stood and applauded. Green was the only one who wasn't surprised by the greeting of the media, the pictures, and the people in the restaurant recognizing him, and stopping their dinner to acknowledge the group.

They enjoyed a nice meal, discussing the progress in their regions, the set-up of the world government offices, and why the visitors called it the Blue World Government. During their dinner, they patiently responded to people as they were approached with questions and requests for selfies. The representatives from the Middle East and the Eurasian regions were caught off balance by the reception, the recognition, and the thanks from a few people who were in New York, but from an area in their region. Green explained that people recognized their work and the positive impacts it was having, and that they wanted to express their gratitude. Satisfied with the explanation, they finished their dinner and left. The driver dropped the representatives off at their hotel, then drove Green and Joy back to the United Nations Building. They said good night as Green escorted Joy to her apartment and made arrangements to meet in the morning.

26

GREEN AND JOY DISCUSS HER NEW ROLE

IN THE MORNING, GREEN AND JOY ENJOYED BREAKFAST IN HER apartment, and she showed him around. He was so thankful that she was with him. After being with the visitors, seeing what they were, and learning they were the caretakers of the universe, he felt that the 'little blue planet' was really just another task for them. We're just biological units that live in three dimensions, and although they seemed to care, Green needed more – he needed to have Joy by his side – someone who really understood his needs. And just by being there she would keep him focussed, on track. So, after enjoying breakfast he was determined to explain more to her about what was going to happen. Joy, on the other hand, was pleased with what the visitors had done for her.

"This is really nice. It's perfect for you, and it looks like a section of your house in Whitehorse. I wonder if they just transported it here."

"That's funny, it isn't like your place, but it has all of the same amenities, and I won't be here all the time, so it's just right for my purposes."

"Absolutely. Boy, the visitors know how to do it right, don't they? Now, shall we go and continue our discussion downstairs after we say hi to everyone?" The visitors responded to Green ...

Sydney, we understand how you feel about us, and for the most part you're right. Although we're learning about humour, emotion is not something that is in our make-up. But please understand that in our own way we really do care about you and your world, why else would we have risked bringing you to meet with us? Remember that we've never done that before. Anyway, it's alright, now go and explain what you will to Joy ... she is with you, and so are we.

Before they left the apartment Green gave Joy a hug and whispered a 'thank you' in her ear. Joy was a little confused but smiled. They went to the world government offices to discuss Joy's role in the plans and so Green could continue explaining some details about the priorities he had discussed with the visitors. As they entered the area, they greeted people who were scurrying around, setting up their offices and decorating the space. They waved, said "Hi" to the staff who were there, and introduced themselves as they headed to Green's office.

After they got into the office, as Joy was getting comfortable, Green paced a little before starting. He knew that if she was to be effective in her role with the new education protocols, she would have to understand what would be happening around her.

"Joy, as I started to discuss yesterday, the visitors propose that we concentrate on several essential priorities. The offices here will be in constant communication, 24/7, with their regional governments to oversee the implementation of the priorities and provide support. This is to make sure that the regions are operating in parallel, are able to share expertise, to effectively communicate in resolving any issues, and take into account the multi-cultural differences that currently exist." Green paused and took a deep breath.

Green stopped pacing and faced Joy. "The first and most important point for all of us is to establish the universal format for education, from preschool on up through the ranks. The visitors have told me that the draft format is complete, which you've had a chance to review, and that you've had discussions and participated with the committee. It seems that it's ready for regional review.

"Joy, this is where you come in. You have an important role in managing and keeping the experts and the regional representatives organized in reviewing and presenting the draft for local input before it's finalized. Then, once the protocols are formally introduced in the regions, we need you to follow up on how it's going, which you can do, for the most part, from your home in Whitehorse."

Green moved behind a chair, gripped the back, leaned forward, and looked right at Joy as if he were talking to his students about the importance of the work they were involved in and the impact they were going to have.

Joy moved forward in her chair, recognizing that Green was about to reveal something important.

"Joy, once the new education programs are operating, you and the leadership from each of the regions have to oversee the work. The team in each regional office must support the implementation of the details in the guidelines and follow up, over time, to make sure it remains consistent globally—that it takes root." Green looked at Joy.

"We have to rely on you to keep in touch and respond to any issues that may arise. I hope you understand the importance of this and how impactful it will be for the youth."

Joy stood up, thought for a moment, and then clearly and emotionally, she started to respond. Green could see she was excited.

"Oh, Syd, do I understand the potential impact of this work? You bet! And I understand the long-term commitment I'm making." Joy started to pace, but Green interrupted her thoughts.

"Joy, Joy, please stop pacing." He could hear laughing in the background.

Now you understand how we feel when you start pacing ... it must be a family thing. There was more laughing.

Then Joy continued, facing Green as if she were a teacher addressing a class. "When I was teaching and started to see the second and third generations coming through my classroom, two things became clear to me. One was that the home environment had a huge impact on the intellectual and social development of the child. And two, I noticed in the kids a yearning, a desire—as if they wanted an ice cream cone—to do well. There was a latent desire for recognition, a look in their eyes that they were focused, interested, but it was to no avail."

Then Joy expanded on the comment explaining how it was, and how before the visitors that she was frustrated with how it took so much time and energy just to keep her students' attention.

Green felt the sadness, and the failure she was now feeling.

"Syd, to this day, I feel that I failed those kids who had a difficult life to overcome, that I wasn't able to compete with the energy and focus they had to exert just to survive their lived experiences." Joy paused and plunked herself back into the chair. As she leaned forward, Green sensed she was going to open up and get really serious.

So, he suggested that they should continue back in his apartment where there was more privacy and quiet. They worked their way through the staff setting up and went back upstairs. Once they got settled in, Joy opened up to him.

"Syd, I saw first-hand the discrepancy in opportunity, in quality of life, between the kids from families that were privileged and those who were not, between the kids who went home to dysfunctional families and those who went home to caring and supportive family units. I saw kids who had academic potential, who were brilliant students, who changed and were lost as they grew into their teens.

"You remember the Mary story, don't you?" Joy stopped, closed her eyes as she wiped away a tear, and covered her mouth as she sighed with memories of what was. "She is a perfect example of what I"m talking about."

Green could see and feel the sadness in her face as she dropped her head deep in thought and leaned into one of the chairs.

She took a moment, then stood up again. "Sydney, those intense feelings of failure, not for all of the kids, but for those that needed my help, and I wasn't able to assist them to go beyond their personal experiences, still affect me to this day. This is part of the reason I want to help now. Do you remember when the visitors took you to their ship, and then you came to school and talked to a rather large gathering?"

"How could I forget that. It was life-changing."

"Tell me, I know ..." and they both laughed, thinking about how Joy had been pulled in as well,

"One of the things you mentioned to the students was that the future was in their hands. That the youth of the world will benefit from and be responsible for the evolution of our world. Sydney, since that day, and the following press conferences and media coverage of your escapades, and the work that happened with the First Nations, those words resonated and started to change the attitude of the students in our school. In my last few years teaching, I constantly thought of those students before who would have benefited from experiencing such a transformation." Joy sat back down in the chair and continued.

"Sydney, the changes that happened in the village with the First Nations membership showed me that the visitors knew what they were doing and how they were directing us. You saw the changes in the village, in the people. Sydney, being part of one's family, a contributor to the community, has become a badge of pride, of honour."

Joy paused and closed her eyes as if she was remembering something, and then she concluded, "Syd, I am totally committed to continuing the work on the education piece with the representatives from the regions, so I can be a small part of bringing that experience to other areas around the world."

Green could see excitement in her face, but realized she needed a short break. "Thank you, Joy. You've no idea how happy that makes me. Why don't I make us a cup of coffee and tea? Then we can discuss a couple of other items." Joy followed Green into the kitchen, and as he prepared the beverages, and a piece of cake for each of them, he continued.

"Joy, I just want to say how important you've been throughout my whole life. You were there for me when we were young, you were there when I was sidelined by NASA, and with the coming of the visitors, you've been amazing. And now, once again, you're there, but for people around the world, for the youth." Green went up to Joy, hugged her, and whispered in her ear, "Thank you, dear Joy. With all of my heart, thank you." He backed off and just stood there, looking at her with so much love and respect.

Joy went up to him and embraced him as she started crying. After a moment or so, she got control, turned and took a deep breath.

"Sydney, thank you! You never recognized it, but even as a kid, I looked up to you. I saw your brilliance, your commitment, and wished I could be like you. And now, oh my God, look at you." Joy shook her head and took a sip of her coffee. "And look at us, a mutual admiration society. Again, thank you, Sydney. Now tell me about the other initiatives as I feel that in dealing with education, it's important to know about what else is happening."

And so Green started, "Joy, what you just discussed about your experiences teaching is so to the point about the next priority. When you talked about some of your students going home to dysfunctional family units, and how their experiences limited their chances of having a good life, and that those experiences, in many cases, forecast their future - was difficult for me to hear." Green stopped for a moment to gather his thoughts.

"What I witnessed all over the world was just that. I saw many families struggling from day to day, and in many parts of the world, the kids suffered under unbearable circumstances. The imbalance in society had, and to a degree still has, a significant impact on the lives of people everywhere."

"Where are you going with all of this?" she asked.

Green took a sip of his tea and then walked around as he continued. "In this next phase, the next actionable priority is to make sure that all people have their day-to-day needs met, from housing to food, healthcare, education ... well, every aspect of life. One step in achieving this is that all money, as a currency—defining one's value, possessions, and quality of life—will be eliminated. The key to success in the new systems, the challenge for everyone, will be to understand that your value is the contribution you make, being committed to family and community, and continuing your learning in whatever field you excel—just like you've explained is happening in the Yukon. And that all people, at all levels, will be treated equally.

"This is why your challenge, and that of all of the teachers around the world, is so critical. Once people are free of encumbrances, especially the children, it becomes essential to work with the new education format so we can identify potential leaders, musicians, doctors, athletes, and educate, recognize, and support our children. As well, we have to teach the history, makeup, and contribution of the seven regions; we have to have inclusion and develop an appreciation of cultural differences and the contribution of individuals."

Green paced a bit, then stretched, took a deep breath, and continued with the visitors' next priority. "Joy, we've talked about education and money, but none of that will happen unless we deal with the governance, co-operation, communication, and sharing between the regional governments, ultimately through the establishment of the world government." Green walked around the room, thinking and reflecting on what to say next when the visitors, focusing their communication specifically at him, interrupted.

Sydney, you're doing great. This is exactly how we'll address the representatives in the world government. By the way, most of them are setting up their offices and seem very pleased with how the space is organized. Now, let Joy know about the multi-cultural nature of your world and what we propose to do.

Green then continued. "Joy, the visitors just explained a bit about the multi-cultural nature of the world as they saw it when they arrived and the resulting prejudice. This lack of acceptance of cultural diversity still exists and has to give way fundamentally to a fair and equitable society. We all have to understand, and accept, the cultural norms of others as we transition to new social paradigms—we have to work together." Green sat down, had some more tea, and took a bite of cake.

"Joy, this part of our future isn't about the power of one culture, of one race dominating others, or one religion belittling others. It isn't about one country, or one region, or nationalism, or political parties, or hierarchical structures ... this is about one world. It's about inclusion, about fairness and meeting everyone's needs, and about the opportunity to succeed. It's about seeing the beauty in others and coming together to help each other as one.

"Is it a difficult process? Absolutely, but that's why education, communication, the levels of government being responsive and accountable are so important. And the right people being 'elected' into positions of authority according to their education, experience, and proven leadership qualities is critical. Joy, our biggest task is to defeat the latent apathy and fear of change that exists."

"The visitors understood," Green said, "that after centuries of living within a social and economic system charged with systemic racism, religious biases that caused conflict and wars, and the abusive control of the elite classes, there would be fear of change. That what people were so used to, so accepting of the way things were, that it would be difficult for the general populations to adjust to new paradigms."

Green let that sink in for a moment as he had more cake and then finished his tea.

"You know, Joy, the visitors explained to me that after we completed the first phase— that we started to see a change in how people viewed the world. Then when people started to see those who got elected to governmental positions actually start to listen and respond to their needs, when they saw the regions sharing goods and services, and when they experienced the new technologies improving their lived experiences, they realized that the changes were beneficial for them and their families. Joy, there is still a lot to do as the visitors have priorities and several objectives for us to implement in order to complete our transition."

"Syd, I feel your emotion, your excitement in what the future holds, and I'm excited to get started."

"We will get started. But right now, as the visitors have let me know, the regional representatives are still busy setting up their offices, and they're very happy with the space. The visitors suggest that we should go back down and formally welcome the regional representatives.

"Just one last thing before we go. As you know, we've had three elections so far, and the visitors have seen a considerable impact of youth moving into positions of leadership. They've recognized the pride of those in the field, helping to build and install the new infrastructure and learning to operate the innovations and new technologies. The bottom line is we seem to be moving in the right direction – and like the Yukon example people are wanting to participate, to help."

"What great news," Joy interjected. "I am so proud of your work so far, now let's go down and meet everyone. I guess the visitors will set up a plenary session for the leadership as soon as possible?"

Just then, the visitors stepped in. *Yes, thank you for mentioning that, Joy. We've set up a meeting for tomorrow morning between yourselves and the leaders of each of the regions. This will be a small group. Sydney, you'll go over the three priorities and the role of the world government.*

Joy, you should discuss what the results have been in the First Nations communities in Yukon and how you look forward to working with educational experts in each region to implement the universal education protocols. Now, most of the delegates will be able to speak and understand English. So, because they're from different areas of the world, they all agreed to have the meeting in English. However, you now have the ability, Joy, that when you speak with a delegate individually—for example, when you're meeting a team from one of the regions—they will hear you in their language, and when they respond, you will hear them in English.

"Now that's exciting ... thank you! And I think that is happening already, although I wasn't sure."

"All right," said Green. "Let's go and meet everyone and welcome them."

27
WELCOMING THE REGIONAL GOVERNMENT REPRESENTATIVES

JOY AND GREEN MADE THEIR WAY DOWN TO THE NEW OFFICES. AS they entered the area, the excitement and energy were palpable. Looking down the aisle on both sides of the "wall of greetings," they were surprised by how the space was taking shape. Joy also noticed that the wall already had two sections, the Middle-East and the Eurasian contingents, showing videos and images of their respective regions.

Then, as they moved down the hallway, they saw people working in each office area, people introducing themselves to others, and lots of goings-on as the offices were being set up. They stopped at a spot where they could witness much of the activity and watched for a moment, noticing the friendly atmosphere, the teamwork, and how the people from the delegations that had completed their work were walking around meeting and helping the others. There were also several people sitting in the coffee shop, enjoying the company of the other delegates. Green and Joy tried to blend in, just watching the activity, but people were starting to point in their direction, so it was time to approach the delegations.

"This is amazing, Syd. I never imagined that so many diverse individuals would come together so quickly."

"I know, and I'm hearing many different languages in the offices as they're getting organized, but then when they interact with other delegations, like here in the coffee shop, they're all using English. It's really something special."

They started to walk around, welcoming everyone—now Green was instantly recognized, and he made a point of introducing Joy. As they interacted with each delegation, Green notified the leadership of each region that there would be a meeting in the chair's office the next morning at 9am for the principal elected representative of each region to discuss the details of the world government. He also arranged for each delegation, as soon as they were ready, to have a quick tour of his office. Then Joy and Green went to the office to wait for the delegations.

As each delegation entered, Green and Joy welcomed them. Each delegation was surprised that both Joy, who was just getting comfortable with her abilities, and Green, spoke to them in their native language. At the end of the tour, Green discussed, with Joy's input, the critical nature of her role in overseeing the development of a universal education system. He also made sure that everyone understood that his door would always be open. Finally, he shared his office contact information and mentioned that if anyone needed help, or had questions, once his office was staffed, it would be open 24/7, and they could come in at any time. When all the tours were completed, the two of them took their leave and went back to Green's apartment.

As they had many times during the past several years in Whitehorse, Joy and Green enjoyed a quiet dinner that they had delivered to Green's apartment. They spent the evening discussing the meeting for the morning. The visitors participated in that discussion.

Joy, Sydney, the meeting in the morning is historic as it will set the direction for the future of your world. Let us be clear with you that you are establishing the first generation of the Blue World Government. The creation of the world government has been the final step with many other worlds as they implement new systems. Just to let you know, in most other worlds, a new calendar is established, celebrating the event of creating a new era.

You both have to be clear, especially you, Joy, as implementing the education piece is most critical at this time. So, Sydney, you have to go through the three priorities we've discussed and touch on the objectives, as necessary. Try to leave the education piece to the last, but once you introduce it, you should turn it over to Joy.

"Understood," replied Green.

Then, Joy, if you could start by introducing yourself and briefly talking about your background and the results in the First Nation's communities and Yukon. Finally, and most importantly, turn your attention to education, how it's been reviewed by specialists in all the regions, why it's important to implement, and how all of the leadership in the room have to work together to make it happen at the local, regional, and world levels. Finally, be clear that you will be there for them if there are questions, and that you will be following up with each region.

You should point to the final iteration of the report, which they should see in front of them as part of their package, and specifically say that this is a final copy ready for regional implementation at all levels. Also, you should mention the need to get on this as soon as possible as the identification of aptitude, leadership, desire, and sectoral interest has to be started at the kids' earliest ages. The point has to be made that these early developmental years predict that interest and are the building blocks that will determine the future of the world. Also, be clear to make the point that this is not to say that children will be labelled—as they grow, and if their interests change, the system will accommodate them.

"No problem, I can do that. I have read, studied the document, and participated in regional meetings to get input. As well, I was involved in formatting the final version and have talked with the authors on implementation recommendations. But, as my work with the report has been primarily academic to this point, if there are questions about details in the report that are specific to a region, such as cultural diversity, will you be there to help respond if I need you?"

Absolutely. If something comes up, we'll be right there with you, listening and ready. Now relax, and we'll be with you in the morning.

Joy returned to her apartment, and the during rest of the evening, both Green and Joy prepared for the meeting.

28

THE FIRST MEETING OF THE BLUE WORLD GOVERNMENT

BRIGHT AND EARLY THE NEXT MORNING, GREEN GATHERED THE packages he would hand out and worked his way to his office. He went to the conference room to make sure everything was ready and he stood at the entrance, looked around, and he thought, *This is it. The time has come.* He had worked with the visitors, preparing the contents of the packages that set out the key objectives and the three priorities, and he placed a folder in front of each seat. Green then walked around the room, practising how he would welcome the delegates. He understood the historic relevance of the meeting he was about to chair and the importance of organizing and leading the world government.

He was thinking of the servant leadership model, how he had to be there for the representatives, to support them. He was also mulling over the establishment of milestones in order to track all of the goals that will be shared. To say he was excited, hopeful, and apprehensive all at once would be an understatement. Just as she was entering the room, Joy saw that Green was taking some pills, as he usually did before an important meeting.

"Are you all set, Syd? Are you okay?"

"I will be," he responded. "I just took the pills to calm me down and they should kick in shortly."

Joy came up to him, took his hands, looked at him and smiled, then she gave him a hug. "It's going to be just fine; I will be right here with you, and so will the visitors."

Absolutely, Sydney. We're here, and you're ready. Just go by the script we discussed, and all will be well. Sydney, you've done this so many times now ... no worries.

"Thank you both." Then, turning to Joy, Green said, "Joy, you should sit here, beside me. I need you close as we get started. There's a folder about the priorities for you. Are you ready for your presentation?"

"Yes, I have a PowerPoint that I'll use. I prepared it with the visitors and it's already in the system. That's why I brought my laptop."

"Okay, so now we just wait for the others to arrive."

The delegates from each region started to arrive, and as they did, Green welcomed them and also pointed out that Joy would be joining the group. Once everyone was seated, he looked around the room. He noticed that of the seven representatives, three were women, and he felt good about that. Getting their attention, he held onto the back of his chair at the front of the room, looked around until everyone settled down, and then he started.

"Welcome, everyone." And to lighten the mood he smiled and said, "As you may or may not know, I'm Sydney Green." Everyone laughed. "For better or worse, I've been appointed by the visitors as the chair of the Blue World Government."

Again, there was some mild laughter, as if anyone didn't know who he was, and there were comments like, "That's a good one, Dr. Green."

"Okay, let's do a bit of housekeeping before we start the meeting. Everyone has had a tour of this space, but just as a reminder ...". Green pointed out where the washrooms were, and indicated to his right that there was coffee, tea, and treats in the room, and whenever anyone needed something to just get it. Then he discussed that the agenda for this first meeting, of necessity, was planned by the visitors, but all subsequent meetings would be held, and planned, at the representatives' discretion, and anyone in the room might call a meeting, which could be held here, or rotating between the regions—it was up to them to decide.

Green repeated that the office had an open-door policy and anyone from any of the regions was welcome to drop in at any time. Pointing in the direction of the technology room, he mentioned the location of the transport device and how it was connected to all of the other devices in the regions. Then he explained that if anyone from the Blue World Government needed to go to a specific area in their region, or anywhere in the world, where there wasn't a transport device, or needed to travel to another region with a group of people, at this time the visitors would have to be notified to make the request happen, and so that they could keep track to make sure that anyone travelling would be transported back to this office, or another location. He then repeated that the office and transportation services were available at any time, day or night or weekend, especially if there was an emergency.

Several representatives put up their hands and asked, "How will we contact the visitors if necessary? Do we go through you?"

"No, good question, though. Please be patient, as we'll get to the role of the visitors very soon, and then you'll have an answer to your question."

Before starting the official meeting, Green sat down, and as he surveyed the group, he noticed they were anxious to get started. He also sensed that they were wondering about the "blue" in the world government. Green stood up.

"Oh, why the blue in the Blue World Government? The visitors explained to me that there were very few planets with as much water as we have on earth, and that two things have been obvious, well, forever: one, that our planet is very small in comparison with others that support life; and two, that when scanning the universe in our area, we are distinctly seen as a little blue planet. So, they decided that as we start to make contact, we'll be introduced as representatives from the little blue planet, and that our organization should then be called the Blue World Government." Everyone understood, and there were no questions, so Green moved behind his chair, took a deep breath as he looked at the people in the room, and started with the agenda.

"Ladies and gentlemen, I formally call this first meeting of the Blue World Government to order."

Everyone clapped.

"The first item on the agenda, for the record," and he paused as he sat down, "is to have a round table with everyone introducing themselves, giving their background, education, experience, and briefly discussing the state of affairs in their region." Close to an hour later, and when everyone had shared their contact information, Green stood, and before going any further, he called for a short break so everyone could mingle, get a beverage and a treat. About 15 minutes later, he called the meeting back to order and began.

"Well, we have quite a varied and knowledgeable group, so let's get started." Green stood behind his chair and leaned in, smiling. "Ladies and gentlemen, coming back to the question that was asked earlier, I have two important announcements. One, within the next few days each of you will have the ability to be in direct contact with the visitors to discuss issues, get direction, and, if required, get help resolving problems. The visitors will be giving you special powers, but we'll be learning more about that in a couple of minutes. We do have to understand that the future of our world is in our hands, and the visitors will be backing off sooner than later, however, they will leave one ship here for a while, until we're fully competent to be on our own.

"The second point that we'll have to discuss as we move forward is, as the visitors have pointed out to me, that on all other planets, as they created their world government, they started a new calendar. So, as we go forward, this will be the first day on the new calendar, but we have to determine how that calendar will look. One example proposed by the visitors was NA 01, standing for 'New Age, Year 01.' The visitors also suggested that we could keep the months, and as well the names of the days of the week, to reduce any confusion. So, think about it, and when we finish this meeting, we'll come back to this discussion." Green paused for a moment.

"Now, before we get to the folders and then hear from Ms. Taller, Joy, the visitors wanted me to discuss something with you." Green surveyed the group, ensuring he had their complete attention.

"There are a few important items: first, we have achieved some successes so far, and we can't ignore that. We have set up the seven regional governments, introduced technologies and infrastructure, and improved the living standards of many people through the SCM system. It is now time for us to work on achieving our independence from the visitors as we move forward.

"That is one of the reasons we're meeting today—to establish how we gain our independence. It is our responsibility to make the world government the link between the regions and set a pattern of communication, partnership, and co-operation. We must recognize and share the positive impact of the social, technical, and infrastructure advancements that have already been introduced and those that will be introduced as we move forward. On that point, there are two essential innovations that the visitors have been working on that will help us with our mandate. We must implement the new communications systems and the education protocols, which we'll discuss soon. I can't overstate the importance of these two innovations.

"The next issue, ladies and gentlemen, is that we have to be relentless in our support of our regions and each other. We have to realize that we must be constant in our communications to alleviate any concerns or issues that may arise. We have to be alert, prepared, and ready to respond."

Green paused as he moved out from behind his chair.

"The final point I have to discuss is really, really important." He smiled as he started to walk around the room. "Just a week or so ago, I met the visitors. Now that was an experience, as I met them in their environment, face to face, so to speak." He smiled at the visitors' laughter in the background, and looked at Joy who heard it as well, then he looked around the room and sensed the surprise. "Now that was an experience, meeting them face to face, so to speak,"

Green chuckled, shaking his head, but he sensed that everyone was anxious to hear what he had to say. "I will try to explain. First, they are not human, nor biological in any way, shape, or form. I needed to have a protective shield in order to maintain an environment that supported human life while in their presence. You see, the environment within which they exist was like being in space … it was vast—actually seemed endless and dark—with just a few flashes of light in the distance. I was literally floating in space." Green paused to let that sink in.

"The visitors explained that they are composed of pure energy and exist in a multi-dimensional environment. It was then that I saw what looked like small bolts of electricity and many rectangular shapes coming into view, again disappearing and then reappearing. The voice of the visitors explained that they have the ability to move between dimensions, which, with the boundless source of power they absorb from dark energy and dark matter, sustains them.

"They also explained that they are one with each other, and merge within and control the technology that makes up their ships. They adjust their technology in order to interact in our three-dimensional existence, to communicate with us, and do the things they do. Ladies and gentlemen, they are the protectors of the universe." Green stopped as he heard some laughter in the background from the visitors.

Sydney, that's enough. They aren't ready to realize the significance of what you're saying and how it's even possible. Good try, though. Just finish by saying that we're here to provide the support and direction to complete their work and give them a couple of examples like the transport devices. Then have them drink the glass of water that will suddenly appear and tell them about the pills to allow them to be able to communicate with us.

"Sorry, everyone," Green continued. "I guess I got carried away. Anyway, let me just finish this part by saying that they are here, because of their role in the universe, to help us achieve success through the next stages in our development. Now, to give you an example of their power." Green was back at the front of the room.

"Ladies and gentlemen, please see in front of you a glass of water." Suddenly, to everyone's surprise, glasses appeared in front of them. "This is a gift from the visitors. Tomorrow there will be another glass of water and a package of pills. You'll take one a day for the next couple of weeks."

The people were puzzled but trusting as they drank the water.

Green then explained, "The water, and then the pills, will give you two skills. As I have mentioned earlier, one skill in the next couple of days will be the ability to communicate directly, telepathically, with the visitors—and the visitors with you. If you have specific issues or questions you need help with, they will be with you as needed and will communicate with you individually or as a group when and if they see the need.

"The second skill, which will expand as you take the pills, will enable you to understand any language spoken to you in our world and respond in the language of the people you're addressing. Joy and I have already gone through this regimen. It's made quite a difference in our ability to have discussions, and as you know, gain the trust of people we work with in all regions. This will be a valuable skill for you as we proceed and deal with different cultures and dialects in each of our regions."

During the next half-hour, Green took the time to respond to the many questions from the representatives. He also explained that this was part of the new communications protocols, so that the world government could take control from the visitors.

"The communication technology, which the visitors have controlled from their ships, will be restored to us. The new communication devices are for our general population, your local, territorial, and regional managers, and for us to keep everyone up to date through broadcasts and respond to situations without delay. They are also a means of acquiring input and sustaining the accountability of all levels of government."

Green paused for a moment as he sat down in his chair. He looked around the room and sensed that everyone was really committed to what was happening. He was excited, got focused, and continued.

"As you know, there are no more political parties, and in that regard we are transitioning smoothly in all of the regions. This is a very exciting time for us.

The three elections we've organized have started to put the right people in positions of authority, managers who are responsible, accountable, educated, experienced, and have the leadership qualities to help us move forward. Along with the changes we'll implement through the new world government, this process will finally prepare us for our future."

Green stood and started to walk around again as if he were presenting to a class. "Ladies and gentlemen, we are a group individually selected by our regional representatives, and as such, we have the mission, responsibility, and accountability for implementing the next stages of our development. We are accountable for overseeing all developments in our regions and sharing with each other our needs, or how we can help each other. We must trust each other; we must be able to speak our minds and be there for each other when issues arise, which they will. Formality is important, but standing as a group supersedes that as we have to end our discussions, even in the next few days, with agreement on our positions as we move forward. We are charged with taking over from the visitors."

Then Green continued explaining that they all had to accept the historic relevance of what they're participating in—creating the world government that would oversee the continued development of their world, a new era, in preparation to represent the earth to other civilizations. He also repeated, slowly, that this was the first day of the new era. It was of historic importance. That was why the new calendar would start with this day, and this meeting, and be remembered as such.

Then he mentioned, "Because of the importance of this meeting, the visitors are recording it and will share that record with everyone at the table. Finally, although we all agreed to speak in English, the visitors have said that they will provide recordings in English, in the primary languages of each region, as well as any other language that is requested. We must practice inclusivity and do what we expect of others." There was silence and then applause. Then Green continued.

"So, let's turn our attention to the folders in front of you." He paused for a moment to give everyone a chance to open the folders. "The visitors have outlined six objectives that we'll work on as we implement three essential priorities. As you can see those priorities are: one, establishing a universal education system; two, finally restructuring our economic systems by eliminating money as a currency and replacing it by establishing a meritocracy, which promulgates the value of human capital; and three, by focusing attention on the residents in each region. We must be able to respond to and listen to the needs of the people by implementing the new communication systems explained in your folders.

"The offices here, and as needed all of you, will be in constant communication, 24/7, between each of your regional governments and the visitors, if necessary. This is to ensure that the regions are operating in parallel and held accountable. It also takes into account that we recognize the multi-cultural differences that currently exist. In all three initiatives, at all levels of implementation and sustainability, is the concept of inclusion, social parity, and fairness."

Green saw several hands go up in the air. They all had the same question, "How can we eliminate money? People work and want to be rewarded for doing a good job. They want to provide for their families."

Green walked around the room as he responded. "Excellent ... I asked the same questions." He paused just for a brief moment. "What is the reward that people want? Why are we working? Why is it that anytime we want, or need something—from a dinner out, to a car, to a home, to insurance, to our kids' education, to medication when we're sick—we all ask the same question, 'How much does it cost? Can we afford it?' All we want is to provide a safe environment and the ability for our children, for ourselves, not to worry about our day-to-day needs – to be successful and have meaning in our lives. And what about those that have nothing, whose children are starving, who are suffering from conflict and war? Ladies and gentlemen, money, and the lust for power, have been the cause of our dysfunctional past. But not anymore."

Green returned to the front of the room and stood behind his chair. "This is exactly what we'll be providing—meeting the needs of all people in all regions. Ladies and gentlemen, money has been an evil product of capitalism, of the plutocracy, being used as a tool in controlling the masses—no more — the greed, the abuses, and the lust for power around the globe, are coming to an end."

He paused for a minute, surveyed the group, and understood he needed to continue. "Soon, very soon, all the goods and services will be available to everyone. It's the same for everything from housing, to infrastructure, to food, to clothing, entertainment, education, and healthcare—everything. No one will need to worry about insurance, about borrowing, about the cost of a family member needing medical care and medications. No more greed, usage, abuse—we are creating a new era for our world.

"Reward, you ask. What more reward can we have than being free to achieve our dreams, not worry about our day-to-day needs? This is how life is on other planets. I have seen it working. The visitors have shown me, and that is how it will be here. Oh my, ladies and gentlemen, we are headed into a new era within which we'll experience a meaningful and fruitful life—all of us." Green turned away from the table to gather his thoughts and regain control.

"In the next few days," he paused just for a moment as his emotions were evident in his voice, "we'll be going through the priorities and the objectives and determining how we'll co-operate to complete our mission. Be patient, and I think you will see how all of this works ... a new age is coming, and we're responsible for framing it. You, me, Joy, our teams here and in the regions."

Green needed a break, so he suggested they break for lunch. "After lunch," he said, "we'll hear from Ms. Taller, from Joy, about one of the most important pieces in this process — education. Now let's have a nice lunch break."

After Green finished, everyone got up, shook hands, and chatted with each other, saying that they felt that the session was a good start. They all approached Green, thanking him as they left the room to have lunch in the snack bar area. Green sensed that they were supportive but not completely on side yet, so he knew he had some work to do.

After lunch, when everyone was back in the conference room and got settled in, Green stood and got everyone's attention.

"Ladies and gentlemen, just a few more comments before we hear from Joy. We are here to show the way, to be the leaders for our world, to bring us all together—to be one global nation made up of seven regional governments—and we, ladies and gentlemen, will represent the blue world to other civilizations and planets. So how do we do that?"

Green walked around as he quickly went through the file he had provided, emphasizing the three priorities, and in general terms, he defined the role of the world government.

"Ladies and gentlemen, we achieve this by working as a unit. I saw all of you and your teams working together, socializing with each other as you set up your offices, so we must do the same moving forward. What I described before lunch will only happen as long as we lead the way, set the example. Nothing stands in our way anymore! We don't have to ask, 'How much will that cost?' Ladies and gentlemen, we just have to put the directives into motion. We are now entering the most critical stage of our development." He paused as he positioned himself at the front of the room.

"As the visitors have said, they will be here to help us if and when we need it. They've been busy in each region, as you've probably observed, in order to develop the expertise needed and to work with all of us on the continued implementation of the SCM systems, developing infrastructure, housing, new education protocols, and providing goods and services." Green then went on to explain, "A big part of our success will rely on the acceptance of our cultural diversity, the uniqueness and equality of all the people in each region, the many wonderful traditions and histories that exist, and unifying our world under one umbrella." He said, with emphasis, "We're not trying to impose any cultural traditions of one area on another or on any region.

"Our power is in our acceptance of our diversity and working together to bring balance and equal opportunity to all sectors of our world. We are to become the leaders of one nation." Then Green clarified that for this to happen, the visitors explained to him that humans must identify leadership qualities in their youth at an early age and then develop that leadership.

"In order for people to achieve their goals and have a meaningful contribution to society, among other elements, we need to have a common educational system in all areas. This system," Green said, "does not mean we don't teach our youth about their heritage. It means we expand their awareness of where they live, who they are, and who we are as one world. It means opening their minds to what they can achieve and challenging them to be the best they can be in whatever field of study or work that they choose to do.

"In order to achieve this goal, our children, our youth, must live without worry, without concerns about their home life, or having money—that, my friends, is in our hands. They must be secure in the knowledge that they can, and will, achieve their dreams. Our children, our youth, have always been the future, and now must be treated as such."

Then Green concluded, "For this to happen, we must identify the skills our youth exhibit, especially any leadership qualities, as early as possible, and then develop those skills. This is where the new education protocols come into play, so I would like to call upon Joy to let us know what has been happening with the experts in education around the world and to open a discussion on the implementation of the educational guidelines and the opportunities that the system offers us. Joy, please."

29

JOY PRESENTS THE EDUCATION PROTOCOLS

JOY STOOD UP, THANKED GREEN, AND GOT THE POWERPOINT display on the screen—there was a picture of two young kids looking through a glass barrier at a huge gorilla, who was looking right back at them, sitting down with his paw on the glass right where the kids had placed their hands. The children had an expression of excitement, of wonder, of a need to know, to reach out as they were looking into the eyes of the gorilla. The word "curiosity" was in bold print right across the frame. Joy turned from watching the reaction of the group, looked at the screen and pointed. Then as she faced everyone, took a breath, and smiled as she started.

"That, ladies and gentlemen, is the essence of education. You can see the curiosity, the excitement in the kids' faces. Our inquisitiveness, our need to find answers, is an essential part of our human nature." She smiled as she looked around the room. "Do you remember your own curiosity, your desire to learn more about … something, anything? Do you remember seeing or hearing something that piqued your interest? Even today, as Sydney talked about the visitors, I sensed that all of us had a desire to learn about them, a curiosity, a need to understand more of what he was saying—to learn? Our curiosity is with us at all times. They call it lifelong learning."

Then, as she walked around the room, she said, "Ladies and gentlemen, I've been a teacher, an educator, for more than thirty-five years. At first, I was an academic and completed a master's degree in education on curriculum development, focusing on developing individualized learning in a classroom setting. However, as I was working on my PhD studies, I lost my husband to cancer, and I ran away from the academic world. After several months and recovering from my loss, I ended up in Whitehorse, Yukon, of all places." She paused as there was some chuckling.

"I became a classroom teacher for the rest of my career. I struggled to find the key to stimulate my students, to nurture that curiosity we just saw, that wonder and desire to learn. What I found was that many of my kids went home to disturbing situations, their lived experience, which profoundly affected them—so many brilliant students were lost." Joy stopped and stood looking at the group at the front of the conference table and then finished her intro.

"Ladies and gentlemen, as I was teaching, I knew that more than half of my students would be fine, no matter what we did to them at school, as they came from good, hard-working families who cared about them. Ladies and gentlemen, it was the other group, the 45–50%, that I felt I had failed. That failure has stayed with me until now. Why now? Because now I have a chance ... no, we have a chance, to make up for how we have failed our kids." Joy stopped for a moment to let that sink in.

"Now, let's talk about education. Sydney, leaders of the world government, as you know, over the past year experts from each region have gathered to review the established educational systems in each region. They went through the programs and curricula, one region at a time, documenting the highlights, strengths, weaknesses, and gaps that needed attention. They studied the disparities that existed within and between each region. During the next year, they took the information they had gathered from the regions and the visitors, and worked very hard to create a format that was acceptable to the group.

"After lengthy analysis, discussions about policy and about fair and ethical curricula, and a peer review, developing an implementation protocol and timetable for key thresholds, they had consensus on where to begin. The executive summary of what the experts came up with is in the folders I handed out to you when you came into the conference room earlier today.

"Let's be clear right from the start, the educational environment, the policies, and the infrastructure we're discussing today are universal in nature and therefore fall on our lap. The co-ordination and implementation of the protocols is the responsibility of the world government, working with and following up on each of the regional and local governments. Expertise has been developed in all regions and is available as we implement the protocols." Joy paused, answered a few questions that arose, and then continued.

"I have prepared a PowerPoint presentation that will take us through the outline of the plan from preschool to university." Joy stopped and asked if there any more questions or points anyone wished to discuss. The representatives wanted a few minutes to scan the folders to get an idea of what was being proposed. So, Joy suggested that they all refresh their coffee/tea, and take as long as necessary. When everyone was ready, she would go through the folders, using the PowerPoint presentation. After about a half-hour, with Joy walking around, socializing and responding to some preliminary questions, the group was ready.

Then, Joy started by turning to the first slide, and she began. "Thank you, so, let's start with the preschool system." She was nervous and apprehensive, and looked over to Green, who gave her a smile and a nod of support. As well, the visitors reassured her that everyone was ready.

"Curiosity," she started, "allowing our children at the earliest stages, to explore, to feel, to grow, to be challenged, to have fun while learning, to be kids, is our responsibility. Our task is to challenge them, to watch them develop, to watch what they're interested in, to watch their skills, and to identify the potential leaders, as well as identifying other skillsets." Joy stood at the front and paced for a moment before continuing. She looked up at the screen, which showed two kids, who looked to be about three years old, playing together.

They were sitting on the floor looking at each other, excited. They were in front of a Lego home they had built—Joy explained that they were indeed three years old. Then she switched to the next slide, which showed a young boy sitting with two adults, but this slide was a video. One of the adults asked the boy, in Spanish, how old he was. He responded in Spanish that he was five. Then the other adult asked him, in German, where he was born. He then responded, in fluent German, that he had been born in France, in Paris. Then the three of them entered into a discussion in French, and the video stopped. Joy bowed her head and then looked up at the people in the room and smiled as she continued.

"Ladies and gentlemen, as most of us know, children between the ages of birth to six years spend their time learning, absorbing knowledge, as the saying goes, 'like a sponge.' They must adapt, learn, experience, and engage with their environment to learn, to understand, to feel. To watch this happen, to look into their eyes and see the excitement, is the most amazing experience in the world." Joy just stood there for a moment, looking at the most recent slide and then going back to the previous one before she continued. "Just watch a two, or three-year-old, and look at their eyes as they see, feel, absorb something new. It's amazing to witness how they cope, adjust, engage, and learn from their environment." Joy looked around the people at the table, some smiling in recognition of what she was picturing, some questioning, and some confused about where she was going.

"Researchers have concluded, and we have known for decades, that 90% of brain growth and capacity happens in the first six to seven years of age.

Regardless of where a child is born, they have the innate capacity to absorb knowledge. Children have the ability to learn languages, observe patterns, learn from their environment, acknowledge the love and support of their mom and dad, and if they are challenged, resolve issues—how to survive and grow.

"Children from birth have analytical skillsets, like how to build a Lego house from scratch or learn music. They have abilities that educational researchers have recognized for many generations. But where we have failed as educators is in not tapping into this intellectual growth and recognizing ability and talent, and supporting its development. Ladies and gentlemen, as I have personally experienced, we have failed many millions and millions of children by them not having a safe environment, by not providing for their needs, by ignoring their circumstances. But ladies and gentlemen of the world government, the intervention of the visitors, and the changes we are implementing will change all of that."

Joy went to the next slide, which was a picture of a father holding a baby in his arms. She drew everyone's attention to the baby's eyes, looking up at the father. Joy pointed out that the baby was learning about feeling safe, comfortable, and loved, which makes her free to grow—to learn, experiment, and ultimately become the best she can be.

"Members of the world government, this is where we start. Providing, not just for our children, but for all of us, a safe environment free of worry, hunger, pain, and anxiety. As you'll read in the report, the education council requires establishing early childhood services in all regions, in all cities and towns. These programs, as designed by the educators, are not only programs that are fun for the children, but are a first stage evaluation process in identifying our future leaders, sports heroes, engineers, trades people, teachers, doctors, artists, and musicians."

She paused as she moved to the next slide and gave everyone a chance to scan it.

"Here we have a video of two six-year-old children, one playing the piano and then another a violin." The group listened for a few minutes. "Now, wait for it ... here we hear a seven-year-old responding to mathematical questions at the university level. Yes, this is unique, but if we aren't looking for this expertise in all fields of study, it gets lost. The point is that as we implement the new early childhood education system, we must develop an environment that promotes creativity, responds to the child's curiosity, and then supports those with special gifts in all fields of study.

"Members of the world government ..." Joy paused for a moment, then in a very determined voice, and slowly, she continued, "... let me be very clear that we'll find children in all regions with special gifts in all sectors of society. We have to work to develop their skills and use the communication systems to be aware of their presence." Joy stopped and let the next three slides, all showing young children with skills in many areas such as the arts, more music, mathematics, sports, and leadership, speak for themselves. The children were obviously from each of the regions and showed ethnic diversity. At the end of the presentation, the room burst into applause, and everyone was saying that the point was being made.

"Yes, yes," replied Joy as she calmed everyone down, "the brilliance we have seen is not unique just to those in the PowerPoint. Our future is identifying this brilliance in all fields of study. We must also support those who want simply to be employees, who will be happy in a supportive role, as they will be the backbone that will allow us to sustain our cities, our schools, and our goods and services." Then Joy walked around the room, as if she were back in the classroom, and went through the files she'd handed out, answering questions and responding to any concerns raised by the delegates. Several times she had to contact the visitors who instructed her on how to respond, especially on the methodology of the global implementation of the plan.

The meeting went into the early evening. Just before they adjourned until the next day, Green stood and thanked them for their patience and participation.

"Thank you all, this has been quite a day, and we'll see you again tomorrow morning at 9 sharp." Everyone chuckled, and as they left, they shook hands with each other and thanked Joy for an outstanding presentation expressing their support for establishing and implementing the education program.

Green and Joy followed everyone and watched as the delegates went back to their regional offices, where the staff were waiting for them, and started discussing with their teams what had just happened. As they walked along the hallway, passing each regional office, they greeted people and then headed up to Green's apartment. Once there, Green made a cup of coffee for Joy and a cup of tea for himself as they went to the living room to relax and discuss the first meeting.

"Joy, my word, you did an outstanding job. So thorough, so well prepared, responding so fluidly to questions, and you made it clear that this was the future of education and the salvation of our world ... thank you." Green got up, went to Joy, and gave her a big hug, but before Joy could respond, the visitors interjected.

Well, that couldn't have been better. Thank you both so much. Joy, your presentation was perfect, and the obvious support of the delegates was a delightful surprise! What a wonderful way to start the next phase of your world's development. You both have exceeded our most desired expectations for the day—congratulations, we are so pleased. Now go into the kitchen and see what we have prepared for you ... and be aware that it took us all day to do this.

Joy and Green quickly moved into the kitchen and there on the table was a huge selection of sushi—they all had a good laugh.

Sydney, are we catching on to humour and jokes?

"Absolutely."

Okay, so go and enjoy the feast and have a restful evening as tomorrow's event is equally important.

"Thank you," replied Joy. And with that, they enjoyed a great meal, engaged in a lengthy discussion about what Green was going to do in the session tomorrow, and then Joy went to her apartment.

After Joy left, the visitors spoke to Green. *Sydney, there is something we must discuss with you.*

"This sounds serious. Is there an issue?"

Well, a potential issue that you and the others from each region have to be aware of. Sydney, as you know, biological units are very sensitive to changes in their social, psychological, and physical well-being and their personal environment. What we're concerned about is how people will react to the new communication protocols and having a device on their bodies. No matter how silly this may seem to us, that innate fear of new technology, in this case, is easily influenced and has a potential impact.

"Thank you, I did sense something like that coming out when I visited and spoke with managers, leaders, individuals, and families about the new education, communications, and money issues during my visits—but it didn't seem a serious enough concern to mention it. I will briefly address it tomorrow. But to reassure you, in my opinion, as we continue with our plans, it will not last. Let's wait until after the meeting tomorrow to see the response from the delegates." Green then went to have a nice rest to be ready for the next day's event.

30

THE WORLD GOVERNMENT DISCUSSION CONTINUES

THE NEXT MORNING, GREEN WAS UP EARLY. HE WENT OVER THE notes he and the visitors had prepared, then gathered up the notes to be added, like the expanded discussion on the communication issue. When he was ready, he went off to the conference room. Once there, he placed the notes on the table in front of each chair and prepared to meet everyone as they entered. By 8:55 a.m. everyone was in their seat and ready to go.

"Welcome. I hope everyone had a wonderful evening and you're ready for today." There were nods of approval, and Green sensed an attitude of "Let's get going. We're ready."

"Good, well, let's begin with your second glass of water and the pills we discussed yesterday."

Then once more, to their surprise, water and pills appeared in front of each of the delegates.

"If I remember correctly, it takes a couple of days for the pills to do their job, so be patient, but when it starts to work, you'll know because the people you're talking to, if they fall into their language, will be surprised that you understand them and are able to respond in their language. As well, the pills, for a specific time, will give you the ability to be aware of what people are thinking. Be ready because it will also allow you to get in touch with the visitors."

Green sensed their surprise with what he was saying. He stood up behind his chair, then walked around the room as the others drank the water and took a pill. Then, back at the front of the room, he started.

"We've been given these skills by the visitors, but we must be empathetic, yet understanding, good listeners, and responsible for guiding each of our regions independently. As I mentioned yesterday, we must also act as a unit, making the world government just that, a *world* government—one nation made up of seven independent regions." Green took hold of the back of his chair and continued.

"Ladies and gentlemen, we have a task in front of us accepting our responsibility to develop and sustain a fair and just society, to provide and sustain, a quality of life for all the people of our world." Green moved out from behind his chair. He brought a podium that was in a corner of the room closer to the conference table. He moved his chair, positioned the podium, and stood behind it, holding onto it with both hands as he started again.

"People, friends, associates ... having completed the recent elections, we have to prepare to maximize the use of the new communication systems that will be introduced. This new system, which is like a tattoo on everyone's shoulder, gives the person access to everything. The technology is harmless to the individual but acts like a passport, a mobile phone, a medical device—it is all-encompassing and even has privacy settings. Do we have the knowledge to understand the technology? No, but we have to trust the visitors, and make sure that everyone understands that this is the key to accessing everything, to making one's voice heard, to voting, to having one's day-to-day needs met.

"We have to show that this is part of the new age that is upon us, that it is part of what gives us the freedom to pursue our dreams and the power to hold managers accountable. Once in place, this device will allow you and your staff to communicate with all of the people in your region, or one person, or groups. It will allow you to give updates, send messages, and allow, as I just said, the people to hold the government accountable, responsible, and to ask questions or report incidents.

"In that respect, we have to make sure government managers, at all levels, use the system to keep the messaging on track about infrastructure development, implementing the educational protocols, and share examples of our successes." He paused as he noticed a number of people shuffling in their seats and that the representatives seemed to have questions.

He moved the podium and replaced his chair. He sat down as he opened the floor for discussion. As the visitors had expected and prepared Green to respond, the discussion that followed dealt with questions about the details of an individual's ability to control the communication systems, their privacy, and concerns about the device controlling people.

Green discussed the issues and proposed that one resolution to the concerns was to use a global broadcast to develop trust in the new world government. "This broadcast," he said, "will be to introduce all of us, the leadership of the world government, to show the advances that have taken place, discuss the priorities, and show how each and every person will benefit as they are implemented." He said, "During the broadcast, they can explain about the new education systems as well as the communication technology, and how the people will benefit from both." The members were satisfied with the plan. It was a lengthy and productive dialogue, so Green suggested a short break.

After the break, once everyone was seated, Green got up from his chair, brought the podium back front and centre, assumed his professorial posture, and continued.

"Ladies and gentlemen, in your folders are the six objectives and three priorities that we have to make happen. We have to message our people about education. We have to make sure that our housing and infrastructure initiatives continue, and although all of this is important, we also have to make sure that we promote sports, theatre, vacations, and entertainment of all types—and focus our attention on the younger generation as they assume control. My fellow associates, after we're finished our discussions, you have to meet with your staff and get to work."

For the rest of the day, Green went through the notes he had handed out at the start of the meeting. When he was ready to discuss the priority about money, he paused. Both he and the visitors expected this to become a heated discussion, so, cautiously, Green stood by the podium as he began.

"People of the world government, the visitors, in observing the functioning of our economic structures, realized that what drove the system, what sustained and controlled the lifestyles of people at all levels—was money. That is why one of the priorities and objectives deals with money. The visitors saw how the myth of capitalism had a hypnotic influence on the masses and that in order for them—no, for us—to create a fair, just, and balanced society, the system must change.

"So, as you know, a couple of years after the visitors arrived, they started the process of eliminating the usefulness of money as a currency and started to replace that with the value of human capital—of people. They had us freeze prices and eliminate interest payments on credit of all types, including loans, mortgages, and credit cards. Then they instructed us to set the remuneration rates and roles of the CEOs in large corporations. As well, there was an adjustment to the prime motivation of industry from profit to service—from gouging the public through their greed, from a profit-driven mentality to one of responding to the needs of the people. Was there confusion, anger, and resistance? Absolutely, but the masses benefited, and big business had to adjust. The transition wasn't, and still isn't completed as there is still money in circulation, but that will soon be fixed.

"Then, with me doing the most of the work, they started restructuring the workplace to recognize performance and to base the decision-making process on servicing clients, rather than cutting corners to save money, or raising prices. At the same time, as you know, we started to implement the SCM systems and developed an ongoing communications protocol dealing with SCM issues between the regions. At that point, education, healthcare, and other essential services became free."

Green looked over to Joy as he continued. He sensed confusion and that the delegates needed to have an example of what he was trying to explain, so he decided to have Joy, who wasn't expecting to be called upon, to discuss her work in the Yukon.

"There was a test," Green started, "of the impact of their proposed actions, in the north of Canada, in a First Nations village in Whitehorse, Yukon Territory, Canada. The visitors organized the test to weigh the potential, and the impact, of what they were proposing."

As he moved the podium back to the corner and went back to his chair, he turned to Joy. "Joy, would you please, as briefly as possible, explain?"

Joy was surprised to be called upon but got up and frowned at Sydney before facing the rest of the group.

"Thank you," she said and then, turning back to Sydney, "Mr. Chair, I wasn't expecting that ..." She pointed and waved her finger at Green as everyone laughed. "Okay I'll try to explain." She took a moment to gather her thoughts. "The First Nations communities in the Yukon, not just the one in Whitehorse, had problems with addictions, family abuse, unemployment, and attitudinal issues, which as you would image enabled persistent social problems. It must be said that the issues were pervasive, and as such, the leadership were incapable of responding adequately to the problems.

"The visitors, directing and supporting Sydney and me, as their representatives, organized meetings with the leadership, first in Whitehorse, to let them know what was about to happen and that their First Nation was about to experience change. The leadership were skeptical, to say the least. That inertia Syd was talking about earlier was certainly a main component of that skepticism."

Joy stopped, moved away from her chair, and stood behind Sydney. She put her hands on Green's shoulders and continued. "Then, with Sydney's help, they changed the social environment in the village, and Whitehorse became the model it has become. Let me explain.

"The first thing they did, in one night, by empowering Sydney, was to get rid of the drug houses and the criminals running them. Then, using a variant of the wave we all experienced when they first arrived, they got rid of the addictions that people were suffering from. The next morning, there was a transformational change in the people. Without the weight of the addictions, they were confused with the new sense of awareness of their individuality, of being free, of feeling good. Their anger was gone, their desire to escape was gone. Now they wanted to do something, to stand up for themselves — and be counted. So, with all of these emotions weighing on them they all made their way to the longhouse to find answers to what had happened.

"The visitors had prepared the leadership, and myself, predicting these attitudinal changes and how to handle them. Meetings were held explaining to the membership what was going to transpire. We explained that every person in the First Nation, adults and youth, everyone, was to go to town and get a new look (new clothing, haircuts, and items for their homes that they needed, etc.) and everything would be free." Joy moved away from Green, leaned in, and put her hands on the table as she continued.

"These actions created a new sense of responsibility, a desire to participate, to do something worthwhile, find a direction and meaning in their lives, and restore the family. I cannot overstate what we witnessed. It was amazing to see the changes evolve. In a follow-up organizational meeting, everyone was offered a chance to go back to school or get training and then help re-establish their First Nation and the village where they lived. People were offered many different ways to help, such as cleanup, landscaping, house renovations, or management ... we struggled to keep up with the demands of the people to become involved." Joy went to the other end of the table, and as everyone followed her movement, she finished.

"Members of the world government, I say to you today that the Yukon has become a model for the rest of the world. You would not recognize the different communities today. Whitehorse, and the First Nation's village, are like being in a paradise, an idyllic community. The people are happy, committed and welcoming. The municipality is clean and lush with vegetation. There is housing for everyone, and there is an attitude of being part of something bigger than oneself, of having a sense of community, of helping each other, of having meaning in one's life. No one, no one in the community has any worries about meeting their needs or those of their family. There is no discussion about and no need for money—it's not the currency that matters. People walk straight and strong. People are thriving because of their commitment, their access to goods and services, the support they're getting, and their participation.

"I am sorry, but I am so proud of what we've accomplished as a community I could go on forever, but I should stop now, and seriously, thank you, Sydney, for giving me the opportunity to discuss this. Are there are any questions?" Joy went back to her seat, responded to the many questions that arose, and led the discussion that followed.

A couple of times, she had to get help from the visitors, and even Sydney, but in the end she clearly made the point that when individuals have opportunity, when they don't have concerns about their safety, their children, and about putting food on the table; when they don't have worries about housing, or about meeting their basic needs; when they have opportunity to make dreams come true—then they have meaning in their lives. Then they, and their communities, can thrive. And she suggested that this is the direction the rest of the world was headed toward, that the story she had just told was like a prologue to what was going to happen.

Once Joy was finished answering questions, Green got up and suggested having a break before continuing. As everyone mingled, all they could talk about was what Joy had presented.

After the break, Green said, "A new age is on the horizon. An age when the populations of earth do not have concerns about their safety; when there is no conflict, no criminality, and therefore no need for police, for military. We're on the threshold of leading our regions, our world, into a global messianic age. An age of peace, of justice, and an age when we're able to reach out and join with other worlds to continue learning from, sharing, and even contributing to other civilizations."

Green then turned back to the folders he had handed out at the first meeting. These contained the instructions from the visitors and the targeted timelines for the missions, such as the implementation of the priorities and the objectives.

During the next couple of days, Green and the delegates continued their work, organizing their approach, the timeline, and how they would respond to any concerns, issues, that arose in their regions. The leaders of the world government had meetings with their staff, as Green had asked. By the time the leadership meetings were ending, each office's staff had completed their initial organizational work and were ready to go.

In concluding the session, Green made a clear point that at every step, the general population had to be kept up to date on what was happening, and the world government leadership had to keep reviewing their accomplishments, and how they were meeting the thresholds on implementing the goals and priorities. "Success will happen," Green repeated, "as people see, and experience progress, and that their voices are heard."

At the end of the session, Green and Joy hosted the staff from each region separately in Green's apartment. Then they had one big party in the area just outside the main entrance of their offices to celebrate and enjoy some time together before the real work began. By that time, the regional delegates had developed the capacity to interact with delegates from other areas in their language and had some initial discussions with the visitors—the pills were taking effect.

During the next few weeks, there was a lot of activity in the technology room with the transport device as the work started. Many of the regional staff also met with Green in his office, keeping him updated on how the work was progressing. He also made a number of visits with the world government leaders from each of the regions to work with and support the officials and meet with various levels of management. One of Green's challenges was to keep everyone, at all levels of government, determined, on track, but patient and aware that their mission would take time and that it was critically important that they target, document, and share their progress through ongoing communication. The visitors were impressed.

Sydney, the actions of the world government, with the obvious commitment of the leadership to guiding the plan's implementation, has been very positive. We feel very confident in what the future holds. Keep in mind, Sydney, people have to see that things continue to happen—that they are becoming the norm.

"Thank you, I understand and agree that the timing was right to establish the world government. Quite honestly, it's wonderful to have all of that support and the responsibility watching everything from a high-level perspective, and keeping the progress on track."

We're glad to hear that. Actually, now you're really starting to replace us. All of the foundational systems are getting in place. Now it's up to you, and the other officials, to make sure the regional governments, at all levels, stay in touch and help each other when and if required. As well, continuing to do the general broadcasts in each region will help keep people involved.

Sydney, because of that, we'll start to focus our attention on the process of training and developing scientists, engineers, and managers to begin the work preparing for interstellar travel—this will take generations, but it has to start somewhere, doesn't it?

The visitors brought Green to his office on their ship to discuss those plans, but he was thinking about what they had said, and once he was settled he spoke, "May I suggest we start right away and hold a global broadcast at the new offices to introduce the offices and the delegates of the world government to all of the regions? It has been several weeks now, and I think we have a lot of good news to report. It's time to show people the world government offices and staff. We can arrange a virtual tour of the offices and have each delegation talk about and show video of their achievements. I can also discuss the priorities, review where we are at, and of course, talk about interstellar travel and contacting other civilizations."

Excellent idea. Absolutely. We'll work with you to set that up right away. It will be a great way to develop enthusiasm, commitment, and pride in seeing the achievements in each region—and the support each region shares with others. We think it'll also create a desire for people to participate—to be part of making the future happen. Thank you, Sydney.

31

PREPARING FOR THE BROADCAST

GREEN SPENT THE NEXT FEW DAYS WORKING WITH THE VISITORS, and discussing the proposed broadcast with each regional delegate and their office staff. They were all enthusiastic, and when he asked them to provide videos and prepare to give updates, the challenge was turned into a friendly competition between the regions. During the prep time, Green called several meetings of the delegates to get updates, prepare an agenda, and go over the details the visitors wanted each of them to discuss. He also wanted to ensure that the regional representatives were on side to go over the plans' thresholds and their progress on implementing the visitors' priorities and objectives.

Those details included the status of the training and implementation of the new educational protocols, an update on the communication systems, and explaining how individuals will benefit from the technology to fulfill their day-to-day needs. As well, it was time for the people in each region to get a reminder, and an update, on the function of the new communications technology and how to talk directly to officials, vote, and be heard if there was an issue. Finally, the visitors wanted each regional delegate to celebrate some examples of the achievements of individuals. Green made himself and Joy available, as well as the visitors, to assist individual representatives as needed.

After a couple of weeks of preparation and before finalizing the agenda, Green called a meeting to deal with any outstanding questions. At the meeting, everyone agreed that Green had to be the moderator, that Joy had to give an update and discuss the key points of the education program, and Green should go over the three priorities and the objectives. Then Green should introduce, one at a time and in alphabetical order, the representatives of the world government to present their videos, updates, and plans moving forward. The press conference, the global broadcast, was then scheduled for one week after that meeting.

In a final meeting, Green let everyone know that the space just outside the offices would be used and the visitors would take the lead in setting it up. As well, the visitors, who still controlled the global communications systems during the implementation of the new technology, informed the delegates that they would take over all communications and broadcast the conference on all media platforms. This would include all social media, news stations, print media, and internet. The day of the broadcast would be a day off work, and it was hoped that everyone would watch.

Green then met with the visitors to discuss any final details.

Sydney, everyone seems ready for the broadcast, good work. As we agreed that space just outside the entrance to the offices is perfect. As well, as we've done for previous meetings like this one, we'll get the message out and bring the appropriate individuals, and media, to the hall to be present. If you agree, this would be a great opportunity for you to discuss the plans we have to develop the orbiting space training centre and the International Space Complex on the moon, where interstellar travel will launch from to begin to make contact with other worlds. And, Sydney, mention that anyone interested in participating in any aspect of interstellar travel and in getting the training, should make themselves known to their local authorities. Finish by saying that this is a multi-year project, so even young people should think about it. There will be many training opportunities and all regions will be involved in these developments.

"Of course. So far, the idea of interstellar travel has been the best-kept secret in the history of the world. What a great idea, and as you've mentioned, I should make the point that each region will have a unique role to play in the development of the orbiting training facility and the complex on the moon. Talk about the opportunities that offers and how it'll help to unify all of the regions working together ... great!" Green was beyond excited about this.

During the next week, the IT specialists and the producers of the broadcast worked closely with each regional office's staff in setting up the program for the day and publicizing the event. Each presenter was given a thirty-minute window for their presentation, including any video they provided. The meeting was planned to start at 9 a.m. with Green doing an introduction and presenting the key elements in the next phase of the world's development. Then Joy was to take the floor to discuss a brief outline and the importance of the educational priorities. After her presentation, the first two presenters from the regional offices would take the floor. Then there would be a lunch break in the broadcast. A light lunch was planned for all guests, media, and staff from the world governmental offices. After lunch, the final five regional representatives would take the floor, and the broadcast would conclude with a short commentary by Green.

The day before the conference Green, Joy, and the representatives from each region met to review the facility, load their presentations with the help of the IT specialists, and review how the system worked. The head of the IT group said that she would be operating the system on stage, that everyone, to be safe, should confirm with her which region they represented before they started, and that she would be there to resolve any issues if needed. Once they were satisfied and all their questions were answered, they agreed to meet at 7 a.m. the following day. Green gathered everyone together ... then he put his hand over his heart, looked at each member of the team and said ...

"We're ready ... we've worked our asses off, but we're ready ... tomorrow we announce who we are, we show who we are, and we celebrate the start of a new era ... now go and get some rest and we'll see you in the morning."

Everyone shook hands, congratulated each other, and left.

32

THE GLOBAL BROADCAST

GREEN AND JOY ARRIVED RIGHT AT 7 A.M. THE NEXT MORNING. They were very impressed with the set-up. The lobby was a large area, with what seemed like more than a hundred chairs set up in a semi-circle around a stage area with the Blue World Government sign as a backdrop. Then the media section, on a slightly elevated riser, was impressive with all of the technology. In addition, there was a cafeteria section, where there was already activity with people enjoying coffee/tea and light snacks. As Joy and Green stood at the entrance, looking around the area waving, smiling and saying *'hi' to people*, a few came up to thank them for their work — a few wanted to take a selfie with Green, which he did.

After a short time, they went over and joined the line-up to get a beverage continuing to greet people. Once they had their drinks, they went to the stage area to prepare. Green put his notes at the podium while Joy decided to hold on to hers. During the next hour, the room filled up and both Joy and Green mingled, welcoming people, answering questions from the media, who were doing the final set-up and test of their equipment. At five minutes before 9, Green went to the podium and asked for everyone to take their seats. Just then, the visitors mentioned to Green, Joy, and the other delegates, that they were there and would assist if needed.

Once everyone was settled, and as he looked around the room, Green saw that the hall was filled to capacity. He estimated that there seemed to be a lot more than one hundred people present, not counting all the media, support staff, and presenters—it was standing room only. He looked over to the media and gave them a welcoming smile and a thumbs-up signal as he was ready to start. Then he looked behind to make sure all of the representatives from the regions were in place and ready.

He took a few deep breaths, got the audience's attention, looked again to the media section to get a thumbs up from them, then took hold of the mic and walked away from the podium. He had a big smile on his face, expecting that this day would go down in the history of the world. He waved to the cameras, then facing the crowd, he began.

"Distinguished guests, ladies and gentlemen, members of the media, and those watching around the world ..." then, turning to face the people on stage, he continued, "representatives from each regional government, and of course Ms. Taller," Green paused for a moment as he turned back to face the general audience, "let me begin by thanking our visitors. Yes, they are our visitors as they'll soon be leaving us, so we can continue with the creation of a new age for our world." Green walked back to the podium.

"The visitors have been here in order to help us understand, and implement, the changes we have to make for the benefit of all the people on earth, and eventually for us to make contact with, to interact with other worlds and civilizations. Ladies and gentlemen, once the implementation of the systems we'll be discussing today have been completed, we'll be on our own to continue." Green paused ...

"People of the little blue planet—" He looked straight at the cameras. "That is how we're known in the universe, as a little blue planet." He stopped for a moment, dropping the mic to his side as he surveyed the audience. He sensed their interest and desire for him to continue.

"People of the little blue planet," he repeated, "the visitors have said to me that we are unique in the universe. From other planets, we're seen as being a small planet compared to others, and with most of our surface area covered in water, we represent to others as being blue, so we are the 'little blue planet'—blue, and unique." Green paused, caught his breath, turned to the delegates, and got a thumbs up from everyone on the platform, and then with confidence, he turned back and continued.

"Ladies and gentlemen, the representatives on the new Blue World Government have determined that as we're entering a new age, as has happened on many other planets, that we have to start a new calendar to celebrate this moment. From this day forward, the months of the year and the days of the week remain the same; however, the year we're in will now be based on this event—the creation of the Blue World Government. A few weeks ago, when the world government held their first meeting, that was day one of the new age. That day was Monday, August 25th, which will be celebrated each year as we move forward as a New Year's Day celebration. So today is Thursday, November 4th in the New Age, year 1." Green went on to explain the rationale in more detail and then stopped by repeating that the New Year would be celebrated on August 25 each year. Then he continued.

"Today, we're going to discuss the three main priorities and the objectives that have been set out for us to work on. We'll hear from Ms. Taller about the progress happening in establishing a universal education protocol, and then we'll meet and hear from the representatives from each region on the progress being made on the priorities and the objectives in their regions. Finally, I have some very exciting news to share with you at the end of our meeting. Please be patient, listen carefully, and I am sure you'll leave today with a lot to talk about."

Green took the mic and went back to centre stage.

"So, as I just mentioned, there are three priorities we're working on, guided by the visitors." During the next 30 minutes, Green slowly went through the priorities and the six objectives, which he repeated a couple of times before finishing. He spent extra time justifying the communication identification system that was being implemented and how important it was for the general population. Then he continued, "Success is meeting our goals and thresholds, and by our commitment, our partnership, and the level of progress we make with this work will determine when the visitors leave." Green then reminded everyone that because of the length of the broadcast, there would be breaks at key intervals. He announced a ten-minute break before they'd start hearing from their speakers.

When Green came back to the podium, he got everyone's attention and then introduced Joy to talk about the establishment of the new universal education system.

Joy got up to a polite reception from the audience, but detected a lack of interest. She spent the next just under thirty minutes explaining the history, development, and introduction of the new systems. She finished her presentation with a new PowerPoint display, talking about how critical it was to identify expertise in all areas and that it all started at the preschool level. There was mild applause at the end of her presentation. Green went over to her and shook her hand as she returned to her seat. Joy whispered to him that she sensed little interest in what she was saying.

"Thank you, Ms. Taller, Joy," As Green looked out at the audience, he sensed people were wondering why that presentation had even been scheduled. He moved to centre stage, then continued, "Ladies and gentlemen, everyone here in this hall and watching around the world, let me be clear, we have never before focused our attention on education, and our youth, as we will now. Throughout our history, we have failed our children—we have basically left them on their own to learn and grow – and oh my so many suffered the consequences of that."

He paced a bit and then looked out at the audience and yelled, "No more! Our future lies in our youth!" Green went back to the podium and replaced the mic. "Our visitors have made it clear that education, lifelong learning, is one of the most important parts of this new age. There is brilliance everywhere in our world, in all sectors, in all regions, and it's our responsibility not only to discover it, but to support it—it's our responsibility to support our children—to be there for them! We must identify leadership, and skillsets in all areas from the trades to music, the arts, sports, medicine, teaching, IT, governance ... well, in every area of society, and discovering those skills, developing that expertise, is the essence of our future." He dropped the mic to his side as he looked out at the audience and then at the cameras.

"Ladies and gentlemen, we've failed our children in not doing that, in not identifying their interests and supporting them, challenging them, developing their skills, providing for their needs and desires and safety, and allowing them meaning in their lives. We're all now responsible, so, once again, thank you, Joy, Ms. Taller." He paused and pointed to Joy. "Ms. Taller has co-ordinated the implementation of this critically important project and we all must participate, and support the effort of the educational community in your region, as the impact it will have is immeasurable." Then he called Joy back up, gave her a big hug to much stronger applause. Green turned back, went to the podium, and introduced the first of the regional delegations.

The delegates from the first two regions got up, one group at a time, and presented their region and the progress they'd made. They were very well received. After the first two delegations finished, Green went to the mic, restated the importance of the education and communication discussions, thanked everyone for the morning session, and then announced a lunch break for the next hour and a half.

After the break, the final five delegations presented, with a short break between each one. Each delegation had a thirty-minute presentation, with a question-and-answer period after they finished. After all the presentations were done, Green opened the floor to questions that had been submitted from the audience. He and the regional leaders moved their chairs to centre stage and responded to questions for close to an hour. Then Green came back to the podium, and as he'd promised earlier, he closed with a special announcement:

"Let me start by saying that part of the next step in this development is the technology that I created when I was working at the NASA base in Florida. Then it was called SORT, which stands for (Standard Orbiting Radio Technology). It was this technology that was responsible for first identifying the visitors' ships. Well, the visitors destroyed my baby when they arrived." Green raised his hands as if to say, "Oh well," and made a face as everyone laughed. Then he continued in a more serious tone.

"Well, the visitors let me know that we'll be bringing a technologically updated SORT back into operation and positioning several of the devices throughout the universe to begin to find and make contact with other worlds." There was mild applause.

"Now, to the main point in all of this," He paused for just a moment, "Ladies and gentlemen, people of the little blue world, with the technical assistance of the visitors, I announce today that in the next few months we will be starting the creation of an orbiting Space Training Centre, and then the building of the International Space Complex on the moon, where interstellar travel will launch from."

There was applause, and then, taking hold of the podium, he looked at the audience, and pointed to everyone in the audience, and then pointing at the cameras.

"Anyone," he started, "anyone interested in participating, in getting the required education and training to help implement these projects, anyone in any region, should make themselves known." He paused again to let that sink in. "Each region will have specific responsibilities assigned by the world government offices. We'll be in touch once that process, to determine what part of the development will be assigned to each region, is completed." Green moved to one side of the podium as there was more applause. He raised his hand to quiet the audience before continuing.

"Ladies and gentlemen, to be clear about the magnitude of these projects, let me say to you that the orbiting station will be home to thousands and thousands of people, and the station on the moon will house close to a hundred thousand people and be like a regular city on earth." He then told everyone that more announcements would be made by their regional delegates as the preparation work would start shortly. He finished by repeating that anyone interested in being part of these projects, wanting to participate and get the appropriate training, should sign up with their local authorities as soon as possible.

"Ladies and gentlemen, our youth, boys and girls, all the people of our world ... we can do this! We *have* to do this! We will work together to become one world, helping each other. We are starting a new age for all of the people of the world, so let's get going. Thank you to all of the presenters today, thank you to all of the people in the audience, and thank you to everyone around the world listening to this broadcast. The future is ours. Thank you!"

Green then closed the broadcast. Everyone who was in attendance, the invited guests, the management that had been brought in from the regions, the leadership and staff from the world government offices, and the media, stayed, talking to each other, meeting with each other, and doing interviews with the media. It took a couple of hours before people started to leave. After the meeting, when Green was back in his apartment, he met with the visitors.

That was outstanding, Sydney ... now, all that remains for you and many others is getting to work and making things happen. So, let's start with preparing for interstellar travel.

33
PREPARING FOR INTERSTELLAR TRAVEL

SYDNEY, WHEN WE ARRIVED HERE, TO OUR SURPRISE, WE HAD TO DO two things: one, we had to clean up the huge amount of space debris that was floating around and blocking our ships from taking positions around your planet; and two, we had to clean up the environment, which included the disgusting amount of waste products and pollution, not only on the surface of the planet, but in the oceans as well—Sydney, you're the little blue world, your water, and your environment, are your most precious commodities. We just couldn't imagine how a population could allow this to happen.

Anyway, we've been holding that back, but had to share it with you as a reminder of how far you've come, and we hope you realize how much had to happen to get your world to this point.

So, let's get going. You know Sydney, that there are several steps to be able to achieve interstellar travel?

"Yes, I assumed so, but let me apologize, again, for our previous behaviour. I think though with your guidance and actions during the years, and the changes we've made, that we proved that we're ready to move forward." Sydney started to pace.

Sydney, the pacing ... yes, you're ready, so here we go.

First, as you know, we've been using our ships as the primary communications systems around the globe. So, we've been working with, and training, a group of scientists to upgrade your previous satellite technology and are arranging to re-establish your global communications systems. Once that is done, we'll transfer the capacity from our ships to the new devices, and you will be in control of all the communication systems, including the new communication protocols for individuals. This is important to keep everyone up-to-date, for each of the research and development centres in the regions to keep in contact, and for finding and training new staff.

Then Sydney, simultaneously, we'll work with you to upgrade your SORT technology and train others on how the new system works. We'll place several of the satellites throughout the universe so you can start to find, and begin to communicate with other worlds that support life. You'll start to learn what is out there, and how you may be able to share experiences and technology—be patient, Sydney, as this takes time. Oh, and we'll also make the arrangements for your first visit to another world once you're ready.

Green stopped walking around the office and just stood frozen in place. "My dreams are coming true." He could hardly believe what he was hearing. "You've shown me other civilizations, but I thought that those images were just fabricated videos for my benefit, and it was just that, a show. Are you saying they were real and that there are life forms out there that are like us, and the videos were true?"

Actually, there are, and the videos were real. Remember when we told you we were eliminating the criminals, autocrats and others, such as the racists, politicians, and plutocrats? That all you had to do was to point, and they would disappear? Well, remember we said that when they disappeared, we sent them to other worlds?

"Yes, I do. Of course. How could I forget all of that? But I thought you were saying 'other worlds' euphemistically and that they were actually terminated. It wasn't easy, not really knowing what would happen to them."

Oh my, Sydney! Surely you know we're not like that. We sent them to other planets. That is what happened. Those other worlds have environments that support biological life forms and are similar to your world, and some of the planets have species that are comparable to your biological species, only much more advanced. Another part of that process, other than just cleansing your world, was that in order for you to eventually make contact with those civilizations, we knew we had to prepare them to learn about you. We prepared those worlds to accept the individuals we sent them, to help the new arrivals to adjust—to acclimate. That was part of the preparation for when you were ready to make contact with those worlds, to have them understand you and be ready. You see Sydney those planets we sent people to, as we've mentioned, are much more advanced than you are.

"You know, this is quite a revelation for me. I've struggled my whole career, wanting to prove that there is life out there, that there are planets that support life, and I was ignored until you came on the scene. So, what you're saying is that we'll re-establish our control over the communication satellite systems, and we'll restart the SORT program, then what?" Green was anxious to hear more, but then, suddenly, he realized something...

"Wait a minute, sending the criminals, autocrats, religious extremists, and leaders of the plutocracy to other planets doesn't represent us very well. How did you manage that?" Green was anxious, and concerned that the arrival of these people would lower the expectations of other worlds and their willingness to accept contacting the blue planet.

Good question, Sydney. We kept them separate from the residents of the new world, and still do. We informed them about where they were, the type of society they were being introduced to, and how they had to act. At first, some were belligerent, and we had to deal with that. We also had to use the "wave" a few times because other planets could be affected by the bacteria in your species. The wave was important to eliminate that threat; that was another reason to keep them separate. We also had to bring specialists from the world they were on to deal with issues, questions, and give us time to prepare them for contact.

During that procedure, we were able to identify some potential leadership among the group and focused on that group as the others adjusted. In time, we started bringing them out in small teams, and invited representatives from the host world, both using the same protective device you use, to visit, observe and interact. Then both groups would return to their communities to share the experience with others. It worked well, and they are all acclimating nicely, but remain for the most part in their own cities. Remember, it has already been more than a decade, and everything is going smoothly. So, let's get back to the main part of our discussion.

Well, interstellar travel means going great distances. The closest planet that harbours life forms close to yours is about four light-years away from earth, so there is a lot of work to do. In the early stages of that process, we have to establish the orbiting space station to train individuals to live in and experience a different environment from earth. An environment that is unique, technological, scientific, and much more controlled than living on earth. We will do our best to develop spaces for grass and trees and open spaces, and to create a cycle of day and night. Also, there has to be a false gravity environment to get used to. This orbiting centre will be a training facility and a bridge between earth and the facility that will be built on the moon.

Then you have to construct the space centre on the moon. It must be built as a launchpad for space travel and have a city-type area with all of the facilities that one would find on earth for support staff. With our help, your scientists have to develop the technology for a spaceship that would sustain human life for extended lengths of time, be powered by an unlimited source of energy, and travel at speeds unheard of right now, all of which is at this time well above your technological capacity. We will also help train selected scientists to develop that technology. The spaceships have to have different areas for food production, entertainment, healthcare, school for the kids, and other necessities. This is because these ships will be travelling for extended periods of time and must support family groups. So, you see, Sydney, there is a lot of work to do, and we have yet to get started.

"So, when can we actually get started with this work?"

We can start with the communications satellites immediately as we've already implemented the system in the regions with our ships acting as the satellites. Once the technology is completed, we can start replacing our ships with the new satellites. We are talking weeks rather than months or years.

As to SORT, we can get going on that with you right away, but between your work as the chair of the World Government. Finally, at this stage in preparing for interstellar travel, we have to start developing research facilities in each of the regions, as each area will have specific responsibilities contributing to the building of the orbiting space centre and the moon base. This way, we'll get the expertise and partnerships we need.

"This is so exciting!" Green could hardly control himself. He sat down on the sofa, buried his head in his hands, and unable to control his emotions, he cried.

It's okay, Sydney. We understand your emotions.

The visitors gave Green a few minutes to get control of himself. Then, he went and got a glass of wine, and some cheese, to celebrate. The visitors started after Green moved to one of the chairs and sat down, sipping his wine and munching on the cheese—he was getting quite giddy with excitement.

We can feel your enthusiasm; however, Sydney, you can't allow the world government delegates to lose focus by concentrating only on the new projects. You must oversee the progress in the regions, have meetings, and keep updated on the modernizing of the education systems, and stay up to date with the other priorities and objectives such as the communications systems. If you don't do that and keep them accountable, the task will be much more difficult and time consuming. They, and you, have to assert leadership. You all must use the communication systems, develop a healthy and competitive atmosphere between the regions, and use the influence of the world government delegates to keep others on track. Do you understand?

"I do. It's clear to me that it's my responsibility, my role, as well as the others in the world government, to eventually replace you. Being involved in the projects will be my reward, such as witnessing the establishment of the orbiting training centre and the moon facility. Everything else is like my dreams coming true—and my pleasure."

Yes, because you're the figurehead, and so well known around the world. Sydney, it's up to you to motivate the others to do their work, to follow up and hold people accountable at all levels. As you establish the interstellar capability, it's critical for Joy to be successful in completing the implementation of the education protocols, and that they are running smoothly in all regions—education is fundamental to achieve success in all other areas. She'll need you to stand beside her, and those working with her in each region. You all have to stand together and have local, regional, and selectively global media broadcasts to support the work being done not just in education, but in all areas.

34

THE WORK GETS DONE

THERE WAS A LOT TO DO.

Within the general populations the anxiety of coping with the new systems, of adapting, especially with the implementation of the communication devices, caused a lot of apprehension. As the visitors had identified many times the stubbornness of the human race certainly came to the surface.

Green met often with the visitors, who were watching the progress being made, not only on the organizational front, but also on the implementation of plans and to deal with any matters that regional leadership identified. To Green's surprise from time to time there were still remnants of groups like al-Shabaab, Boko Haram, the Taliban, al Qaeda, and the Lord's Resistance Army (LRA) in Africa. There were still religious, political, and economic groups in the North American and European regions, as well as in the Middle East, trying to disrupt progress and re-establish their authority. In the Asian and Eurasian regions, remnants of the previous political elite threatened the achievement and aspiration of the general populations, and they continued, stubbornly, to try to assert power.

Green had no more patience. When a hot spot was identified, he would visit the area, focus on the troublemakers, and send them away. He had an agreement with the visitors that if he sent someone to their ship, they would deal with the person or group. In other circumstances, when one of the ships detected a problem, and Green was busy, the visitors simply removed the troublemakers from the cities or villages and either sent them away, or transported them to the "communities" they had previously established in each of the regions.

In China, for example, the lieutenants from the previous communist state, frustrated at being just one part of a regional government, tried to reassert themselves and regain some of their authority over other nations in the region. The visitors couldn't understand the persistence of groups like this, but it was obviously unacceptable, and they had to be sent away. In India, the entitled groups of what was once the caste system also tried to reclaim their standing, prestige, and entitlement at the expense of what they called the lower castes, even though the caste system had supposedly ended decades ago. They, too, had to be sent away. Then, using the communication systems, broadcasts, face-to-face meetings, and even new elections, things started to improve. In other areas of the world, members of the elite wealthy classes, the plutocracy, all had trouble dealing with the abolition of money as a currency, their lack of influence, and fitting in socially.

Green would meet with the visitors to discuss these situations, and they explained to him, *Sydney, these people lived a privileged life, and in many cases, had others doing the work for them. They just told people what to do and felt that this was just the way it should be. They can't understand how, suddenly, they have to participate, that they aren't better or entitled, and that they have to treat others with respect and pull their weight. Sydney, this isn't unusual, and that's why normally, as we have mentioned, it requires generational change, but in this case, we are acting more quickly by separating them from the general population, or sending them away.*

Green understood and continued with the plan.

• • •

It took several years to finally eliminate the impact of these groups and make the issues, if they appeared, isolated and therefore much easier to deal with. As time passed, the remnants of the older generations gave way to the youth, new leadership, and the belief that all people are equal. The new paradigms of governing by having a fair and just society took hold. The greatest impact on creating this new age came from the leadership of the world government and the focus on the youth. The visitors had many conversations with the leaders of each region, with Sydney, and with Joy, whose teams in each region had completed the new education procedures and were starting to see the results. On this occasion, they were discussing the progress with Sydney.

Sydney, the management of the world government, with the transitions in leadership, with new elections during these years, has become the trusted authority. Your work, with all of the managers in each region, and of course your partners at the world government, has been excellent—congratulations. The communications of the world government with each of the regions have produced outstanding results. The SCM protocols and the demands of that system have developed a skilled and focused global community. Accountability has become the norm.

And Joy's work with the educational teams in each region has led to the universal education system being fully functional. After a few years of implementation, support, supervision, and continued training, it is running smoothly in all seven regions and is having a considerable impact. The early identification of potential leadership, of expertise in all areas of science, sports, arts, medicine, trades, and technology, and the ability to develop that potential, became the rule, not the exception. Sydney, we are pleased.

• • •

After several years, with the passing of the previous generation, the acceptance of the new systems just seemed to happen naturally. As well, this new normal unified the regions around the world. The exchange of expertise, sharing, and using the regional and global communication systems, made things much easier. Then the SCM programs, because of the need to communicate and organize, turned into an ongoing dialogue with the regions and the world government, creating a new era of peace, co-operation, sharing, and positive results in many areas, including sports, entertainment, tourism, and technology.

The new and ongoing communication systems led to the immediate identification and resolution of issues and problems, and more importantly, the finding and development of expertise globally. The meritocracy, which demanded accountability, developed the regions' abilities to educate and promote people with leadership skills, education, and experience. The transportation technology allowed global sharing of expertise and produced a new level of co-operation, acceptance, and respect for people's culture, knowledge, experience, and education. In terms of the issues, there was a new resolve and capacity to deal with and find solutions to any problems as they arose anywhere in the world.

The visitors explained to Sydney, and the current world government representatives, that the work was getting done because of their leadership and co-ordination! Housing developments, infrastructure, health and social services, cultural exchanges and awareness, technology, and even vacations showed results. The population of the little blue planet was finally achieving equality and finding meaning, fulfillment, and happiness in their lives. The direction and support between the regions and the world government solidified as the new age of peace, of opportunity, of achievement, of sharing, became accepted as how things were. What the visitors had shown Green years ago on other worlds was, by NA 15, being successfully implemented on the little blue planet, and he was starting to witness the results.

During these years, there were two more elections for the changes to become the new normal, continuing to put the right people into positions of authority. By this time, the idea of electing, and promoting people with leadership skills to increased levels of responsibility, experience, education, and a servant leadership management style became the norm. And the idea of promoting people from municipal to provincial and regional positions of responsibility was understood. Finally, individual skillset identification, access to technology, and all the communication data receptors were in place within the first five years. This helped instill in society the idea that all people must be treated equally, that they had the ability to communicate with those in power at all levels, and that those in power were accountable and responsible. The visitors made a point of mentioning more than just the governance side of the progress—there was also the fun side.

Sydney, during these years, activities in the arts, entertainment, sports, and general activities outside of work increased exponentially, and people's ability to enjoy life, to experience that which was previously reserved for the wealthy and powerful, just happened. Also, with the new technical innovations and training in transportation, individuals and families in all the regions are now able to enjoy vacations and experience other regions anywhere in the world. This aspect of life, being free of burdens, of the worries of the past dealing with money, and of the entitlement of the wealthy, powerful elements in society, opened everyone to achieving their dreams.

So, Sydney, what else has been achieved? The visitors discussed that they made themselves available full-time to develop the ability for interstellar travel. They were heavily involved in training the scientists, the development of the required technology, and the construction of the orbiting space centre and the moon base, and through all of this in assigning specific projects to the regions. The visitors then went on to share more successes.

Projects such as the next stage in the development and upgrading of SORT, and the manufacture of a number of the devices. They were called SORT, out of respect for Green, but they were much more advanced and had little in common with his original design. Then, with the help of the visitors, decisions were made on the proposed locations of SORT—these were decided in part by considering if any of the planets had humans from earth transported there by the visitors during their early intervention years. The new SORT technologies were positioned in those locations, and a few were positioned in other areas of the Milky Way. The scientific community on earth, and the world government representatives and staff, were kept up to date about the discoveries of the SORT devices.

Other projects, such as the orbiting space training facility, housing more than 20,000 people, was built by NA 10 and immediately started operating. The orbiting platform was a training facility and the launching pad for the development of the space complex and facility for interstellar travel being constructed on the moon. That facility was a phased construction. It started with the living facilities and support departments to sustain human life, such as medical facilities, food services, a technology department, schools, and an entertainment centre.

The final stages, still in the works, were the construction of launching pads where interstellar travel will launch from, the ongoing training of astronauts, and the construction of the ships that will travel to other planets. By NA15 the facility on the moon had more than 100,000 staff living there.

Sydney, we're pleased to report that you're now in a position to reach out and begin to make first contact!

35
PREPARING FOR FIRST CONTACT

DURING THE YEARS OF GETTING THINGS DONE, GREEN WORKED closely with the representatives of the world government. Together, they visited each region, got updates on the progress made, and resolved any questions and concerns. Green and the representatives made themselves available to mingle with people, listening to them and supporting their efforts. Typically, they would use the new communications technology to hold a broadcast where all community members could get updates and ask questions. Green also spent a lot of his time dealing with the construction of the orbiting space training station, and then the establishment of the facility on the moon.

His pet project, of course, was the updated version of his SORT technology. He spent many hours studying the new technology and learning from the visitors why they positioned the devices in the locations they did. He was amazed by the innovations he'd never thought of in his original design. The visitors notified Green that a few of the SORT devices had already made initial contact with other worlds, but they notified those planets that the little blue world was not yet ready to engage in any discussions. The visitors remained in control of these systems and contacts.

During the past few years, the visitors would leave earth for periods of time, which lengthened year by year. They would return for short interludes to see how things were going. They did keep in constant communication with Green, beginning on a daily, then weekly, then on a monthly basis. They said it was just in case they were needed.

As to his sister, Green got together with Joy during her visits to the world government offices in New York, and he would periodically travel to Whitehorse to visit and get caught up on what was happening with her, and in the Yukon. Green made a point to keep up to date with Joy's work discussing the progress and the impact of the educational protocols.

Recently, however, at Joy's eightieth birthday, Green noticed that she wasn't doing so well. She had difficulty getting around and seemed weak. He was concerned when she spoke with him about her decision not to travel anymore. He knew he had to do something soon if Joy was going to be able to witness him making first contact with an alien race—or even be part of it. Ever since that first session at Joy's school, Green needed to have Joy with him as much as possible, and now, getting ready for first contact, he saw that slipping away. As well, he, too, was beginning to feel his age.

The visitors had mentored Green as he trained and prepared to make initial contact with other civilizations, and they helped lay the groundwork for that happening. They identified a world for first contact that they said was populated by a similar biological form to humans. It also had a number of people on their planet who had been transported there during the early days of the visitors' intervention, and that was an important element in making a decision for first contact. The planet chosen was just over 4 light-years from earth.

Recently, after visiting Joy and seeing her condition, Green called upon the visitors to return to earth to brief him in more detail about first contact. He also indicated he had a number of organizational questions. The visitors understood that Green was anxious to actually meet with the representatives of another world and to reconnect with the people from earth who were sent to various planets to see how they were doing. They also knew he wanted them to help Joy so that she could be with him to witness the event when it happened.

Because of Green's request, the visitors returned. The first thing they noticed was that Green had grown older. It was nearing NA 16. They had been following the progress being made through the years and the continuing dedicated involvement of Green, but they had assumed their anti-aging pills would have lasted longer, and so they hadn't paid much attention during the years to Green's visual appearance and his physical well-being. They didn't know that he had stopped taking the pills years ago. They were surprised when they brought him to their ship and realized they needed to do something quickly. They gave Green the pills again, but they knew that his time on earth was limited, not only because of his age, but also because he now had to turn the office over to someone new. Therefore, they had to act quickly for him to fulfill his legacy of making first contact.

"Thank you for coming back, and for the pills," said Green as he settled in on the visitor's ship, in the replica of his living room in New York. "Can you do something for Joy? She's not well. I would really like for her to be able to witness, if not participate, in first contact."

The visitors sensed he was not asking, rather this was a request that Green needed to be fulfilled. "She deserves that, after all she's done, and I need her to be there." Green stood up and covered his face with his hands as he asked, "I would also like to have one last visit with her, have dinner together, perhaps take in some theatre, talk, reminisce, but just to enjoy each other as we used to do." Green dropped his hands, closed his eyes, and raised his head, hoping for a positive response.

He, too, had been feeling his mortality this past year, and the feeling that Joy wasn't going to last much longer was having an effect on him. He wanted her—well, the two of them—to have one last fling with life. He knew they could, but he hoped the visitors would give him that wish.

Sydney, we'll bring Joy to meet you in your apartment at the world government headquarters as soon as we're finished here.

The visitors were careful in their response. *We'll be able to honour your wishes by giving Joy more time. We did check in with her and helped her feel better, but please understand that there is only so much we can do with biological units. Sydney, when she arrives, it will all be like it used to be, and you two can enjoy some time together. We'll make sure that you have fun, some entertainment, nice meals, and reminiscences before we set up a meeting with you, Joy, and the leaders from each region, and finalize the details for first contact.*

"Thank you for that." Green felt the pills starting to have an effect. He was beginning to feel his energy and excitement returning, and his thoughts turned to what the aliens would look like on the planet chosen for first contact. Feeling better he smiled, and hoped it would be the same for Joy. "I'm ready to complete this last historic event and then let the others take over for me."

Okay, Sydney, we understand. Sydney, that's not what they look like. And as he once again heard laughter in the background; he joined in and had a good laugh.

Now, because of the distance to the planet, we'll have to transport your delegation there as your technology is not advanced enough to travel the more than four light-years in a reasonable time. We'll set the preparatory meetings with your delegation for next week, giving your world government leadership and you, of course, time to choose who will join the delegation. You all must understand that we cannot bring a more advanced alien race here because of two reasons: one, your world is not ready to host a foreign delegation—it is close, but more work has to be done, and it will take another generation or so to be ready; and two, it will help for your delegation to see what the expected end result of the work you've been doing looks like, and how the people who were sent there have acclimated, and hear what they have to say.

"I understand," and with that, Green found himself back in his living room at the world government headquarters. He saw Joy standing in the living room, waiting for him. She looked much better, came up to Green, crying, and gave him a big hug—she didn't want to let go. After a few moments, she backed off, took a deep breath, and smiled.

"Sydney, it's good to see you again so soon after your last visit, and oh my God, I may not look the part, but I feel like a kid again, thanks to the visitors." She started to laugh, and as she had done so many times before, went to the kitchen to make herself some coffee and tea for Green. Later that evening, as they were sitting in the living room, the visitors suggested they go to the kitchen. They did and started laughing when they saw a sushi dinner fit for a king and queen. Then the visitors said they should have a good rest as there were some events scheduled for the next couple of days. Joy went to her apartment, which was still there for her as that was where she would stay when visiting New York working on the education protocols. They had a good rest.

In the morning, Joy came to get Green, and they had a nice breakfast in her apartment, chatting about the plans for the next few days. Then they headed down, as the visitors had suggested, to the world government offices to say hi to everyone. By the time they went down to the offices, it was close to the noon hour. As they approached the doors to the offices, they heard noises coming from inside which was very unusual as people were typically working quietly in their offices. What they didn't know was that the visitors had been working with the leaders of the regional governments organizing a surprise. Cautiously, Green opened the doors, and as soon as he did, there was an uproar of clapping, and everyone was yelling, "Surprise!"

All of the representatives from each of the regions were there, excited to congratulate Green and Joy on the announcement that they would be making first contact in the next week or two. The leaders from each region came forward and suggested that everyone move into the foyer where there was a lot more room. As they did so, they suddenly noticed that there were tables set up, a small riser just to the side of the doors with a podium and a microphone, and even some media had started to set up, and many others were arriving. Both Green and Joy noticed that previous heads of the regional offices were in the group and came up to congratulate Green and say hi to Joy. The leaders from the seven regions went to the riser and invited Green and Joy to join them. Once all of the others had gathered, and the media had set up some cameras, with others taking pictures, the leader from the North American region stepped up to the microphone.

"Ladies and gentlemen, members of each of the regional offices both present and past, members of the media, guests, and of course ..." he turned and brought Green and Joy to be beside him, "our guests of honour, Dr. Sydney Green and the wonderful Ms. Joy Taller." There was loud applause and shouts of "Yes" and "It's happening" and "Congratulations."

"We are here today to celebrate the announcement that we'll be making first contact with another civilization in the next week or two." Again, there was clapping. "Dr. Green, Ms. Taller, and the leaders of each of the seven regional governments will be transported by the visitors to a planet that is just over 4 light-years from earth. I would now like to call upon Dr. Green to address us."

Green moved up to the mic and took hold of it. "Thank you, Dr. Kapinsky, and thank you to all of the delegations from the regional governments for your hard work preparing us, and our world, for this meeting. And thank you, Joy, for your work organizing, implementing, following up, and keeping everyone on track implementing the educational protocols. As well, I notice that we have a number of people who were here at the beginning to set up the world government ... and I thank you! Come on, we've all worked so hard during these years, and even though some of you are relatively new, come on, let's give ourselves a huge round of applause." The gathering broke out in loud applause, shaking hands with each other and patting their neighbours on the back. Then when everyone had calmed down, Green went on to discuss some of the details for first contact and explained why their delegation was going to be welcomed on another planet, rather than hosting the first meeting.

There were a number of questions from the group, and the media, that Green and the regional leaders responded to; specifically, the media asked about the aliens and if the visitors had shared with Green what the alien race looked like. He responded that they had not as of yet, but he was sure that they would not be sending them to meet with a hostile race. There was some laughter from the group, but Green, Joy and the leaders of the regional governments also heard some laughter in the background. Then they heard directly from the visitors.

Each of you has done an amazing job. Congratulations. And although there is still work to do, the next few years look very promising for your world ... you should be proud of your accomplishments so far. Thank you.

Green, Joy and the leaders looked at each other and smiled as Green took the mic and got everyone's attention.

"Ladies and gentlemen, we all know the work continues, but please know that ..." Green pointed to Joy and the leaders who were standing beside him. "Please know that we are so proud to have had the opportunity to work with all of you, past and present, through thick and thin, and through the successes of these years. And let's not forget all of the managers and leaders in your regions." Green walked to the far end of the platform, looked out over everyone, and then concluded. "We have achieved so much and have advanced to the point where our progress is self-generating, so now we'll begin to expand our horizons and make contact with others. Let's enjoy a nice lunch and then get back to work."

Everyone was clapping and making noise as Green and the others on the platform rejoined their regional groups and took seats at the tables while lunch was served. After lunch, everyone mingled, congratulated each other again, took pictures with Green, Joy, and other leaders, and then went back to their offices.

During the next few days Green and Joy enjoyed themselves, visiting restaurants, going to theatres, and entertaining people in Green's apartment. They also spent a lot of time reminiscing about their early years and all that had happened since the arrival of the visitors. On the last day or so they spent time going over the many highlights of their life saying how they had lived and participated in an extraordinary time in the history of the world, and now they were ready for whatever was to come.

36

FIRST CONTACT

THE DETAILS AND PREPARATIONS FOR THE TRIP WERE FINALIZED during the next couple of days, and then the day arrived. Green was dressed in the same outfit he had worn when he'd met the visitors face to face. Green, Joy, the leaders from each region, and two others who were responsible for recording the event gathered in Green's apartment. Joy had to work hard to keep Green calm. She had never seen him so animated, so eager, so nervous, and so exasperated all at the same time. As the visitors made sure that all of the participants had the little black device that Green had been carrying for many years now, Green was pacing. Then the visitors explained what would happen.

Welcome, everyone. First, we'll bring you to our ship. The visitors stopped and spoke directly to Green. *Sydney, please stop pacing, as we have to go through all of the details, and we need your attention.*

We sense your excitement, but please be patient as it won't take long.

Green stopped pacing and sat down in a chair, holding on tightly to the arms. Joy moved over to him and put her hands on his shoulders as the others smiled.

Then the visitors continued. *We will first bring you to our ship, but please be aware that the space will be a replica of the room you're in now. We'll then discuss the actual process of sending you to meet with some of the people who were sent to the alien planet more than twenty-five years ago. When you've recovered from that trip and you've met the settlers, they'll show you around, and prepare you to meet the aliens. When that discussion has concluded and the host group feels you're ready, they will bring you to actually meet with the alien leadership of the planet.*

The visitors paused for a moment as they transported the group. "You're now on our ship, so let me continue. As this world is more advanced than your earth, the primary goal is to experience what is to come for your world—to see how things work. We want you to know two important things before you go: one, the civilization you'll be meeting are biological units, and they look a lot like you do; and two, it may be difficult for you to accept right now, but your DNAs are very similar."

There was shock in the group as they looked at each other, trying to understand the meaning, and the depth, of what they were just told.

Let us try to explain. The visitors paused as the delegates were still in a state of shock, but they started and got the attention of everyone. *You see, when we first noticed its existence, millions of years ago, your planet was just like a ball of fire, so we ignored it at first. But after the planet settled down, we then watched how the blue planet was developing. Eventually, when we discovered that there were various types of basic life forms thriving, it drew our attention. Then ladies and gentlemen, about 300,000 years ago, we noticed that the environment would support human life forms. And because of that, we began to understand that we could use your world and populate it with humanoid beings from other planets. So, we transported biological units to your world. We watched their development and noticed that as time passed, they not only survived, but multiplied, moved around the globe, and started to develop societal norms.*

The visitors gave the delegates a chance to cope with what they had just heard.

So, that is how you evolved and in actual fact, you're returning to your roots, as the individuals from your world realized after we transported them to this planet years ago. The bottom line here is that you are distant relatives to the biologicals you will be meeting.

The implications of what they were hearing were overwhelming to the group. They were speechless, in shock, and went to the sofa and chairs and sat down, not knowing what to make of what they had just heard. Once he gathered his senses, Green stood up, started pacing again, and when he was ready, he turned to address everyone in the room.

"Well, I guess that answers a lot of questions and theories about how we got to our world and where we come from, and the questions about creation vs. evolution." He then addressed the visitors. "Tell me, are there other worlds that developed religious factions that believed we, biological beings, were created by a god? What about the people we'll be meeting? What do they think?" Green started pacing again.

Sydney, the pacing ... please, stop and give us a chance to respond. To answer your question, as time passed on your planet, your species developed quite differently than it had on other planets. We followed our guidelines of not interfering once a species has established itself and is surviving, refraining from contact until they reach out to contact others. Your world, in an attempt to understand and answer questions, was unique in turning to religious and mythical beliefs as an answer. The civilization you will be going to did not—and please understand that they are much more advanced than you are. When you meet, you will be seeing your future selves. So, just to make sure everyone is ready, are you all set to go?

Green looked to each of the people in the room, who nodded yes.

"We're ready."

Good, so five things to keep in mind and always remember. One, please check right now that you have the little black device on your person and keep it with you at all times; it will protect you, and it will protect the people on the planet from you. Two, the device will protect you during the trip as you will be travelling through various time and dimensional distortions, so when you arrive at your destination, you will find yourselves in a room specifically designed to acclimate you to the new environment. Three, we will be there watching you. It won't take long for you to acclimate, and when that is done, we'll bring others to the building to invite you out to go on a tour of their city and facilities. Four, the first people you will see are those who were sent to this planet from your earth during the early stages of your transition. They live in a large city of several million and will show you around. And finally, the fifth point, when that is completed, the leaders will bring you to meet with the leaders of the planet to learn and listen to how it operates. So, everyone, ready for the trip of your life? Keep your device in your pocket, and please take hold of it now.

With that, which seemed to be instantaneous, they found themselves in a large, brightly lit room. The walls were an off-white colour and had beautiful pictures of a countryside, of various cities, and of what seemed to be people. There were a couple of sofas, chairs, a few ornate wooden tables, and a small kitchen area. It was very comfortable atmospherically. The air felt so, for lack of a better word, clean, fresh, even healthy. Once they took in the visuals, everyone noticed that they felt a little dizzy, so they sat down on the sofas and in the chairs and just waited. After a few minutes, Joy felt better and got up.

"I'm going to see if I can make something to drink. I'm sure the visitors have provided us with coffee, tea, various beverages, and even something to snack on ... I don't know about the rest of you, but I'm hungry." Joy walked over to the kitchen area, and as she had done in Green's apartment, noticed that there was everything she needed. She laughed in awe of the visitors. Others joined her as she put the kettle on. The rest of the group started to gather, looking at what was to snack on. Just as they were munching on the muffins, cinnamon rolls, and Green's favourite cocoanut/vanilla cake, there was a knock on the door. Green turned to answer the door, but the visitors interrupted him and spoke to him privately.

Sydney, this is a small group of leaders who represent the people that were sent to this planet from your world. They will welcome your group, bring you all up to date, and show you around. They are also very interested in getting an update from your delegation. Once that is done, they will brief you and transport your team to meet this planet's alien leadership. So, go answer the door and let's get started.

Green went to the door and cautiously opened it. He was nervous and wondered what had happened to the people sent here more than twenty-five years before. As he peered out the door, he was apprehensive, thinking of the circumstances of how and when they had been sent to this planet and if the residents here treated them well, knowing why they had been sent there. He was also concerned if they had residual anger about what happened. As he looked out and surveyed the group, he saw nine individuals standing there with big smiles and outstretched arms—he sensed their calm, their happiness, and that they were more than content—they were exhilarated. He noticed they had a glow about them, a welcoming aura that said everything was fine, so he stepped out.

One of the women in the group stepped forward and came right up to Green and gave him a hug.

"Welcome," she whispered in his ear as everyone else stepped out of the building and stood beside Green. They were greeted with hugs and welcoming comments from the group. As this was happening, they had a chance to look at their surroundings and the distant landscape. The whole setting was so calming, so amazing. Then the group stepped back to give them time to take in what they were seeing.

As they surveyed the area, they noticed that they were on a hill, slightly elevated from the rest of the area. Right in front of them were fields of lush green grass landscaped with several areas that had picnic tables and flowering plants. The air had a wonderful calming effect as they breathed in, with a scent of flowers somewhat like roses. Beyond the field of grass, and circling the area were trees—a forest of trees. Then, looking beyond that, they noticed mountains, and to the right, they saw a trail between the trees that led to a lake. It was a breathtaking sight, that seemed so sculptured, and well looked after. The air was fresh, the scent of flowers comforting, and the sky—not a cloud to be seen. After a few minutes of quiet time to give Green and his associates a chance to take in the scenery, one of the women started to address the group.

"Welcome to you all. My name is Liron." And then, turning her attention specifically to Green, she said, "Dr. Green, to answer your question, we are not angry. Quite the opposite. Look around you." As she turned, she pointed at the scenery in all directions. "How could we be anything but euphoric?" She paused just for a brief moment. "Oh, and as you can tell, I have the same powers as your delegation, only more advanced." She was speaking to them telepathically.

"Anyway, when we arrived, we didn't know where we were, and of course, we were concerned, but we learned very quickly that we were in a place where we were welcomed, and now we're part of this amazing world's organizational structures, but we'll explain all of that a little later. First, let's say hi to each other, have another cup of tea, and then please let us know how things are progressing on the little blue planet. We do get reports from the visitors, but something from the 'horse's mouth'," she had to pause as there was considerable laughter, "would be great." Green and the team turned back to go into the building where they thought they would sit and get caught up when Liron called to them and got their attention.

"No, no, please everyone, follow me." As soon as they turned back a vehicle appeared. "Come with me. We'll make a treat for you all and we'll get to know each other, get updates and answer questions. Then, when you feel ready, we'll take you on a tour and prepare you for meeting our world government leadership."

Green and his group were surprised at the sudden appearance of the vehicle, but looking at each other, they shrugged, knowing that this world was much more advanced and this was probably the first of many surprises.

"Thank you," said Green, and everyone headed into the ship, which they noticed was hovering just above the ground. Once inside, they were in a large reception area similar to the conference room at the world government headquarters in Green's office, but much larger. There were drinks and treats ready.

"Please, help yourselves. Take a seat at one of the tables, and we'll get started in a moment." Once everyone was seated and enjoying their beverages and treats, Liron got up and got everyone's attention.

"Again, welcome," she started. "As I mentioned, my name is Liron, but I go by Lori. My name is followed by a series of numbers that identify the city I live in, the province, and then the region." Lori then pointed to a small patch, like a tattoo, that was on her upper right arm and explained. "This patch is not only my identification, but it is also a communication system that gives me access, well, to everything and everyone. Each person on this world is connected through a communication system—but we can control the level of communication. For example, if we want to talk to an individual, a group, vote, report issues etc., we can do that." Lori paused as she saw the delegates looking at each other. "Oh, so the visitors are just implementing the system on earth. I understand, but please be aware that you can trust them implicitly." Then she continued to explain.

"The reason for this type of communication is that after we arrived, we realized that the primary form of communication on the planet was telepathic as the residents were much more advanced than we were. It took time, but with their help and that of the visitors, our telepathic, indeed our brain function, started to develop—now we have the capacity to get along and participate. And as you have experienced, Dr. Green, we can also shut it off so we can be private.

"This technology also gives us access to all the services provided, from education to medical and health care services, housing, entertainment, and travel, and anything we need. Do we understand how it works? No, but do we benefit from it? Absolutely!"

Lori stopped for a moment and answered a few questions. One, in particular, made her and the others in her group chuckle. The question was asking how they kept track, how Lori, as an individual, kept all of the information organized that must be shared. Lori turned it over, smiling, to someone else in her group ... he was an elderly gentleman.

"Hi, my name is Albert, but I typically go by Al. Let me try to explain. As Lori mentioned, when we first arrived, we were advised that humans on the world we came from have accessed only about 10 - 12% of our brain capacity, and one of the first things that had to happen was that we had to increase that percentage. As you all have experienced, we were given medications that did just that. There were only just over one hundred of us in the first group to arrive here. After we had acclimated and the medications took effect, we could communicate with the local government officials, be trained, and learn about our new lifestyle. By the end of our training, we were not the same people who had arrived here just a few weeks before. Then we became responsible for and were kept busy welcoming the many others who arrived.

"Right now, just in this city, we have over two million people. And there are ninety-two other cities like this one." He paused for a short break to let the group absorb what he had just said, for everyone to refill their beverages, and to answer some questions.

When he started again, he explained to Green and the group, "The residents of this planet, as you will see, are far more advanced than we are, and because of that they were able, almost like a simple operation to fix a broken arm, to increase our brain function so that we could get along—to understand, to communicate with them, and to answer your question to keep everything organized and available when needed. I am sure you have felt the effects of the pills the visitors have given you. It's the same thing for us, only much more focused and advanced. In time, this is what will happen on your world, on earth as well." Al stopped to take a drink of tea.

"This planet," he continued, "is more than four times the size of earth. When we arrived, the visitors told us that there were just over 6 billion people living here. Their technology is unbelievable, like this ship and our city that they established, as needed. And there was, and is, a lot of space for us, and others who arrived later, to settle in, to learn, and when feasible become part of this world's organization ... back to you, Lori."

Lori smiled and thanked Al before continuing the discussion. "Well, I think that's enough from us for now. So, tell us a bit about how your world is coping; then, we can take a quick tour and show you what it's like here. After that, we'll transport you to the capital city, and you can meet the leaders of this world. Al and I will accompany you when you meet them."

Lori turned it over to Green who brought the group up to date with what had happened and what was happening on earth. Lori, Al, and their group asked a lot of questions and were surprised about the state of affairs on the blue planet.

Then Green posed the obvious question. "You know, it has always bothered me that the visitors so arbitrarily sent so many people away, rather than trying to work with them as they did successfully in some regions of the world, such as in Yukon, Canada." Lori and Al raised their hands, stopping Green, and then another representative responded.

"Representatives from the little blue planet, my name is Yoshi. Of course, as Lori and Al mentioned, my name is followed by a series of numbers further identifying me. I will try to answer your question. You see, on your planet during the start of the intervention, the visitors, as you call them, saw conflict, they saw abuses that they couldn't tolerate, they saw social and economic dysfunction that they could not permit to interact with other planets—they knew they had to act and act quickly. They had experienced the same situation on other planets, and the solutions they had developed they implemented on earth. There were too many people to operate as they did in the Yukon. So, what happened to us, you ask?"

Yoshi paused as he positioned himself so that behind him was a view of fields, of trees and mountains, and a beautiful blue sky—it was calming, to say the least. Then he smiled as he explained that they had been transported to a large room on one of the ships that were positioned around the earth. There seemed to be hundreds of people, but he explained that later he learned there were one hundred on each ship.

"We were angry, anxious and scared, not knowing what was happening. Then we heard a voice reassuring us that all would be well and explaining our situation and what was to happen. Before we could react, something did happen, and when we came back to our senses, we found ourselves here." Yoshi turned and pointed to the scenery behind him, raised his hands, and took a deep breath. "We were met by representatives of this world. Obviously, at first sight of the aliens, we were shocked, but again, before we could ask any questions, the building behind you suddenly appeared, and we were asked to enter. When we did, we saw beverages and treats just as if we were at a meeting at home. We were left alone for a time and soon became more relaxed, still wondering what was happening.

"Then two of the aliens entered. Of course, they got our attention, and they commenced to explain what had happened, where we were, and what was going to happen. They made a point of saying that we had to be kept separate from the general population of the planet for two reasons: one was that as this planet is a sterile environment, we had to be 'cleansed' of any potential bacteria we might be bringing from our previous environment, and how they had a protective shield around them; and two, we have to be acclimated to how things work on this planet, to be educated, to have us join the communications systems, and to develop our brain function. They also said that we were to have responsibility to work with the others as they arrived. They explained that any resident coming to help us get settled, as they were, was protected by a force field and that this whole area would also be enclosed in a force field.

"During the next few weeks, we were educated, given wonderful accommodations, and treated, well, as you would say on earth ... like kings and queens."

He went on to explain the communication patches, and how they worked. He concluded by discussing how they became the greeters for the many, many people who came after them and how the cities were created, as needed, and then how they started to interact with the world government and become part of their world. Now, after a couple of decades, they consider this to be their home, their world. Then he stopped, and Lori took over.

"Okay, let's show you around, and you'll see where your world is headed. Then we'll go to meet with the world government." With that, they all took a seat, and just like the visitors had shown Green years ago, the delegation saw what to expect once everything would be established on earth. They travelled all over the world to many of the cities that were established by the migrations from earth. At the end of the tour, another elderly gentleman got up and faced the group.

"Hello, welcome, my name is Arthur. Of course, as the others, my name is followed by numbers and the patch that the others have mentioned, for further identification. You need to know for when you go home that this communication system is seamless, supportive, and it is not intrusive or controlling.

"I will be brief, as my task is to prepare you to meet with this world's government delegation. First, protocol dictates that even though the 'aliens,' as you call them, can read your thoughts, you must introduce yourself by first and last name, and your current position on the Blue World Government. Then you have to thank the government officials for accepting, training, and including the people from the little blue planet to become active members of their world. Then Dr. Green, as president of the little blue planet, you have to step forward and ask for permission to begin developing communication and dialogue with members of this beautiful planet to help your world develop. At this point, the president of our world government will respond to you and your delegation." He paused to answer a few questions and then addressed the one question in everyone's thoughts—what do the aliens look like.

"So, you want to know what the aliens look like. Well, here we go. They are physically similar to us; however, you'll notice a couple of things, one, they are not of various sizes. They are all what you would consider of medium structure, averaging about 5'8". Their eyes, ears, and nose are larger than ours as they have developed advanced sight, sound, and smell more than taste and touch. But the most notable difference is that their skull structure is much larger than ours as they have evolved to their greatly increased brain function. They don't speak. They use telepathy to communicate, and because they have a much higher percentage of brain activity than we do, their abilities are still well beyond our understanding. To them, we are like primitive cavemen. Until we can develop, which they are helping us do, we live in our own cities and don't mingle that much, but they're patient, caring and have provided us all the necessities, as you witnessed in the cities we visited. I am not sure how they will respond to any requests, as they have already done so much for us. By the way, that was at the request of the visitors, so they aren't obliged to do any more.

"I think we're ready. Let me be clear, the devices and the pills the visitors gave you will help you communicate, but you must wait for them to make the first attempt to communicate. They will be quiet at first as they probe to make sure your protective devices are protecting them, and as they probe you to understand your motivations. Here we go."

And with that, without responding to the questions that Green and the others had, they found themselves in a small but elaborate foyer. There was only Lori, Al, and Green's group. Lori went up to what seemed like a door and knocked on it. The door instantly disappeared, and the group found themselves in a beautiful and ornate room, almost like a court room, but welcoming. There were tables, an area for beverages and treats, and at the front of the room, they noticed a table with a few chairs. Then they sensed something, or someone, talking to them.

"Please make yourselves a cup of tea or coffee or a beverage, and we are sure you could use a little snack. The visitors have informed us of your dietary habits. Please, help yourselves, and we'll wait until you get settled at the table." Once everyone was seated and had some refreshments, they calmed down. Then, at the front of the room, the aliens appeared. They seemed to be all the same. They were all wearing the same clothing—white shoes, slacks, shirt, and a jacket. Green could not determine male from female but didn't say anything. As Arthur had already described them and their facial structure, it was not a surprise to see how they appeared. For Green, he was pleased as they appeared to be like one of his conceptions in his apartment.

"Dr. Green," one of the aliens addressed Green. "We cannot discuss the male/female questions you have right now. Perhaps when your world matures. Dr. Green, is this what you were expecting?"

Green stood up as he heard laughter, and even he had a big smile on his face as he responded. "Well, actually, one of my visions of what an alien race would look like was very close to what I am seeing now, thank you for asking." He was beyond excited with anticipation about what would happen, and he was hopeful.

"Please, introduce yourselves."

Then, as Arthur had instructed them, and starting with Green, each person stood and introduced themselves, finishing with Joy. There was a pause. Green and the others sensed something was happening, but Lori and Al kept them calm, explaining that the aliens were probing them and discussing what their responses would be.

"Dr. Green, you have something to say?" Green stood and quickly followed Al's directions, thanking the aliens for welcoming the others and providing for them. Then he outlined what was happening on earth and that they were there because of promises made by the visitors that he would, at the appropriate time, meet an alien race and make first contact with another world. Then he asked if they could begin discussions to help earth progress. There was another pause.

"Dr. Green, did you actually meet with the visitors in their environment?"

"Yes ... why do you ask?"

"Because we have never heard of this happening before—never."

There was a pause.

"Dr. Green, members of the Blue World Government, Ms. Taller, the answer to your request Dr. Green, is yes and no. Let us explain. Only because of your interactions with, and the recommendation of the visitors and their respect for you, Dr. Green, and for some reason to a lesser degree, the regional leaders, and of course you, Ms. Taller. We will set up a system where we can watch your progress and, from time to time, welcome a delegation here to assist in your continued development by focusing on specific goals and gaps. We will only do that with absolute secrecy until your world progresses to a much more acceptable situation. I sense that you, and the others, are asking, why do they have to wait?" There was silence in the room as the aliens looked at each other and then seemed to come to a conclusion and addressed Green and the others.

"Please understand that the devices the visitors gave you to carry on your persons at all times are meant, as well as protecting you, to protect us from you. You see, as Lori and Al, and all of the others who were sent here have experienced, they had to go through several, shall we say, isolation and cleansing stages, before we could meet face to face. Your species is still at a stage of development where you carry diseases and perceptions that would decimate our populations, so we have to control contact. Those perceptions, Dr. Green, representatives of the Blue World Government, are dangerous to us as your world is still primitive. It has a long way to go to complete all of the social, educational, political, philosophical, and technical requirements set out by the visitors before we can actually visit you, or have an extended contact here. Although you're on the right path, there is still so much for all of you to do.

"So, Dr. Green, and members of the Blue World Government, the other answer to your request at this time is no, we must limit the contact with your world. We will, however, through the visitors, keep an eye on your progress and when applicable and beneficial, we will dialogue with your world representatives as we have done today. Now, go back with Lori and Al and enjoy a day or two to learn more about us, have a good time, and then back you go to continue your work."

With that, they all found themselves back in the building in which they had originally arrived.

During the next couple of days, Joy, Green, and the others got a lot of information and directions from Lori and her group. They also had more tours and receptions, and enjoyed their visit. On the assigned day to return to earth, they said their goodbyes, and expressed their thanks for the hospitality and all of the valuable information. They were escorted into the building within which they had arrived at the planet, and the locals shook hands, wished them luck, and left. As before, they seemingly instantaneously found themselves, disoriented, back in Green's apartment. It took a few minutes to regain their sensibilities as they just stood there in awe of the technology. Once recovered, they decided to rest that evening and meet to debrief during the next few days to go over the trip and assign specific tasks to each of the leaders from the regions. The visitors assisted them in forming the direction the world government was to take and how future meetings with the aliens would happen.

The visitors made a point of cautioning the leadership many times, explaining that it would still take another generation, or more, and new leaders as they presented themselves, to complete the tasks set out for the world. *Remember what you've seen on the planet you visited and what you learned, and share that information.* The visitors also made it clear that these changes, this new era, were not simply for contacting other civilizations, other worlds, other species—it was for the benefit of the people of earth. Soon after first contact, Green retired from his position with the world government, but retained his apartment and would welcome visitors.

He would also visit Joy in Whitehorse many times, spending weeks with her reminiscing about their youth and anything that came to mind. They loved talking about the first time Green was taken to the visitor's ship and then appeared at her school to talk to a school assembly, which had turned into a worldwide broadcast. They had a great time the first couple of months back, but then Joy's health declined, and she required increasing care.

Joy made sure Green understood that she'd had a wonderful life and was ready to go. She passed away one year to the day after they made first contact. Green was right there with her, holding her hand and continually thanking her for everything she had accomplished. At the last moment, he felt her tighten her grip on his hand as if to say, "It's okay," and "Thank you," and then she passed away.

After word got out about her passing, there were celebrations of her life and her contributions—especially among the education community worldwide. In the school where she had taught, a permanent display in her memory was established just inside the entrance to the school, and at the world government offices, her portrait was hung at the entrance to the chair's office.

After he had retired, and Joy passed, Green spent his time as a keynote speaker, travelling the world, supporting the efforts of the regional governments, and he wrote two books about the coming of the visitors and the first years of creating a new age for the world. Finally, the visitors met with Green.

Sydney, we think it is time for you to leave. We want your world to remember you, to have memories and stories to tell as a vital, strong, active, and healthy person who has achieved so much for the people of earth. We want to have a final broadcast within which the world government leaders present you with a special award, acknowledging your lifelong work and celebrating your life. At the end of the broadcast, you can speak, thank everyone, and as you have done for many years, step to the side and disappear. We'll bring you to a special planet, reserved for people who have made exceptional contributions on their planets, to live out your life. How does that sound?"

"I'm tired, and I feel it is time for me to go. I have done all that I can do, so I think that is a wonderful idea. As Joy said to me that she had had a wonderful life and it was time for her to 'go,' so I feel the same. I miss her, but I have so many fond memories. Will you set it all up?"

Yes, Sydney, and although we'll continue to meet periodically, we want to be the first to say a profound thank you for all you've done and to make sure you understand we will continue our work with the little blue planet. Remember this. You are the only biological unit to have ever met with us, face to face, so to speak.

Green laughed with his friends.

It was a week later that the broadcast was made, and at the end of Green's emotional speech, he simply disappeared.

Several more years would pass—with the world government representatives working with the visitors and the people of the world Green and his associates made first contact with—before the visitors suggested that they could arrange a visit to other alien worlds and have an alien race visit earth.

SUMMARY, AND A FEW LAST WORDS

SUMMARY:

In the beginning of their relationship the visitors showed Green a dysfunctional, violent, and corrupt world, with an abusive, greedy and entitled leadership in control. They exposed him to the suffering and the day-to-day struggles of the majority of people – they laid bare the dark side of humanity. The dark side, that included images of the terror, racism, and abuses in our past and present history. Because Green was reaching out to find other populated worlds the visitors had to act to protect other civilizations from having contact with us.

The visitors told Green that they had hoped, even expected, that with all of the suffering, pain and torment throughout our history, that at some point in time we would have come to our senses, and would have worked together to find solutions. They expected, as it is on other planets, that we would help each other by tapping into the caring side of our humanity. But they found the opposite was true.

They explained that with the creation of nation-states, the development of hierarchical social structures, the industrialization and urbanization of the world, that much of that caring side of humanity was ineffective against those in power. What replaced it was a lust for money and dominance – greed, ambition, and selfishness ruled the day. And those in control asserted themselves, and felt entitled to do as they pleased, living in luxury, while the vast majority struggled, yielding to their power.

During the early years the visitors had to implement many foundational changes, with Green as their agent, to begin the evolution to a fair and just society. The first stage culminated with the establishment of the seven regional governments. However, for the Little Blue World to evolve to an acceptable level, there was much more to accomplish.

Then the visitors, after reviewing with Green the existing situation in the world, outlined the next phase in our evolution. They shared with Green how he, and others, had to implement the new priorities and objectives in order to complete the process of establishing a new era for our world, and preparing us for first contact. Once completed, the transition to a fair and just society would change our world.

The work got done, a new era was established, and Green was able to make first contact.

A FEW LAST WORDS:

So, what does this teach us in our world today? How do we start putting that puzzle together? We can no longer be indifferent to the needs of the world's populations, to our environmental crisis, to the greedy and selfish nature of those in power. For example, we are the little blue planet with 70% of our surface covered in water, and yet 2.2 billion people, 1/4 of our world's population do not have access to clean drinking water, and other infrastructure that we take for granted. We must ask, 'who are we to allow this to exist?' Collectively we are responsible for the world we have created. Now we have to stand up and work together to make change – to fix it!

We have to fix our politics, our socio-economic systems, and establish a stable universal order that is balanced and fair for everyone – inaction is not an answer for us anymore if we are to survive. Green understood that it requires a parallel effort globally; which seems at this time to be something we're incapable of doing. So, we must step up, overcome our hesitancy, our fear, and our complacent, self-serving nature. It will take determination, communication, education, and co-operation, but we can do it, we must do it – one step at a time.

Green came to the understanding that no longer can one person in power, or one small entitled group, direct the future of a nation, control the socio-economic structure of a country, simply for their benefit. The era of aggressive and competitive countries must end – corrupt leadership, divisiveness, conflict, and greed, must end. The people of the world must come together and act as a single, united force, demanding change.

How can we possibly do all of that, you ask? The answer is not complicated! We can discover our inner strength, our empathy and awareness of others, and stand together to make change. We the people are the majority, and have the power. We don't have to wait for an alien intervention; we can act right now!

And we have a good example, one of many that exists, of people standing up, demanding, and producing change by using their collective power. That example is in South Africa. It wasn't until the Black majority stood together and boycotted all the white businesses that apartheid ended - and it happened very quickly. Likewise, we have to stand together and demand change, leaders can only lead when their followers follow, blindly giving them the power to do what they will – think about that.

First, we have to eliminate the corruption in political parties, and the self-serving mentality within the corporate sectors – their lust for money and power. This must change so we can have leadership that is accountable – 'for the people by the people'.

To achieve what happened in South Africa globally, one of the first things we have to do is to change our political systems, and how we elect people into positions of leadership. As the visitors explained to Green, we have to elect the right people into positions of responsibility. People who have education, managerial experience, and proven leadership qualities – people who care about working to create, and then maintain, a social and economic balance in the world, meeting the needs of all people, not just the rich and powerful. We have to create a system that is accountable to the people, and unified globally by a World Government. It is through a World Government that stability will be established – the thought of having a united nations government was on the right track, but the way it was organized and how it operates is not the world government model proposed by the visitors

There are currently examples of governments where there are no political parties. Rather, the people vote for a person in their district to represent them, then, after the election, those elected to office choose who will assume the positions of leadership based on their education, experience, skillset, and previous performance.

With leaders who care about being part of creating a new socio-economic model of governance, change will happen. What a thought, get rid of the influence of the lobbyists, and those that use their wealth, their power and influence, to assert control from behind the scenes - the so called 'old boys club'. Now that would be something.

But, to achieve this another important step in modernizing our outdated social, political, and economic networks, and moving us into the future, must happen – and that is eliminating money.

As we all know, in our world everything, everything, is based on money. Regardless of what we want, or need, regardless of the discussion, the first thing we ask, or think about, is 'what does that cost?' But like the visitors pointed out to Green, on more advanced worlds, nothing is based on money – there is no money to interfere with the needs of people. In these more advanced worlds people work and are rewarded for their contributions by having all of their day-to-day needs met. This system creates a socio-economic standard within which everyone contributes to the system through their work, and in return the system looks after them. They can go out to a nice dinner, dance, celebrate, enjoy sports, music, theatre, get an education, go on a vacation, be content, and have meaning in their lives. This is the era that the visitors, with Green as their emissary created - it is not beyond our reach – we can do it.

By creating the World Government, with representation from the seven regional governments, with the power to plan and oversee the universal ecosystem, and sustaining the new paradigms, we become one nation – the Little Blue World. And with a strong representative World Government we can achieve the leadership, the partnerships, and get the results we are seeking. We can accomplish this by implementing a true meritocracy, and getting control of the corporate and industrial sectors. As well, by creating a global supply chain management system that would provide goods and services, housing, technology, and infrastructure to the world's populations; our world would be well on the way to establishing a fair, just and balanced society.

As Sydney Green discovered, by working together we can create a compassionate, responsible, and balanced socio-economic model, and a governance system that is fair and just for the people of the world. People will be heard, and free to achieve their goals, their dreams – and be safe.

Finally, as Green witnessed, a universal education protocol is a critical part of the process for sustaining that balanced and fair world. A universal education system that celebrates and encourages curiosity, the desire to learn, to be compassionate, to grow, to excel, and that supports excellence in all fields of study. This is how we find our future leaders, our scientists, our doctors, teachers, our sports heroes, artists, musicians, and support workers. As well, by having a communication system that joins the world together, we can also cherish our cultural diversity and learn from each other. We can do it all as Green discovered – one step at a time. It's in our hands now.

Think about it,

Rick Karp

Printed in Canada